Loyalty's Betrayal

Masters' Admiralty, book 2

Mari Carr and Lila Dubois

ISBN: 9781790332397

Editor: Kelli Collins

Cover artist: Lila Dubois

Loyalty's Betrayal

Masters' Admiralty, book 2

His redemption comes with two conditions.

Mateo failed in his duties as Head of Security for the world's most powerful secret society and people died. His chance for redemption comes at a price.

The conditions: Mateo is partnered with Cecilia–a brilliant woman, and Dimitri, an arrogant spy.

The deadline: They have one week to find the traitor.

The ultimatum: Mateo will be the third in an arranged ménage marriage with Cecilia and Dimitri if they don't find the traitor in time.

When enemies become lovers, no price is too high.

Acknowledgements

Special thanks to Lexi Blake for allowing us to "crossover" briefly between with her Masters and Mercenaries world. This was done so with her permission. She rocks!

Prologue

There was something wrong.

He knew it the moment he walked in the front door. The house was too still, too quiet. Typically, the smell of dinner was the first thing he noticed upon arriving home, but today the only scent he could detect was the tanginess of the pomegranate blossoms in the bouquet of fresh flowers his mother always kept on a side table in the foyer.

The silence was unnerving and unfamiliar. He was an only child, something his parents seemed to overcompensate for by constantly filling their large house with noise—be it from the radio, the television, laughter, or conversation—and constant activity. They were a family in perpetual motion. It had been that way for as long as he could remember.

He had stayed after school for *fútbol* practice, having made starting midfielder on the team during his final year of *Educación Secundaria Obligatoria*, a fairly substantial feat in a city like Seville, where everyone ate, drank and dreamed *fútbol*.

His father hadn't been surprised by his success on the field. After all, Papa had declared him a born runner, swearing his first steps hadn't been made walking, but rather in a mad forty-meter dash.

He was going to continue his education next year in *Bachillerato*, before following in his parents' footsteps and heading to university. Like him, they'd been born and raised in Seville, leaving only to attend university and medical school in Barcelona, then returning home to accept residencies at the local hospital. Both of his parents were renowned surgeons, esteemed in their fields. His mother was a neurosurgeon, Papa's specialty vascular surgery, and their aspirations for him were the same, both of them certain he would follow in their footsteps to pursue a career in medicine.

The three of them had spent a great deal of time discussing which discipline he would pursue, perusing the medical journals, discussing the pros and cons of each. His parents were peaceful, loving people. To them, a life well lived meant saving lives through medical care, not through force or politics or financial gain.

They lived close enough to his school that he walked each day, enjoying those few minutes of solitude. He was an alert, astute boy, constantly taking in the world around him. He'd grown more quiet with each passing year and had begun to master the art of blending in. His father was boisterous, lively, typically the life of every party they attended, so Papa wasn't sure what to do with a brooding son. Lately, he'd begun resenting his father's comments about him needing to speak up, to share what was on his mind, so in a typical act of teen rebelliousness, he'd gone even quieter, simply to annoy Papa.

Glancing around the front foyer, he spotted his mother's purse, overturned on the floor. It looked as if she'd missed the table when setting it down, and it had fallen, the contents scattering on the hardwood. A tube of lipstick, pack of tissues, two pens, several credit cards. He catalogued the items in his mind, noting the details. Mama often made a game of his ability to see everything at a glance. Whenever they were driving somewhere, she'd tell him to close his eyes, then ask him to describe something that lay ahead of them—a billboard, a building, a person walking on the sidewalk. She'd ask random questions and he always knew every exacting detail perfectly.

He thought it strange that Mama had left her purse lying there that way. She took tidiness to new heights, something he thought indicative of a slightly obsessive-compulsive nature.

"Mama?" he called out, his voice echoing slightly, thanks to the tall ceiling in the foyer. The door on the right, which led to the formal dining room, was usually open, but he noticed it was closed. In fact, all the first-floor doors were closed. He pondered if he'd ever seen them so.

He called for his mother again. No response.

He briefly considered heading straight upstairs to drop off his school bag and grab a quick shower, but there was something about the silence that told him all of this was wrong. Terribly wrong.

He opened the dining room door.

It took him a moment to understand what he was seeing.

The room was awash in red, the splatters covering the off-white walls in a style reminiscent of a Jackson Pollock painting.

He was the sixteen-year-old son of two surgeons. He'd seen pictures of bodies, cut open on the operating tables, in his parents' medical journals and textbooks. Blood didn't scare him. It was as necessary to life as water and air. The walls held his attention for far longer than they should have. Perhaps because he wasn't emotionally able to turn his gaze toward the table.

Peripherally, he could see what was there. Understood that his entire life had changed in the blink of an eye.

He was an intelligent boy, perfectly capable of reasoning things out. He'd always been proud of his ability to analyze a situation and see the next fifteen steps. His papa told him that would make him an excellent surgeon.

He sucked in a deep breath, swallowing heavily to dislodge the bile in this throat, then turned his eyes to the table.

There, lying side by side, their chests ripped apart with one long, deep gash down the center of each, as if by a machete, were his parents. Both of them had died with their eyes open, their final expressions the perfect blend of horror and pain.

It was nothing like the images in medical books. In those, neat, clean incisions were surrounded by sterile blue cloth. It hid the person, made it easier to treat the body as a puzzle or a machine, his father had explained once.

He could see his father's heart. At least he thought that was what the mangled lump was. The powerful blow that had opened his father from chest to belly button had broken some of his ribs, leaving his chest cavity open. There was a gray mass under all the blood, and he thought it might be the lungs.

His mother's wound started lower, at the bottom of her sternum, but it cut deep into her belly, and things that looked like half-formed sausage links trailed out of her.

The screaming in his head made it hard to think. To breathe. He took the source of those screams, shoved it in a box and closed the lid. Later, he would let it out. Later, he would dream of this. Nightmares, no doubt.

Whoever had done this had staged the bodies, placed them in their current positions after killing them. His mother hadn't died here but by the front window, the trail of her blood starting just below the damask curtains she had purchased last spring to replace the heavy velvet ones that had been gathering dust in the room since before his birth. Had their killer reached into her, pulling out her intestines to drape them over the table?

His father had been killed in the kitchen, his own bright red trail beginning beyond the closed swinging door that separated that room from this one. They were murdered and dragged here by their killer, placed on their own dining room table, their bodies displayed to mirror the looks of the patients they treated in the hospital.

His eyes lingered on his mama's face, her pale, lifeless blue eyes. Every part of him longed to run to her, to hug her, to kiss her, to beg her not to be dead.

She was his beloved mama, the woman who understood him, loved him, made him laugh.

He reached out to her, but stopped. He couldn't touch her, couldn't destroy any of the evidence that might lead the *policia* to find her killer.

He forced himself to look at everything. To commit it to memory. It was easy, given the numbness, the shock taking over his body. The emotions would come later—pain, grief, fear, anger. For now, all of it remained at bay, his own soul as lifeless as those of his beloved parents.

He forced himself to scan the room once again. All of this mattered. Every detail needed to be noted, filed away. He would have to call the *policia* soon. They would take him from here, probably place him in a home with some distant relative—a cousin or great aunt. It was the one unusual thing about his parents.

Unlike his friends at school, he wasn't constantly surrounded by an extended family.

He turned to go back to the foyer, to place the call. That was when he saw it.

Written on the back of the door he'd just passed through, in his parents' blood, were two words.

Comienza aquí.

It begins here.

A chill ran through his body and he shivered violently.

Walking to the phone, he dialed the authorities, then went into the living room on the opposite side of the house to wait. He left the doors between him and his parents open, the way they were supposed to be, so he could watch over their bodies.

Sirens blared, lights flashed through the front windows and within minutes, the house was filled with men. Several of them came into the room where he remained, one at a time or in pairs, and asked him the same questions, over and over.

What time did you get home?

Was anyone else in the house?

Did your parents have enemies?

Had they received threats?

What do the words comienza aqui *mean to you?*

He answered them all, his responses never changing. He knew nothing. He saw nothing. The words meant nothing to him.

Hours passed as the *policía* took photographs, gathered evidence, removed his parents from the house.

Through it all, he remained a statue on the couch, his eyes taking it in.

He listened to the baffled detectives and knew deep in his heart that these men would never be able to solve the mystery, to bring the killer to justice.

Finally, at the end of the evening, a stranger approached him, placing a firm, strong hand on his shoulder.

He looked up into the man's gaze and saw something he hadn't in the eyes of the *policía*. Confidence, strength, answers. And then, looking deeper into the man's face, he also saw the same pain that he felt. The man may be a stranger to him, but it was clear he was grieving. How could the stranger feel the death of his parents as keenly as he?

"It will be alright, son. I'm sorry I wasn't here sooner, *chiquito*," the stranger said.

Chiquito? He wasn't a little boy. But the man's tone hadn't been patronizing. It was affectionate—the term of endearment used almost habitually.

That couldn't be. He'd never seen the stranger before.

No. That wasn't the truth. The stranger looked terribly, sickeningly familiar.

A sense of otherness gripped him, and the world seemed to tip as if the ground under him had suddenly gone sideways. The man's eyes...

That was when he recognized they were same eyes that stared back at him in the mirror each morning.

This stranger looked like him. Just like him.

"Who are you?" he whispered, a sense of awe and fear washing through him.

The stranger gave him a sad smile. "I'm your father. I've been watching over you your entire life."

"No, you are not my papa." His father was dead. Dead and now gone from their house, never to return. He swallowed down the pain.

"Not your papa, your *padre*." He used the more formal word for father.

"What does that mean?" A thought occurred to him, and he stiffened. Was this man the murderer?

As if sensing the direction of his thoughts, the stranger held up his hands. "I am here to help you. I will take care of you."

"Why? Who are you?" This time the question was harsh, the tears he hadn't cried tightened his throat.

"I told you. I am your father."

"Liar!" He leapt for the stranger, who stepped back, putting a chair between them. "My papa is dead! You are no one."

"I wish we'd done things differently. I wish we'd told you."

"Told me what?" His throat hurt, but he would not cry.

"The man who died here today was your papa in every way, except one. You are my blood. Look at me, and you will know the truth."

He frowned, confused. He wanted to dispute the fact. To scream from the rafters that his father had just been brutally murdered. But the words didn't come. Because he saw the details. Saw the truth.

"What do you know about the Masters' Admiralty?" the stranger asked.

The words were foreign to him.

"Nothing, sir."

The stranger gave him a kind smile. "I will teach you. You're coming home with me, Mateo."

Chapter One

"I don't mean to question your authority, sir, but—"

"The very nature of that sentence implies a question, Arthur," the fleet admiral interjected.

"I understand that, but I would be a very poor leader in my own right if I didn't question something that gave me pause, caused me concern."

"You have...concerns...about what I've ordered you to do?"

Arthur considered whether it was wise to forge on. Eric Ericsson was the new fleet admiral, installed shortly after his predecessor had been murdered. Arthur had been there, had witnessed that brutal killing.

As admiral of England's territory, Arthur had to walk a fine line with his new boss. He was honorable and believed in rules and order, things that had been ingrained in him since his days as a knight. There were codes and traditions that had to be protected and honored. The most important one was that ultimate authority of the Masters' Admiralty rested with the fleet admiral. He should obey Eric without question.

However, his new position required more of him. Suddenly, every decision made for the territory of

England rested with him, which meant speaking up in times like this.

Of course, a smarter man would also know which battles to pick, and Arthur wasn't sure he wanted to die on this hill.

"Arthur?" the fleet admiral prompted. "If you're going to question me, do it. Do not prevaricate." The carefully enunciated English word sounded odd coming from the Eric. He was a huge blond man who looked like a Viking king. His nickname—"the Viking"— though unimaginative, was fitting.

Arthur considered his options, and then took up the figurative sword. "I do have concerns about this request, Fleet Admiral."

"Why?" Eric turned the tables on him, and suddenly he was the one faced with answering questions. "This doesn't involve anyone in your territory. Just do what I've ordered."

"It's Mateo Bernard. I've had the opportunity to get to know him over the course of the past few weeks. He won't be happy about this, and I—"

"Happy? Bernard's happiness has no bearing on my decision."

"I understand that. I'm simply concerned he will view your actions as punishment."

Arthur met Mateo when the former fleet admiral, Kacper Kujakski, had been poisoned. They'd worked together further as they hunted for the sniper who had used the murder of the fleet admiral as an opportunity to take out two more admirals and one of his fellow knights. Mateo, head of the Spartan Guard, felt he'd failed in his duty to protect their leader, and he was anxious for an opportunity to redeem himself with the new fleet admiral.

Obviously, Eric Ericsson didn't give second chances. "He is head of the guard and he allowed the fleet admiral to be poisoned and then murdered. Mateo was standing right there, and the fleet admiral was shot. You think I should trust him to be my head of security?"

Arthur took the fleet admiral's words as an insult. Because Mateo hadn't been the only one standing there when the fleet admiral was killed. What made the man's comment sting even worse was that wasn't the only murder Arthur had witnessed in the past few months. "I was a knight in this territory, sworn to protect my own admiral. He was gunned down in front of my eyes. As a result—"

"As a result, you were made admiral of the England territory. Are you saying you don't feel as if you were punished?" Eric's tone was morose. There had been a rumor Eric hadn't wanted the job of fleet admiral.

A smile crept onto Arthur's face, and he was glad the fleet admiral was still on the Isle of Man and this conversation was happening through speakerphone.

Regardless...he gave credit where credit was due.

"Touché," Arthur muttered.

"I'm not placing Mateo in this alliance to punish the man."

"Alliance? Is that what we're calling this? I thought it was a marriage."

"Unless I get to start watching the new trinities have sex as a perk of this fucking job, they're alliances first, marriages second."

Arthur tried to hide his laugh, turning it into a cough.

Eric's sigh was audible. "We're part of the Masters' Admiralty. Trust me, for us, marriages and alliances are the same."

"Have you told the three admirals of the territories where these members live?"

Arthur was fairly certain he wasn't imagining the humor in Eric's voice when he said, "I told the admirals of Castile and Ukraine that I'm calling people from their territories into a trinity. I thought I'd leave the other one to you. After all, you have a family tie to the admiral of Rome."

Yep, Arthur thought with a sigh. He was definitely being punished. Giovanni Starabba, the admiral of Rome, was his new father-in-law and that "family tie" was so loose, it wouldn't bind a kitten to a feather.

"Thank you, I'll do that." Arthur made sure his tone was polite.

Eric laughed. "I love you English. You're good at saying 'fuck you' while sounding polite."

Arthur winced, feeling guilty that he hadn't had better control of his tone. "My apologies, Fleet Admiral."

"Don't apologize. And don't be so...British. I don't trust many people right now, Arthur. You, James and Sophia are at the top of a short list."

Arthur felt for Eric. They'd both been thrust into jobs they weren't prepared for, despite the fact that they were technically qualified. Eric needed...not a friend, exactly, but a comrade in arms. Someone who understood him.

"I'll contact my father-in-law, but I'm not happy about it," Arthur said begrudgingly.

Eric laughed, and Arthur smiled.

Then his smile turned to a grimace. He was not looking forward to that phone call. Giovanni took his job as admiral very seriously, and he *definitely* created alliances when forming trinities in his territory. It was the primary reason they'd gotten off to such a bad start.

Arthur had been bound in marriage to Giovanni's daughter by the previous fleet admiral. His relationship with Giovanni was still strained due to his sudden, unexpected, and unapproved marriage to Sophia. She was referred to as the Princess in the Roman territory, and Giovanni had intended to form a powerhouse alliance with his daughter's trinity.

Kacper had taken that privilege away when—with his dying breath—he'd bound Arthur to Sophia and James.

Arthur smiled when he thought of Sophia. He adored his beautiful, opinionated, headstrong wife. She was everything he would have chosen in a bride had the decision rested on his shoulders rather than with his admiral.

Rising from his desk, Arthur moved to the window of his office on Threadneedle Street, looking down at the street below. He'd only just recently returned to this office from his home one, as England's Admiralty headquarters had suffered a great deal of damage, thanks to the barrage of bullets that had pierced through the roof, destroying it and the large conference room on the floor above.

The sky was gray, spraying down the cold mist that seemed to hover over the city constantly lately. London needed more sunshine. The weather was affecting his mood, making him question every move, every decision.

Although that shouldn't be surprising to him, considering the last few months. Within the blink of an eye, the fleet admiral—as well as England's admiral, one of the knights, and the admiral of Castile—had been killed, the latter three shot right here in this building. The Masters' Admiralty had been thrust into outright chaos for a brief time.

Arthur had been promoted—if he could call it that—from his role as a knight and took over as the admiral of England. And to make matters worse, the

Masters' Admiralty was fighting a foe as old as the organization itself.

The Domino was back. And the villain was hell-bent on bringing down everything Arthur had spent his life fighting to protect.

Aware that he was losing the fight on Mateo's behalf, he changed course. "Sir, perhaps we should discuss the other, much more pertinent matter at hand," Arthur suggested.

"The Domino."

"Yes. There's been no further information discovered about the dead American sniper. Perhaps it would be easier to uncover more about the man if we contacted the Trinity Masters. However, given our recent..." Arthur paused, trying to find the right word for their troubles with the Trinity Masters.

"Altercation? Disagreement? Go on, say something British."

What the hell did that even mean? Say something British? "We forged an unsteady peace. But I'm not certain they'd be willing to help us."

"There it is." Eric sounded satisfied, then started to chuckle.

Arthur stared at the phone, unsure how to respond. He reached for his cup of tea with his right hand, then stopped. He swallowed hard and sat back in his chair.

The fleet admiral's laughter faded. When he spoke next, his tone was cool, his voice low and serious. "You have friends who are members of the Trinity Masters. You know their Grand Master."

"I do." Arthur truly liked Juliette Adams, the Grand Master of the Trinity Masters. However, there had been some strong words, as well as some not-so-veiled threats leveled from the Masters' Admiralty in their last meeting. He couldn't imagine Juliette would be too keen to hear from him so soon.

Eric took that concern off his shoulders. "If it becomes necessary, I'll contact the Grand Master."

Now, instead of worrying about how he'd talk to Juliette Adams after what had happened in their last conversation, he could worry about just how badly a conversation between Juliette and Eric would go. Brilliant.

"However," the fleet admiral continued. "I will need actionable intelligence, something useful, before pursuing that course. For now, we keep our interaction with that other society as limited as possible."

"Of course." He hoped Eric couldn't hear his relief. "But that leaves us with precious few leads."

"I can think of several."

Arthur paused, waiting for Eric to illuminate him. It became clear he didn't intend to.

Mysterious silence.

Of course.

Eric played his cards very close to his chest. Which reminded Arthur of this unorthodox trinity the man wanted forged.

Eric had left Mateo in England, cooling his heels, ever since the American sniper had shot Manon, the former fleet admiral's wife, and then taken his own life. A man of action himself, Arthur understood that Mateo had felt like a caged animal, forced to remain in London rather than return to his proper place on the Isle of Man.

The knight in him—the man he'd become after joining the Masters' Admiralty—wanted to obey the fleet admiral without question.

The young man he'd been—a man who'd struggled for years to prove himself worthy of both being a member of the Masters' Admiralty, and of being a knight of England—felt for Mateo. Understood how he was feeling.

"Sir, I really think Mateo should be given a chance to prove his worth."

There was a long pause on the other end of the line.

Great, Arthur thought. A few months in and he'd already pissed off his new boss.

Eric grunted. "Fine. Contact Mateo privately, before calling in the other two members of the trinity. Tell him he has one chance to redeem himself."

"What do you want him to do?"

"Find the traitor."

"Traitor." It was a heavy word.

"There's a traitor amongst the Spartan Guard. It's making living here, surrounded by all of them, very exciting."

That startled a laugh out of Arthur, but he smothered it. "I'm sorry, Fleet Admiral, I assure you that I do not think your safety is a laughing matter."

"And I like breathing. But I'm going to stick my finger in the soil before I do anything."

He was going to what? Arthur made a mental note to ask someone if that was a Scandinavian idiom, or if the fleet admiral was actually going to do some sort of soil testing.

"Someone made sure Kacper received tainted medication," Eric continued. "Someone knew he was on the balcony that day."

Arthur remembered the feel of the sea breeze, the tension and fear in the moments following Kacper being shot. A drone had shot the fleet admiral with a dart full of an otherwise non-fatal chemical. The deadly reaction had come when the compound in the dart entered the fleet admiral's system, interacting with the chemical agent already in his body from the tainted medicine.

Eric was right. There was no way all that happened without help from someone inside the stronghold of the Masters' Admiralty.

"Tell Mateo I want a name." The fleet admiral's voice was hard. This was an order, and from his tone, if Arthur objected again, Eric would not take it well. "If he is able to expose the traitor, I'll dissolve the trinity. He has a week."

"Very well, sir." Arthur was torn, trying to decide if he'd done Mateo a favor or not. Discovering the identity of the traitor in the Spartan Guard wouldn't be easy, and the fleet admiral hadn't given Mateo much time.

"I'll share that same information with—"

"No one except Mateo is to know the trinity may be dissolved."

Bloody fuck. This was bad. Members of the Masters' Admiralty agreed to an arranged ménage marriage when they joined. It was the price of membership to a secret society that offered members security, wealth, and power. Because of that, when members were placed in a trinity, they worked hard to begin forming emotional ties as soon as they met their spouses.

Having a trinity dissolved, even if it was only a week later, would mean that people might end up emotionally wounded.

A week after he'd been married to Sophia and James, he'd been in love with them. If someone had tried to take them away, to dissolve the trinity...

Arthur opened his mouth to say he'd changed his mind, that this was a bad idea, but Eric started speaking once more.

"The other two should help him in his search. I want the three of them to remain together until they report to the Isle of Man. Under no circumstances is Mateo allowed to investigate alone."

Arthur didn't like misleading people. He was still, at heart, a knight of England, beholden to ideals of truth and justice.

Too bad that those ideals had no place in the real world, or in his role as admiral.

"Do you understand me, Admiral?" Eric's voice was hard and formal, his Scandinavian accent adding a crisp formality to the words.

"Yes, sir. Is there any—"

Before Arthur could finish his question, the door to his office flew open and his husband, James Rathmann entered the room, limping quickly. Typically, the mountain of a man strolled with an easier, slower gait, as a way to offset his size.

Arthur reached for a sword that wasn't there, with a hand that also wasn't there.

Another casualty of the attack on the admirals.

"James," Arthur barked, heart in his throat. "What's happened? Where is the attack coming from?" He yanked open a drawer in his desk with his left hand, pulling out a gun. He'd been practicing with it. "Is Sophia safe?"

"What? Of course she is. She's at home, fine and dandy. I've got an idea I want you to run by the fleet admiral," James said excitedly.

Arthur dropped the gun on his desk so he could raise his hand and wave it in a desperate signal for James to shut up. After all, the fleet admiral, unbeknownst to his husband, was on the other side of the speakerphone. "James, wait—"

"I've been thinking about the Domino."

In all fairness, that was all he, James and Sophia seemed to think about...when they weren't wrapped around each other in bed. They *were* still newlyweds, after all.

Regardless, Arthur didn't want Eric to know how much he shared with his spouses. The admirals were supposed to be masters of keeping secrets. Now if he could just get his very excitable spouse to not out him...

Arthur started making a slashing motion across his throat, while keeping his voice level. "Why don't we discuss—"

"It was Cecilia who actually came up with the idea," James forged on.

Arthur dropped his chin to his chest. Great. And now the fleet admiral would know that James was discussing the Domino with other people. It was not exactly a sterling example of secrecy and security. "James, please—"

"It's a brilliant idea, Arthur. That cousin of mine is a clever one."

Arthur wasn't sure he'd ever seen James so excited about something that wasn't a coin. Or sex. Newly united in their trinity, it had taken Arthur some time to get used to James' love of old, rusty, decrepit pieces of metal. He and Sophia preferred to spend their evenings together listening as James regaled them with stories about his glory days as a tighthead prop with the New Zealand All Blacks, both of them enthralled by rugby stories over dry tidbits about numismatics. Unfortunately, the coins usually won out as James' topic of choice.

"She's in England?"

James nodded. "She's in the Lake District, helping our family with a few things. She called me this morning after you left the house."

Cecilia St. John, James' cousin, was a member of the territory of Rome. Due to some inter-territory marriages a generation or two ago, James' family tree had roots and branches all over Europe.

The fleet admiral hadn't said anything. Maybe he'd hung up. No, the light was on. Maybe he could get James out of the room before this hole got any deeper. "James, listen—"

James had a full head of steam, and it was clear he wasn't going to stop talking until he'd said what he'd come to say. James had once complained that he didn't have a weapon, to which Arthur had reminded him that he *was* a weapon. Once James got going, either physically or intellectually, stopping him was like stepping in front of a train.

"You remember how I went to Cecilia for help when we were still chasing down the person who killed those three people in Rome?"

Arthur didn't reply, wondering if it would be bad form to disconnect the phone call. He could lie and claim the call dropped. Instead, he started jabbing his finger at the phone, hoping James would see the light indicating a call was active.

Despite Arthur's lack of verbal response, James continued, "As you know, I called Cecilia because of her knowledge of the Masters' Admiralty. That woman's mind is a history book when it comes to the society. Not a rule she can't quote verbatim."

"I really think we should—" Arthur tried once more.

"Well, Cecilia thought as long as the Domino and—let's face it—probably even the apprentice, are still out there, we should form a group of thinkers, of historians and experts in their fields to study the clues to try to capture them once and for all. If we don't outthink him, then the body count will only continue to rise."

Arthur couldn't argue with that assessment. Too many people had already lost their lives to this Domino.

Arthur asked, "What are you talking about? A brain trust?"

James nodded enthusiastically. "Cecilia and I have already come up with the list. Five of us. We think it's important the group remain small. Each name on the list is a foremost scholar, the top of their field, and a member of the Masters' Admiralty."

"Who is on the list?" Eric asked, causing James to jerk back in alarm.

"Bloody hell!" James looked at the phone, and then at Arthur.

Arthur sighed. "The fleet admiral and I were in the middle of a call when you stormed in. Without knocking." He added the last because it had become James' habit of late and something they'd discussed several times before.

"Who is on your list?" Eric repeated his question.

"Well, uh, it would be Cecilia and me. Oh, and hello, Fleet Admiral."

"That's two, who else?"

"Then we wanted to invite Karl Klimek, the anthropologist, Hugo Marchand, who happens to be one of the leading minds of the day in the field of political science, and Nyx Kata, the religious scholar."

James, a renowned numismatist, had a vast knowledge of ancient coinage and modern-day currency. Cecilia St. John was a financial analyst by day, currently living in Singapore, but her knowledge of the history of the Masters' Admiralty was undisputed. It was her information that helped them discover the former fleet admiral was in danger. Unfortunately, it hadn't changed the outcome, as Kacper was killed anyway.

Eric was silent for a moment. "I see. I'd like you to include Josephine O'Connor. She's an accomplished linguist, and I think she'd be a valuable addition to your collective. When and where would you meet?"

"Cecilia thought, given the danger involved, that we should start with monthly meetings. She proposed meeting somewhere in Rome."

"No," Eric said. "You'll meet in the Long Room at Trinity College. After hours."

"Uh, sure. I mean, yes, Fleet Admiral. I'll see if Cecilia knows someone who can get us in there."

"Very good. Arthur, I want you to give James all the information we've gathered on the Domino thus far. And, James, I need you to impress upon your think tank that secrecy is of the utmost importance. Nothing they learn in those meetings can be shared with others outside the group."

James realized he'd perhaps said a bit too much in front of the fleet admiral and made an apologetic face at Arthur before speaking to the phone. "Absolutely, sir. That was one of our first considerations in making the list. None of these people—except for me—are in trinities, so that removes the temptation to share with spouses. Plus, these people can be trusted. I will personally vouch for them. Besides Josephine."

"I will vouch for Josephine," Eric said.

"Right. Of course. This will be—"

Arthur once more made slashing motions, hoping this time James would take the hint and stop talking.

"I'm glad you approve," James finished rather lamely.

There was a pause, then Eric said, "We won't catch the Domino by force alone. The knights and security officers will continue the hunt, but your group, the keepers of knowledge, our…librarians…will work on the history of this adversary, and perhaps even find a motive for the Domino's actions."

James grinned. "I like that name. The librarians. We won't let you down, sir."

Arthur smiled. "It's a good idea, James."

Arthur was pleased the fleet admiral was willing to listen to and accept new ideas from the membership. Their society would flourish under such a man.

Assuming he wasn't assassinated.

The Masters' Admiralty was one of the longest standing and most powerful secret societies in the world. Formed during the Black Plague, the society spanned nine territories—including the whole of Europe, Turkey, Scandinavia, even the westernmost borders of modern-day Russia—and had been instrumental in forming governments, guiding history. They used to control most governments, but now their power was exerted in other ways, financially and politically.

"I have other business to attend to. I look forward to progress reports from the librarians, James. And, Arthur, I trust you will take care of that other matter as soon as possible."

"Of course, sir." Arthur disconnected the call and sank down into his seat.

James was kicked back in the chair across from his desk, his injured leg stretched out while he absentmindedly rubbed his knee. James had suffered what was still referred to as one of the worst injuries in rugby ever, and clips of the break that had left James unable to bend his left knee still circulated on social media outlets and sports programs.

Meanwhile, Arthur ran his left hand over his prosthetic right arm. He was still getting used to it.

"What other matter?" James asked.

Arthur really should learn to hold back from his partners, rather than sharing so much of the day-to-day things that came across his desk. The problem was, the job was still too new and he trusted them, valued their input. More than that, they'd forged a strong partnership working together to catch the Domino, before they were married. That habit was proving difficult to break.

"The fleet admiral is forming his first trinity."

"Really?"

Arthur understood James' surprise. While not unheard of, it was fairly unusual for the fleet admiral to form the alliances—dammit, marriages—leaving that task to the admirals of each territory. Typically, marriages were made between people in the same territory. The only person with the power to bind trinities between territories was the fleet admiral.

Arthur wondered why the fleet admiral had chosen these three. He knew why Mateo had been chosen, but what about the other two?

"He wants me to call this trinity and tell them they're getting married. Then he wants the three of them to travel to the Isle of Man, where he will perform the ceremony."

"Who are the lucky trio?"

"Mateo Bernard, Dimitri Bondar, and Cecilia St. John."

James let out a long whistle. "My cousin Cecilia...and Mateo?"

"And the fleet admiral expects me to inform the admiral of Rome."

James winced. "Make sure you wait to call Giovanni until after I'm gone. That man is still pissed we took his *principessa*. He won't be pleased to find out Cecilia is off the market as well. She's brilliant and very well-connected in the finance world. Giovanni likes that about her."

"Thanks for pointing out the obvious. If I didn't think it would make me look like a coward, I'd ask Sophia to make the call."

James chuckled briefly before sobering up. Arthur recognized his look of confusion. It was the mirror image of his own a few minutes earlier when Eric made the request.

"Why Cecilia and Mateo? And who is that other guy?"

"Dimitri Bondar. He's the wild card. I have no idea who he is."

"Doesn't this marriage mean that Mateo will have to step down as head of the Spartan Guard?"

Arthur nodded slowly. "It does."

He didn't tell James about Mateo's opportunity to save his job. Cecilia was James' cousin, and he wasn't sure his partner wouldn't tell her about the caveat to protect her feelings. Arthur would keep that piece of information a secret, as an admiral should.

Too bad it made him feel vaguely ill to lie to his husband. Perhaps he'd grow used to the feeling.

"Won't Mateo be upset about giving up his position?"

Arthur nodded. "I suspect he'll be very upset."

"Well, while I realize I may be prejudiced, I can't imagine any man would be disappointed to marry my cousin. She's as beautiful as she is intelligent."

Arthur gave James a disbelieving look, one eyebrow raised. "Are you practicing that line so you can deliver it with ease to Mateo? Because I believe the word you used to describe her to me was 'ballbreaker.'"

James chuckled. "How did it sound? Convincing?"

Arthur nodded. "Actually it was. I'll admit I'm looking forward to meeting Cecilia St. John, given the things you've told me about her."

"Well, it sounds like you're going to have the chance very soon." James rose slowly, putting his weight on his good leg, holding the stiff one out at an angle as he did so. "Of course, you have to call our father-in-law first. I'll leave you to that."

"Coward," Arthur muttered.

"I'm headed back to the museum. You mind bringing all that information about the Domino home tonight? Given Cecilia's upcoming nuptials, it sounds like the librarians would be wise to hold their first meeting sooner rather than later."

Arthur nodded, chuckling at the name James had clearly adopted wholeheartedly for his brain trust. "I'll gather it and bring it home. God willing, the six of you can discover something we've missed before anyone else is killed."

"Amen," James said sadly, limping out of the office at a slower pace than he'd walked in.

"Amen," Arthur whispered.

Chapter Two

The Old Library at Trinity College in Dublin made regular appearances on lists of the most impressive libraries in the world and was the permanent home of the Book of Kells. During open hours, it was a hive of activity, filled with tourists from all over the world who came to peer into the glass cases at the famous illuminated manuscript, or to walk through the second-floor Long Room. Velvet ropes kept visitors confined to the center aisle, and aware from the old, rare, and delicate books that filled the two-story shelves. Normally, access to the Long Room was limited to paying visitors and the occasional scholar who had very special permission to access the books.

They'd begun arriving twenty minutes earlier, entering one by one through a side door and making their way up to the Long Room via an old, creaking elevator that was closed to the public. The path they took showed the too-modern, behind-the-scenes parts of the Old Library, including staging and storage areas, heavy concrete and steel that had been used to retrofit the old building, and the cleaning supplies used to keep the place from looking like thousands of tourists tramped through every day.

It was an effective setting for these meetings, as nothing got an intellectual's brain churning more than being surrounded by thousands of delicate, precious books. The fleet admiral and Josephine, the person he'd recommended to be their sixth member, had pulled a few strings in order to use the Long Room for their secret meetings.

There had been promises of dire and painful deaths if they so much as breathed wrong on one of the books.

They were gathered around a narrow scholars' table between two of the stacks. The Long Room also functioned as a museum, featuring rotating exhibits. The current exhibit included large banners bearing replicas of stained-glass panels from a cathedral in Northern Ireland. A banner hung across the entrance to the stacks, further hiding them in the narrow space between. It was intimate, with the window on one side looking out over the well-lit green lawns and pale stone of Trinity College, two-story high bookshelves looming over them like friendly giants, and the stained-glass banner filtering the light that fell over their small assembly.

"Okay. If I could just get everyone's attention, we'll get things rolling." James had to speak up to be heard, despite the fact there were only six of them in the room. He was speaking English, which, along with French, everyone spoke fluently. Still, he should be careful not to use colloquial phrases. He cleared his throat. "We'll begin once everyone is quiet."

It took a minute, but they quieted down. Nothing worse than a bunch of academic types getting together. Everyone was talking at the same time and clamoring to be heard.

"I assume everyone had an opportunity to read over the file I had delivered to you."

They nodded.

James grinned, pleased that every person he'd invited to join this special brain trust had accepted without reservation. They really had pulled together some of the best minds of this generation.

Looking around the room, he noted how diverse the group was. Cecilia was seated next to him, and while he'd joked about her powerhouse personality to Arthur, the truth was, she was his favorite cousin— intelligent, interesting and truly beautiful. Her chestnut hair was cut in an efficient yet stylish shoulder-length style that frame her heart-shaped face nicely. She had expressive, bright blue eyes that could pierce through anyone who came up against her more efficiently than a laser. She was tall—everyone in his family was—and slim. She ran five miles every single morning and practiced yoga.

Beside her sat Karl Klimek from the Germany territory, though he himself was Dutch. He had dark curly hair and wore frameless glasses. The glasses seemed more like a disguise than anything. Karl was heavily muscled and had a stern, serious face. He was an anthropologist, specializing in urban settlement. He was the man governments called when construction and renovation projects turned up an ancient city or unexpected pile of bones.

Nyx Kata, their religious scholar, had pale white-blond hair, shades lighter than her medium-tone skin. Her eyes had an almond shape and tilt, and were a blue so pale they were almost translucent. Her pupils stood out stark and black in contrast. She was lovely, but not in a traditional way. She looked like an artist had taken features from a dozen different cultures and ethnicities and combined them into one unsettlingly beautiful whole. She was one of those people who made you feel stupid when you talked to her, not because she was condescending, but because she was just that intelligent.

Hugo Marchand sat at the other end of the table from James. The man's field of study was political science, which seemed to fit. He had devilish good looks—dark hair with piercing blue eyes, a strong jaw with a dimple in his chin—which would have served him well if he'd chosen to become a politician rather than merely study them. James had caught Cecilia, Josephine and Nyx all giving him sidelong glances when he'd entered, and his cousin had murmured "hello, Superman" under her breath. Hugo seemed entirely unaware of his appeal to members of the opposite sex, not noticing their slight blushes when he'd introduced himself and shook their hands.

Josephine O'Connor had claimed the spot next to Hugo, and while she was sitting, James could hardly call her still. Her hands gestured wildly whenever she spoke, her expressions reflecting every word, every emotion she felt.

"As I told each of you when I issued the invitation, the fleet admiral has entrusted this information to us because he believes it will take much more than brute force to bring the Domino to justice. The Domino is responsible for the deaths of at least four members, two admirals, and the late fleet admiral.

That was a sobering thought, and around the table, the faces of the gathered scholars reflected that grim reality.

"So far, it feels as if he—"

"Or she," Cecilia interjected.

James nodded. They truly didn't know if the Domino was a man or a woman. "True, but for our purposes, Cecilia, I think it would be easier to simply use the pronoun *he* in discussion."

"It would be just as easy to use *she*."

James folded his arms. He loved his cousin to pieces but...she never gave an inch when it came to gender equality. Or anything else she felt passionately about. Normally, him folding his arms made people think twice about pissing him off. Unfortunately, Cecilia was related to him, so the nonverbal threat was less than useless.

"You know, there's been a great deal of discussion about the importance of pronoun usage in the transgender community," Karl added. "Misgendering an individual is viewed as disrespectful to many for whom the male/female binary—if you'll forgive that description—does not work."

"I've read about this." Hugo leaned back in his chair, and James considered the man's confident, easygoing demeanor. He looked too bad boy pretty to be a political scientist. Of course, that was probably the pot calling the kettle black. Not that James considered himself a hot ticket, but it wasn't every day a former New Zealand All Black found his way into a job at the British Museum, studying old coins.

"Isn't the preferred pronoun 'they,' in that situation?" Karl asked.

"Oh, that's just one possibility," Josephine said excitedly, pushing her oversized glasses up on her nose. She was the one member of their merry little band of brainiacs James and Cecilia had never met. He'd been curious about her when the fleet admiral asked that she be included. She was a tiny little sprite with bright, curly red hair and a face full of freckles. Cecilia had spotted her when she'd entered the Long Room and noted under her breath that the woman didn't appear to walk, but instead skip. He'd chuckled quietly at the accurate description. Even now, she was practically dancing in her chair as she continued to speak.

"Linguistically, pronouns have become a hotbed of discussion lately in terms of gender fluidity. *They* is a common one, but there are others like ze, sie, co, and ey that have been used as well. Personally...I prefer ze."

"Oh?" Karl said, clearly curious. "Why is that?"

"The simplest solution would be to switch to a better language," Nyx said quietly. "English is inelegant at best. Perhaps one of the Austronesian languages?"

"Oooo, Tagalog is fun," Josephine chimed in, pushing her glasses up.

James wasn't sure where he'd lost control. Then he remembered—and shot Cecilia a dirty look. She gave him a sheepish grin that said she was enjoying his discomfiture, even as she mouthed the word, "sorry."

"I'm afraid we'll never accomplish anything," James said loudly, continuing to speak over Josephine and Karl, who clearly weren't finished with their discussion. Nyx was staring into space, probably figuring out the meaning of life. They quieted down reluctantly when he continued, "If we don't try to remain on the topic at hand. For our purposes," he gave Cecilia a pointed look, "we will refer to the Domino as *he*."

She shrugged. "Fine. Though *they* may actually work better."

James started to growl, but she raised her hands in a conciliatory manner.

"I'm simply saying history has taught us there is always a Domino—a master-slash-mistress—and an apprentice. This is a two-person operation. *They* are responsible for these killings."

James couldn't fault that observation at all. And since it was on topic, he took the ball and ran with it.

"Exactly. As we know, the Domino has been an enemy of the Masters' Admiralty for centuries."

Everyone nodded, and James was relieved by their easy acceptance. When he'd first mentioned his opinion that the Domino was in play again to Arthur and Sophia, it had taken a lot of effort—and more proof—to convince them.

Cecilia, never one to mince words or waste time, gave a very succinct summary of hundreds of years of terror wrought at the hands of their enemy.

"It's typically one person per generation who takes an apprentice, who in turn becomes the Domino in the next generation. Each Domino has their own signature, which is one reason it's been so difficult to expose and stop them. They leave different calling cards, which are essentially taunts to let us know they've acted. In the early years, half masks were left at the scene of the crime. In the first World War, two black dots were drawn on victims. In the second World War, the actual domino game pieces were left behind—snake eyes, typically. Seven years ago, a black mask was left behind after a bombing in the Ottoman territory."

James added, "And in the case of the killings in Rome, it was the coins."

"None of that makes much sense," Hugo said. "The calling cards appear to change with each new crime, but surely there aren't countless Dominos. Just a master and an apprentice, right? And the apprentice does the master's bidding, rather than acting alone."

"The pieces don't fit together in these more recent crimes," Cecilia confirmed. "This current Domino and apprentice don't stick to the same routine. They're highly organized, but nonlinear, using different methods to keep us guessing, confused."

"We're using the present tense, but I thought the person who killed the fleet admiral, and the one who shot the other admirals, were all dead." That information wasn't exactly secret from the members of the Masters' Admiralty, but there had been details in the file James had sent to everyone. Hugo's point was another good place to start the discussion.

"They are, but—" James was interrupted by Nyx.

"Do you believe in fairy tales, Hugo?"

"What?"

"Fairy tales." Nyx's voice was calm and level, as if her question had been totally normal and not a non-sequitur.

"I know a trap when I see it." Hugo cocked an eyebrow at her.

Cecilia and Josephine made an appreciative noise.

Nyx was as calm and mysterious as a sphinx. "It is a fairy tale to believe that something as complex as this took place, and then, conveniently, all the people responsible died. The Domino killed three people in Rome. From what we know, it appears that was done to put the focus on Rome, and perhaps, given the coins, as a form of greeting or warning.

"The Domino had someone in place to deliver the fatal additive to the fleet admiral. Perhaps that death was also no more than the move of a pawn, in order to gather all the admirals. If the plot hadn't been discovered when it was, would all of the admirals have died?" Nyx looked at each of them in turn. "All that, and we are to believe that the three people who were identified—the drone operator, the sniper, and the fleet admiral's wife—were the only ones responsible?"

Heavy silence descended, and even Josephine was still.

"No," James said quietly. "My husband doesn't believe it. The new fleet admiral doesn't either. They have knights and security agents from all the territories out looking for accomplices. Tracking movements, paper trails. They're handling that side. We're here to come at it from a different way."

"We assume the Domino and their apprentice are still out there." Cecilia's brisk tone helped to dispel the lingering tension. "We assume the others were all pawns, and just didn't know it."

"You know, the word domino comes from the Latin *dominus*." Josephine leaned forward, hair bobbing, and tapped her fingers on the table. "Which means lord or master. In the late seventeenth century, the French adapted it to domino to refer to a hood worn by priests. It's a very interesting word because, with the invention of the game of dominos, it's taken on a vast array of meanings."

"So many, in fact, it's allowed the Domino a way to cover his—or her—tracks for centuries." Cecilia's disdain for the villain was obvious. Thanks to her love of history, she'd immersed herself in the study of the Domino and was more familiar than the rest of them about the true atrocities wrought at the hands of these men—or anarchists, as she'd referred to them from time to time.

"Do we know the source of the Domino's hate of the Masters' Admiralty? What provoked this generations-long assault?" Hugo asked.

Cecilia grinned. "That's why you're here, Nyx. The earliest stories of the Domino indicate he was a priest."

While Cecilia knew the history of the Masters' Admiralty front to back, James suspected Nyx could recite, chapter and verse, every word of every religious scripture ever written for the top five or six world religions.

Nyx sighed. "Religion is both a source of unification and the greatest divisor in human history."

Cecilia gave Nyx a nod, agreeing with her assessment. "Originally, the Masters' Admiralty was formed in Venice in 1347 during the height of the Black Plague. The third member of each trinity was always a priest."

"Why?" Josephine asked.

"To counter the influence of the church," Cecilia replied.

Josephine considered that for a moment. "So where does the Domino come into play?"

"You mentioned the hood, Josephine." Nyx took over the explanation. "It is that clue that led a prior scholar—and I would venture to say we're not the first such collection of scholars to gather and discuss this threat—to connect the original Domino to a priest in seventeenth-century France. He was invited to join, but balked not at a secret marriage, but at the thought of being intimate with another man, should his third be male and not female."

"Poor guy probably missed out on some good times," Josephine joked. James liked her. With so many intellectuals in the room, it was nice to have someone with a sense of humor, someone to keep things real.

"*What has been will be again. What has been done will be done again.* Ecclesiastes 1:9." Nyx's words rang with quiet authority. She would have made an incredible priest or pastor, though looking at her, James got the feeling she might have been a high priestess for some merciless goddess in a past life.

"A man who knew about us, because he'd been offered membership, decided we were, how do you say…perverts?" Karl looked around, and several people, including Nyx, nodded.

Nyx continued, "The presence of a master and an apprentice, and only those two individuals, is what has allowed this ideology to persist. Religion mellows the larger it gets. That is why cults and fundamentalist sects are usually small. There have been other religiously motivated foes in our past, but they have faded, their fanaticism exposed by time. I surmise that the Domino survives because there are only ever two. That's also why the attacks and assaults are sporadic and opportunistic."

"Not this time," James said quietly.

There was a brief silence, each member nodding solemnly as they recalled those horrific attacks.

"According to the file," Hugo began, "the first evidence we have that the Domino was active again started seven years ago, with the bombing in the Ottoman territory. And then nothing until the brutal killings in the cave in Rome? Is that correct?"

"Starting at the beginning is a wise decision." Karl had the file open and was perusing the information. The files had been sent out heavily encrypted, and cyber security within each territory had decrypted the files and then hand-delivered them to the people around the table. They hadn't taken any chances with the security of this information.

"Where was the Domino for seven years?" Josephine asked.

"Planning," Karl and Cecilia said at almost the same time. Karl nodded to Cecilia, offering her the chance to explain, but she waved at him to continue.

Karl adjusted his glasses. "The fleet admiral was being fed one half of a two-part poison. That meant that the Domino was planning this for a long time. And more importantly, it wasn't enough that the fleet admiral died; he wanted to control exactly *when* he died. It would have been much simpler to slowly poison him. Something like arsenic could be given in tiny doses and it would build up in the bloodstream over time."

"Simpler but not precise." Cecilia looked troubled.

Karl nodded. "We must then assume that they were waiting until their plan was in motion—the murders in Rome, then the piecing together of the clues. I think the murders were a warning, as Nyx said, or a greeting. The Domino wanted us to know what was coming. Once James arrived at Triskelion, the mystery of the coins decoded, they killed the fleet admiral. That, in turn, meant the territory admirals would gather to choose a new leader."

"More people would have died if Arthur hadn't figured out what was going on." There was no small amount of pride in James' voice. His husband had thrown himself in front of literal bullets to protect the admirals, and kept the body count from being higher. He'd lost his arm in the process.

"Executing a plan like this takes fortitude, patience." James thought he heard the slightest amount of respect in Nyx's tone.

That was terrifying.

Everyone looked at Nyx for a disconcerting moment, but she simply stared them down.

"She's not wrong," Josephine muttered.

"How does the master find the apprentice?" Hugo asked. "And if we assume that Manon wasn't the Domino," Hugo inclined his head to Nyx, "what if either she or the American sniper was the apprentice?"

"Arthur doesn't believe Manon was the Domino. Or the apprentice."

"And the American sniper?" Hugo asked. "Was he one or the other?"

James shrugged. "Possibly the apprentice?"

"Impossible," Nyx said. "The apprentice will be someone disillusioned and disassociated from society. Someone who feels like an outcast. The master will give them a sense of belonging. The same people who are at risk of joining any sort of religious fanaticism are those at risk of being the apprentice."

"So every possible suicide bomber, al Qaeda member, school shooter, abortion clinic massacre..." James trailed off.

Karl held up a hand. "*That* we cannot know or control. But the Domino has left us clues. Clues only we can read."

All eyes turned to him.

"Each Domino has a signature, as you said earlier. But this time the clues were far subtler. More layered. We focus on that."

"The coins," James agreed, happy to be on a subject he knew and loved. "I put in my notes about those."

"Consider the complexity." Karl leaned forward, eyes bright behind his glasses. "This is the first time the Domino has been so obtuse. It suggests that he thinks himself smarter than us. That he is challenging us to understand him."

Josephine bounced out of her chair, pacing the length of the table on the balls of her feet. She did indeed appear to be skipping. "How can there be so much information in that folder and yet it feels like nothing? We need more."

Cecilia sighed. "We need to work with what we have. Waiting for the next clue could prove to be deadly."

Nyx was the only person who didn't appear frustrated by their lack of substantial leads. "We study the situation as if the master is still alive, since to assume they are not is hubris. We form a hypothesis about the Domino."

"A profile of the perp," Josephine said with relish.

"Assignments," Karl said. "We each work on some aspect of this, as fits our knowledge. When we come back together, we pool our new information."

"Homework," James said. "Good."

Another hour of discussion and they had their respective assignments. James was going to try to trace the rarest of the coins. It was something he'd been planning to do anyway, but with everything else that had happened, he hadn't had time.

Cecilia was going to draw up a concise timeline of the current Domino's actions, drawing parallels to past Dominos to look for connections and similarities.

Nyx was going to look into any online discussions about the Masters' Admiralty. Rather surprisingly for a religious scholar, she was an expert at finding hidden chat rooms and infiltrating otherwise closed online communities. Maybe she'd find a likely recruiting platform.

Hugo planned to speak to Aslan Polat, the Ottoman territory's security minister. He and Aslan had attended university together. They all wanted more information about the bombing.

And Karl was going to search for other possible crimes or action that might be related to the Domino. He was a professor, and so he had a bevy of indentured servants—otherwise known as grad students—whom he could task with searching records both modern and ancient.

"Want me to talk to Eric?" Josephine resumed her seat, though James wouldn't say she was sitting. Bouncing like a two-year-old in church was a better description. "To see if there's any information he has that isn't in those files?"

"Eric?" Cecilia glanced at Josephine curiously. "The new fleet admiral?"

"Of course. James said all this information came from Arthur. Knowing Eric, he's probably got more he didn't want in the file. I'll try to weasel it out of him."

They all stared at her.

"You, uh, know the fleet admiral?" James certainly wasn't going to call their new leader "Eric" to his face.

"Sure." Josephine's casual response made it seem like she thought everyone was comfortable enough to walk into Triskelion Castle and have a beer with the man. "And maybe I can talk to the Archivist."

The way she said "Archivist" made it clear there was a capital letter.

"The who?" Cecilia asked.

Josephine looked perplexed. "The Archivist."

James walked over to Josephine, spun her chair around, and gently took her head in his hands, hoping if he held her still she might make sense. "Josephine. Who is the Archivist?"

"He's in charge of the archive."

James stepped back. "I'm out. One of you try."

"Josephine," Cecilia started. "What archives are you talking about?"

"You know. Our archives. The Masters' Admiralty archives."

Nyx shook her head. "There is no such thing."

"Sure there is. But it's neutral."

There was a beat of silence then Nyx rose smoothly from her chair, walked calmly over to Josephine and leaned down, caging the other woman in by bracing her hands on the sides of the chair. "You will tell me about this archive." Nyx bared her teeth. "Now."

Yikes.

Josephine blinked rapidly. "There...there's an archive. All our membership records, information, some artifacts... But it's neutral. The archive, and the

Archivist, don't belong to any one territory. It's like Vatican City."

"Where?" Nyx purred.

"About five minutes that way." Josephine pointed to the window. "Merrion Square."

"It's here?" Cecilia asked. "In Dublin?"

Karl and Hugo started to get up, clearly ready to go.

"But we can't go there," Josephine said. "The Archivist doesn't let anyone in."

"I'll have Arthur make him let us in," James said.

"You're not listening." Josephine leaned to the side to look around Nyx. "The center of Dublin is neutral territory. The admirals can't tell the Archivist what to do."

"That makes no sense." James couldn't understand the purpose of a Masters' Admiralty archive that members of the society couldn't access. The historian in him was completely baffled by such a concept.

"It's always been that way. Well, no, okay, I mean in the past, the archive was more like a library combined with a bank. Pre-World War I, it was in Brussels. After that, they split it up, and the information, the archive, went to London, and the treasury went to Switzerland."

"There's a treasury?" James wondered if he could shake the information out of Josephine. Nyx looked like she was ready to beat it out of her.

"But then during World War II, they moved the archive to Dublin. It turned out that Ireland was, surprisingly, not really obeying the admiral of England anyway, and they had all this real estate and resources, so they were able to take on the archive."

"How does she know all of this and you don't?" James asked Cecilia.

"Why don't you just pick up a knife and drive it into my heart, James? I honestly had no idea any of this existed. How do *you* know about it, Josephine?"

"Eric and I talked about it once. It's not really a secret. It's just one of those things no one really discusses. The Archivist and the fleet admiral are the only people with access to the information there."

"Of course," Cecilia murmured. "You and *Eric* talked about it." James could tell from her tone she was uncomfortable using the fleet admiral's first name, even in jest.

"I will have the name of the Archivist," Nyx said.

"Um…"

"Tell. Me."

"I guess I could invite him to our next meeting. If you think it's that important."

Karl stared at Josephine. "Should we ask someone with access to secret historical records to join us as we try to find and identify the Domino? Yes, perhaps we should."

"Don't all of you look at me like that." Josephine shoved Nyx out of the way. "The Archivist might not come. He's neutral."

"Even when we need help?"

"*Neutral*," she insisted. "Like, really, philosophically neutral. Like Switzerland. Where the treasury is," she added, clearly trying to lighten the mood in the room.

"Josephine?" Nyx said.

"Yes?"

"Get him here." Nyx was trying to smile, but it looked like she wanted to bite the other woman. "I don't care what depraved sexual favors you have to offer; you make him come."

"Okay, so I'm a bit worried that's where your brain went." Cecilia was leaning away from Nyx. Karl's and

Hugo's expressions were somewhere between horrified and aroused.

Josephine crinkled her nose. "There is such a thing as *too* depraved. Incest is out."

"Incest?"

"The Archivist is my brother."

Nyx was clearly annoyed. "We've been here for hours, while she has access to information that could prove vital."

Josephine still looked confused by Nyx's comments. "I'm not sure we'll find anything there, but I will ask my brother, see if he'll come to the next meeting. He's kind of a pain in the ass, so don't expect much."

"I think this would be a good place to adjourn." James realized things were only going to continue to escalate at this point.

Thirty minutes later, James walked out with Cecilia. They were the last to leave, and made sure the unobtrusive side door locked behind them.

"That was an interesting ending," Cecilia mused.

"I think we certainly got a good feeling for who we're working with. Nyx is a little scary, and Josephine is…I have no idea what she is. Still not quite sure I can wrap my head around it all."

"Me either," Cecilia agreed.

They continued to walk in silence. When they reached the front steps of the chapel, Cecilia's phone pinged. She glanced at the screen. "I just got an email from your husband."

"Oh?" James feigned surprise. He wished Arthur had waited a bit longer before sending his missive.

"He's requested a meeting with me in his office tomorrow morning." She leveled a hard stare. "What's going on?"

James shrugged and lied. "No clue."

There was no way he was dropping the old marriage bomb on her. He already had one bad leg. God only knew how Cecilia would react to the news she was being bound to two men who were not members of the Rome territory. Her life was about to get very interesting. And complicated.

"Mmmhmm." Her response proved she didn't believe him, but mercifully she didn't press for more. "I'll have to go to the airport and see if I can change my ticket to a London flight. I've already checked in for my trip back to Singapore." She looked annoyed, but then shook her head. "It was a good first meeting, James."

He grinned. "Yeah. It was."

"I think we stand an excellent chance at finding the Domino. We're stronger when we work together like this."

"We'll find him—"

Cecilia glared, and he corrected himself.

"We'll find *them*, and then we'll tell the guys with swords and guns and they'll go get *them*."

They walked out the main gate onto College Green, heading down far enough so she could get a taxi headed the right way to take her to the airport. He was planning to stay for a day or so. There were some excellent coins in Dublin Castle he'd gotten permission to see. He'd start his homework there.

"Thanks for suggesting this, Cecilia."

She gave him a quick kiss on the cheek. "Goodbye, cousin."

Stronger together.

James hoped they were strong enough.

Chapter Three

Mateo paced the small hallway outside Arthur's office, his mind whirling over the admiral's phone call earlier.

"You heard him wrong," Mateo muttered to himself. It was the only explanation that made sense. Arthur had told Mateo that Eric, the new fleet admiral, was giving him a task, an opportunity to prove himself and to make up for failing in his duties to protect his predecessor. That part was the answer to Mateo's prayers.

However, Arthur contradicted all of that by announcing Mateo was being bound in his trinity.

Spartan Guards didn't marry until they retired at forty. They couldn't. It was a direct conflict of interest. While in the employ of the fleet admiral, protecting the society's leader was their only duty. Marriage was considered a distraction.

He'd asked Arthur what he meant, but the admiral wouldn't explain, insisting that Mateo meet him at his office to discuss it further.

Mateo couldn't get married. At least…not yet. He was only thirty-two, and his plans for the future, the immediate one, included one thing. To serve the fleet admiral of the Masters' Admiralty as head of the Spartan Guard.

To prove himself. To show the territory admirals and the new fleet admiral that he was worthy.

As a child, he'd dreamed of being a surgeon. Those plans changed the night his parents were brutally murdered and his father, the previously unseen third in their trinity, came to take him home. His narrow vision of the world had changed overnight as he was introduced to the secret society.

His new father taught him about the Masters' Admiralty, opening his eyes to a way to make better use of his talents. Growing up, he'd wanted to save lives, but after the death of Mama and Papa, he felt it was more important to *protect* lives. Stories of the Spartan Guard set his heart aflame as he realized he was destined for a much higher purpose.

He hadn't been able to protect his parents, so he'd dedicated his life to protecting the fleet admiral.

I failed.

Mateo hadn't slept a single night since Kacper Kujakski was brutally murdered, poisoned, right in front of him.

I failed.

Those two words had become his mantra, keeping him focused, determined.

He would not fail again.

"Mateo," Arthur said from the doorway to his office.

Mateo had been so lost in thought he hadn't heard it open. His head still wasn't quite in the game. His reflexes slow, his senses dull. He needed to get back on track if he planned to succeed in bringing the killer to justice. "Yes, sir."

"Please come in." Arthur stepped aside, gesturing for Mateo to enter with his good arm.

"Have a seat," Arthur invited, walking around his desk to claim his own chair.

Mateo would have preferred to stand. Sitting was a weaker position. "Sir—"

"Please, Mateo," Arthur insisted. "Sit down."

Mateo dropped down, using only the front edge of the seat while maintaining an "at attention" pose, the balls of his feet supporting him, allowing him to rise quickly if the situation demanded.

"I know that you have questions about my phone call earlier."

"Yes, sir," Mateo started. "I'm conf—"

"Allow me to offer a more detailed explanation, and then you can ask questions if you still have them."

Mateo nodded.

"The fleet admiral has set up a trinity for you. In fact, the other two will be here shortly, which is why I need to say this quickly."

"Sir, if I marry, I can't—"

Arthur held up his hand. "Please. I will explain. The fleet admiral feels that you were derelict in your duties in protecting the former leader."

Mateo opened his mouth to defend himself, but was silenced by Arthur's short shake of his head.

"I was there, Mateo. No one saw that shot coming. No one *could* have. I understand how you feel. I also saw my admiral murdered. I was there as his knight. I should have protected him. Instead, I was helpless to save him."

Mateo's eyes instinctively drifted to Arthur's prosthetic arm. He may have failed, but it was clear Arthur had been prepared to die in the attempt to save Winston Hammond. In the end, he'd lost his arm *and* his admiral.

"I know you're anxious for a way to prove yourself to the new fleet admiral. I see a lot of myself in you. I spoke up on your behalf, and the fleet admiral has offered you a chance. One chance."

"Anything," Mateo said.

"As you know, the shot that killed the former fleet admiral was just the final piece of a larger puzzle. Someone was slowly poisoning Kacper. Giving him the tainted medicine that led to his death. Additionally, someone allowed the man who operated the drone that delivered the death blow to our former leader on the grounds of the castle."

Mateo had considered this. In fact, it was much of what kept him up at night. "There was a traitor amongst my guards. It's the only explanation. We, the Spartan Guard, were responsible for picking up Kacper's medication, and we control the entrances to the property."

Arthur nodded. "The fleet admiral wants to know who it was so that we can question the man about the Domino. With Manon, the sniper, and the drone operator dead, this traitor is our only chance of knowing for sure if Manon or the sniper was the Domino, and why there's been a change from just one apprentice to two. Or possibly three, if this traitor was also a devotee to the Domino's cause, rather than bribed or blackmailed."

"I'll find him," Mateo vowed, grateful to be assigned the very task he'd intended to request to undertake once returning to the Isle of Man.

"If anyone can, I'm sure it's you. However, there are conditions to this…" Arthur paused as if struggling to find a word. "Reprieve," he finished at last.

"What conditions?"

"You will work with the other two people assigned to your trinity to uncover the traitor."

"I think I would work better, faster, alone, sir."

"That is nonnegotiable."

"Who are—"

"That will be answered in a moment. Fail to deliver the turncoat within one week and the marriage stands. The fleet admiral will bind you in this trinity and you will be relieved from your duties with the Spartan Guard."

"One week?!" Mateo rose, throwing his hands up into the air. If this was the fleet admiral's idea of a reprieve, it was obvious he didn't want Mateo to succeed. "Sir, please."

"There's another condition."

Mateo didn't care if it was a sign of weakness. He was feeling deflated, defeated at the moment. He sank down onto the chair, leaning back, slouched. "What is it?"

"The other members of your trinity cannot know about the time limit or the possibility the union could be dissolved."

"He doesn't think I'll succeed, so he sees no reason to worry them unnecessarily."

Arthur didn't reply. His silence response enough.

"In one week's time, you and your partners will report to the fleet admiral with the traitor's name or to be bound in marriage. Understood?"

Mateo didn't answer for several moments, wondering if there was anything he could say on his behalf to change this command from a superior officer.

In the end, he realized he'd probably been given more leniency than he deserved.

I failed.

"Yes, sir."

Arthur hit some buzzer on his phone and a minute or two later, there was a knock on the office door.

"That will be them."

Arthur rose and opened the door, allowing his vice admiral to enter with two people Mateo had never seen.

"Thank you, Lorelei, for entertaining my guests while I handled my business."

Lorelei gave him a sharp, pointed glare that said she didn't appreciate being used as a babysitter, but she said nothing in return as she left.

Arthur invited the people—a man and a woman—to claim the other two seats across from his desk. The woman was a pretty brunette, tall and slim. Mateo suspected she was about his age, but the way she carried herself made her seem older.

The other man was dressed in dark jeans and a plain black T-shirt, and he carried a duffel bag, which he placed on the floor next to his chair.

The woman looked in his direction. "Cecilia," she said by way of introduction as she sat down.

The other man followed her lead. "Dimitri."

"I'm Mateo."

Once all three of them were seated, Arthur began. "I'm sure you're curious about your presence here. It would seem you have the distinct honor of becoming the first trinity formed by our new fleet admiral."

Mateo glanced at the other two, seeing the same shock he'd had a few minutes to adjust to on Cecilia's face. Dimitri, Mateo noted, seemed to take the news in stride, which sparked his curiosity.

"The fleet admiral created this trinity?" Cecilia asked. Mateo detected a slight accent in her voice, but in truth, it felt like a strange blend of Italian and British, and he got the sense she was fighting against both.

Arthur nodded. "Yes, Cecilia."

"Why?"

Dimitri snorted at her direct question, earning a glare from Cecilia. "You aren't curious?" she asked point-blank.

He shrugged. "Not sure it matters why. Our membership in the society means we give up the choice when it comes to choosing our mates. The fleet admiral is well within his rights to do this. Questioning it won't change it."

Dimitri was easier to figure out, his features and accent betraying his Ukrainian background. He possessed jet-black hair, dark eyes, heavy brows and a strong jawline, and when he spoke, his words resonated from the back of his throat with a slight nasal sound to it. Mateo had taken up the study of accents with his second father, who insisted there was knowledge to be found in knowing where a man came from.

Cecilia was clearly not the type to blindly follow orders. "I'm aware of that, but traditionally, trinities are formed within territories. Neither of you is from Rome, are you?"

Mateo shook his head as Dimitri snorted again, saying, "Mercifully, no."

Dimitri's response did not endear him to their future wife.

Mateo wiped that thought away. He wasn't going to marry these two. He would move heaven and earth to get the traitor's name. He would question the villain, then see that justice was served. After that, Mateo would resume his position of head of the guard. His job was his life, his identity. It was everything. Without it, he was nothing.

Arthur cleared his throat, drawing their attention back to him before Cecilia could give Dimitri an earful. She certainly looked like she was ready to do battle for his slight to her territory.

"The fleet admiral holds his own counsel, so I'm afraid I can't answer your question, Cecilia. My role in this is a small one. I was asked to inform you of the trinity, to introduce you to each other." Arthur paused as if realizing he'd forgotten that part. He pointed at Mateo first. "Normally, a trinity formed by the fleet admiral would be called to the Isle of Man, and you'd hear this directly from him, but these are not normal times."

Arthur stood up, clearly trying to make this announcement feel more formal than just three strangers meeting in an office on Threadneedle Street. "Mateo Bernard from the Castile territory. Cecilia St. John from Rome. And Dimitri Bondar of the Hungary territory. The three of you are to report to the Isle of Man in one week, at which time the fleet admiral will bind you in marriage. In the meantime, he has requested that you take the next week to get to know one another. You are to remain together and not return to your homes. Mateo will fill you in on a task you've been asked to attend to as well during this week."

"Task?" Cecilia looked at Mateo and then back to Arthur. "What's going on here? None of the traditions regarding the forming of trinities are being observed. I realize trinities between different territories aren't unheard of. In fact, they were more the norm than the exception during the second World War, when it was necessary to form allegiances that would keep the world from crumbling under Hitler's regime. However, that is no longer the case. I still don't understand."

"I am simply relaying the fleet admiral's wishes." Arthur's face revealed nothing. Mateo wondered what else the admiral knew.

"How is this supposed to work?" Cecilia looked at Mateo then at Dimitri. "I live and work in Singapore. And you?" she asked Dimitri, a tinge of hostility in her voice. She hadn't forgotten his earlier slight.

"I work in Kiev. Paper pusher for the government."

Mateo was surprised by that answer. Dimitri didn't look like the type of man who'd be happy sitting behind a desk day after day. He wondered exactly what Dimitri did for the government.

Dimitri seemed completely at ease in this office, his casual, relaxed posture giving him the appearance of a man without a care in the world. However, his eyes said something else entirely. They were focused, alert—and for some inexplicable reason, locked on Mateo. During the entire conversation, Mateo had felt the other man's gaze on him, assessing him, sizing him up.

"And you?" Cecilia asked, turning her eyes toward Mateo.

"I'm the head of the Spartan Guard."

His response took Cecilia aback. There was no missing the astonishment on her face. He allowed himself a split second to acknowledge it before glancing in Dimitri's direction. It was his response that interested Mateo most.

Again, the man was unsurprised, unrattled. If Mateo didn't know better, he would believe this man had known every word that was going to be said in his office before he walked through the door. Which was impossible.

"Sounds like you're out of work," Dimitri said drolly.

Mateo narrowed his eyes, filled with the desire to set the man straight. Sadly, he couldn't.

Arthur distracted him before he could speak again.

"What I'm about to tell you is completely confidential. None of you is at liberty to share what is said in this office. Do you understand?"

Peripherally, he saw both Dimitri and Cecilia nod. The admiral had captured their attention. Belatedly, Mateo nodded as well.

"The former fleet admiral was killed. I'm certain you are all aware of that. What is not common knowledge is the means by which he was murdered. There was a traitor among the Spartan Guard. One of the guards tainted Kacper's medication with a chemical that remained dormant, harmless in his system, until the second agent—delivered through a dart—was introduced into his bloodstream as well."

"Clever killer," Dimitri murmured.

Mateo's ire rose at what sounded very much like appreciation in the other man's voice. "You think that's something to be admired?" Mateo asked hotly, resisting the urge to pull the arrogant man out of his chair and teach him a lesson.

"A plan like that would take time and careful execution. Evil or no, this traitor in *your* guard has proven himself a worthy foe. He's calculating and patient."

Mateo hadn't missed the way Dimitri stressed the word *your*. It was an intentional jab. He was too angry to let the insult slide. "And I will find him. The punishment will fit the crime, believe me."

Arthur shook his head. "No. The punishment isn't yours to mete out, Mateo. You are simply to uncover who the traitor is and deliver his name to the fleet admiral. What happens to the man after that is up to our leader."

Mateo swallowed the bile thickening his throat. Someone on his squad had turned against them all, had broken his vow to protect their leader, and had tainted the sanctity of the guard. Mateo couldn't step aside.

Arthur recognized that determination. His eyes narrowed. "Just the name, Mateo." Each word was said slowly, enunciated clearly.

Mateo gave one quick nod, working hard to school his features. That wasn't an order he could obey. He understood their need to question the man, but once that was done, the information acquired, Mateo would finish the job.

"One week isn't very long. What happens if we can't uncover who the traitor is in that time?" Mateo was impressed by Cecilia's intelligence and forthright nature. She would have made an excellent Spartan Guard.

"The binding ceremony will occur and you will be relieved of the task. Someone else will take up the hunt. Discover what you can, Cecilia. Use *all* the resources at your disposal."

Originally, Mateo had thought Cecilia and Arthur strangers, but now he got a sense there was some familiarity between them. That was confirmed when Arthur smiled at her. "It's very nice to finally meet you at last, cousin."

She shared his grin. "I never had the opportunity to congratulate you on your nuptials. I suspect my cousin is keeping you on your toes."

"Cousin?" Mateo asked. "You are related to the *principessa*?"

Cecilia shook her head. "No. Though that's a logical assumption to make, given my membership with the Rome territory. My cousin is James Rathmann."

Dimitri sighed loudly. "And while this is a touching family reunion, perhaps the three of us should be on our way. Bad guys to catch. Honeymooning to do. Right, Cece?"

"Cecilia," she corrected. "And there will be no honeymoon if you continue to use that ridiculous nickname."

The animosity Cecilia sent Dimitri's way seemed to rival Mateo's outright disdain for the man. Finding the traitor had felt like a life-or-death task for him before as he considered losing his position. Now the stakes were even higher. There was no way he could spend the rest of his life in a trinity with this cocky, obnoxious man.

Dimitri took Cecilia's threat in stride, dismissing it without concern as he stood, picked up his duffel, and gestured toward the door. "Shall we, wife?"

Cecilia rose as well, rolling her eyes. "That's even worse."

Mateo followed the two of them to the door, but all three stopped when Arthur called out to them. "Remember. You are to remain together for the next week. I suggest you use that time wisely to..." Arthur paused. Obviously, the admiral had his own strong reservations about the three of them succeeding at anything together. In truth, they'd probably kill each other before they made it to the sidewalk. Finally, he said, "Get to know one another."

Dimitri turned toward Cecilia, intent on placing his hand on her lower back to guide her out of the office. She shrugged off his touch, walking ahead of them quickly.

Dimitri followed with an amused snicker. "She's quite a woman."

Mateo didn't reply as he followed him down the corridor, the three of them walking single file until they reached the street.

Once there, Mateo glanced both ways, then at Dimitri and Cecilia, both of whom were looking at him.

Now what?

Chapter Four

Cecilia glanced around the busy street, not really seeing anything. She was shell-shocked by what had just happened. She wasn't the type of person who could accept anything at face value. Her mother swore her first word wasn't mama or dada, but "why?"

There were reasons for trinities created across territories. Always.

And so there had to be a reason here.

But Cecilia would be damned if she could figure it out.

Mateo was the head of the Spartan Guard, a job he would lose the moment they were bound in marriage. Given the fact the previous fleet admiral was murdered by a traitor in Mateo's guard, it seemed to indicate this marriage was a way to relieve him of his duties. Which meant she was here as part of his punishment.

I'm part of his punishment.

She dismissed that as a reason. The new fleet admiral didn't strike her as the type of man to be that petty. From all the stories she'd heard, Eric Ericsson was a shrewd, calculating, clever man, the type to always see the big picture.

His was an unusual story. Sixteen years earlier, he had been a knight, and in a trinity, when one of his wives was appointed admiral of Kalmar. She served for one year before she was assassinated, and he was forced to become admiral. Not long after, his second wife, a prominent politician, was also murdered. After that, he asked to be excused from the role of admiral after serving one year. Typically, admirals served in their position until death or until they were no longer mentally or physically able to do so. No one was allowed to simply walk away.

Until Eric.

After the brutal murders of his wives, it seemed only fair that he, of anyone, be allowed to step down. However, Masters' Admiralty tradition stated that only an admiral could rise to become fleet admiral. With two territories in chaos after the murders of their admirals, it was decided that to pull one of the admirals who'd survived the attack from their post to be fleet admiral would cause too much upheaval. Which left just one man for the job.

Eric.

She knew that much about him—it wasn't exactly public knowledge, but she collected information like this about their membership. A strange hobby perhaps, but after a day spent looking at numbers and finance, she enjoyed history and human-interest stories.

What she didn't know was where Eric had been, or what he'd been doing, in the fifteen years since his wives' deaths.

"Should we book a room somewhere around here?" Dimitri asked. "I came to the meeting straight from the airport and didn't have time to find a hotel."

Mateo shook his head. "No. We don't have time for that. We need to start searching for the traitor."

Dimitri scowled. "I caught the red-eye to get here. The only place I'm going is to bed. We can start tomorrow."

Mateo's hands clenched into fists and Cecilia decided this continual animosity was going to have to stop. The three of them had been thrown for a loop with the announcement on their trinity and then the assignment of a seemingly impossible task, given the short time frame. She understood Mateo's impatience to begin. He, as head of the guard, would obviously feel guilty for his failure to protect Kacper.

"Where do you want to start, Mateo?" she asked.

"Stranraer."

She tilted her head. "Scotland?"

"Yes."

Dimitri scowled. "Seems to me you'd want to root your traitor out where he lives, on the Isle of Man. Unless, of course, there's a reason you're avoiding the place. Not ready to face the new boss to answer for your actions? Or lack thereof?"

Mateo took a step closer to Dimitri. "If you have a prob—"

Cecilia cut him off before this turned into a proper brawl in the middle of a public street. "Isn't Stranraer where the Spartan Guard's training facility is?"

Mateo nodded, shooting Dimitri a smirk. "Not many people know that."

"The Masters' Admiralty is very good at hiding their secrets in plain sight." Cecilia was still smarting over the news there was an archive in Dublin she'd known nothing about, even though the place wasn't exactly a secret.

"I agree." Mateo went on to explain his reasoning. "Records regarding the guard are stored there in the off-site backup servers. Background information, work details, castle assignments. I need to see who had access to the fleet admiral's medicine. Who was standing guard at the gates the day the man entered the grounds to fly the drone that fired the dart."

"Shouldn't you also ask who on the guard had access to the fleet admiral's daily schedule?" Dimitri asked.

Cecilia was pleased by his astute question and sudden interest in helping. Maybe now he'd stop leveling accusations at Mateo.

Her first impression of Dimitri wasn't good. His arrogance and disinterest in basically everything turned her off. Given his paper-pusher job description, she could only assume he was content to follow the status quo without question or comment—he's certainly taken Arthur's announcement about their trinity in stride—but that was something unusual to find in a member of the Masters' Admiralty. Which meant there had to be something more there. There was nothing worse, in Cecilia's opinion, than a mindless drone, and that felt like the impression Dimitri was trying to project.

"I already know the answer to that. His wife, Greta." Mateo paused. "And me."

"No one else?" Dimitri asked.

Mateo shook his head. "Someone could have hacked into my personal account. Or Greta's."

"They could have." There was no denying Dimitri's tone indicated he didn't believe that.

"That's it." Mateo clenched his fists and took an intimidating step closer to Dimitri—who changed into someone else entirely, right before her eyes.

Dimitri didn't back down. Instead, his casual, almost slouching stance stiffened and he grew broader, stronger, more threatening as he dropped his duffel to the ground. His T-shirt tightened as previously unnoticed muscles bunched.

"Come at me. I dare you." Dimitri had done an excellent job concealing his true strength. The man worked out. Hard.

She glanced at Mateo, who wasn't backing down either and was a mirror image for Dimitri in beefy biceps. In certain places—namely, her bed—that would be hot. Right now, it was fucking terrifying.

Both men looked intent on doing the other serious bodily harm and they were completely capable of it.

What a wonderful way to start their lives together. With suspicion and bloodshed.

She stepped between them. Accustomed to typically being one of the tallest people in the room at five foot eleven, she was surprised to find herself looking up at both her future husbands. Regardless, she wasn't about to let their sizes intimidate her.

After a lifetime spent in the presence of Italian men, Cecilia should have a higher tolerance for this sort of alpha male chest beating. She didn't. It was one of the reasons she'd jumped at the career opportunity in Singapore. She'd been with them a total of twenty minutes and she'd already had enough of their macho posturing to last her a lifetime.

"We're not doing this here," she said through gritted teeth.

"Doing what, sweet Cece?"

"Get out of the way, Cecilia," Mateo said. "I'm not going to stand here and be accused of being a traitor."

Cecilia stood her ground. "I've rented a car." She pointed to a silver Renault Kadjar parked several cars away on the other side of the street. "We're going to get into it, grab your suitcase from wherever it is, Mateo, then stop by my hotel to gather my things. Then we're driving to the Lake District."

"No. I told you—"

"You want to go to Stranraer. I know." She pulled her cell out and opened her GPS map. Just as she suspected...Stranraer was a fair distance. "My family owns a B and B in the Lake District, which is about five hours from here. You can sleep in the back of the car, Dimitri, while we drive there. Tomorrow morning," she consulted the map on her phone once more, "we get up early and travel the rest of the way to Stranraer. Should only take us another couple of hours and we'll all be well rested and refreshed."

Mateo looked as if he wanted to finish what Dimitri had started, but Dimitri backed off, bending over to retrieve his duffel. "As you wish, wife."

He walked toward the car, not bothering to see if she and Mateo followed.

"We don't have a lot of time," Mateo stressed. Then he looked over his shoulder at Dimitri. "And that man..."

She nodded. "I understand. Truly. We'll find the traitor who betrayed the fleet admiral and the guard. But you heard the English admiral. We have to do it as a team. There's a lovely little private kitchen in the B and B. We'll grab some bread and cheese and a bottle of wine for dinner. It'll give us tonight to talk and get to know each other. We're about to embark on a lifetime together. This is no way to start."

Mateo studied her face for a moment, and she got a sense there was something else he wanted to say. Whatever it was, he must've reconsidered because, like Dimitri, he too started walking toward the car.

They stopped at Mateo's and Cecilia's hotels to grab their bags and then they were on their way.

Dimitri had remarked he was tired, and while he'd claimed the backseat as she suggested, he didn't close his eyes to rest.

"You're from the Castile territory?" Cecilia asked Mateo, fighting like crazy to figure out how three people living on separate corners of Europe—and Asia, in her case—could make a marriage.

"I have not been home in many years. The Isle of Man is my home now."

"Was," Dimitri murmured.

Mateo shot him a dirty look over his shoulder. It was clear Mateo was unhappy about giving up his position with the Spartan Guard.

"Have you considered what you will do after you leave the guard?" she asked, thinking perhaps he had skills that would allow him to live somewhere closer to her. She didn't relish the idea of a long-distance marriage.

"No. I have not," Mateo confessed. "I'm only thirty-two. I expected to have another eight years with the guard."

Dimitri leaned forward. "How old are you, Cece?"

She sighed, annoyed by his insistence on using that silly nickname. "Thirty-six, Dim."

Mateo snickered at her appropriately shortened version of his name.

"How about you?" she asked, looking over her shoulder. Dimitri was grinning at her joke. He winked at her as he said, "I'm thirty-eight."

"What do you do in the Ukrainian government?"

He shrugged off her question. "Told you. Logistics."

She waited for him to follow up with more details. He didn't.

Cecilia let her eyes drift to the scenery while seeing nothing, her mind racing over everything. This trinity felt like a mistake. The three of them were a complete mismatch, none of the pieces connecting.

Then Dimitri decided to take the lead on twenty questions. "What do you do for a living, Cece?"

"I work for a multinational import/export company in Singapore."

Dimitri leaned back, trying to stretch his long legs—an impossible feat, given the size of her rental car. "Sounds boring."

"*Stronzo,*" she said, miffed about the way he'd evaded her question. "I thought it sounded like a real answer, no?"

Mateo glanced at her, drawing her attention to his kind smile. She'd just given him a lecture about the three of them trying to overcome this…God, this constant antagonistic way of communicating they'd formed. Now she had fallen into the same bad habit.

She decided once more to offer an olive branch. "It's probably not the most fascinating job on the planet, which is why I tend to focus on my hobbies more."

"What hobbies?" Mateo asked.

She started to answer, then threw Dimitri a grin over her shoulder. "He'll no doubt think this is boring as well. I'm a historian. Spend a lot of time reading and researching the Masters' Admiralty."

Dimitri ran his hand over the stubble on his jaw. He was an attractive man—both of them were—though not in the traditional way. She noticed Dimitri's hands were rough, covered with calluses and scars that didn't indicate he spent much time behind a desk. There was a long, thin white scar just below his right ear that she'd only noticed a few moments ago when he turned to look out the window. She was dying to ask him how he got it, but knew he'd merely give her another nonanswer.

"So impress us," Dimitri dared her. "Tell us something interesting about the society."

At least fifty things popped into her head at once—she really did find the history of the Masters' Admiralty fascinating—but she decided to feel out her future husbands about their knowledge of Domino lore. After all, Arthur had looked at her point-blank in his office earlier and told her to use everything at her disposal to help Mateo. He'd invited her to pull the librarians in to help find this traitor.

"The most interesting—as well as horrifying—is the history of the Domino."

She paused, wanting to catch their reactions.

"That is who killed the fleet admiral," Mateo said. "I was there when we captured her."

"Her?" Dimitri asked with more interest than he'd revealed at the announcement of his future trinity. "The Domino is a her and she's been captured?"

"Manon. The former fleet admiral's wife. And she's dead. Shot by her lover."

"Didn't she have access to her husband's daily schedule?" Dimitri leaned forward once more.

Mateo shook his head. "She hadn't lived at Triskelion Castle for quite some time. She was…unhappy there."

"What do you mean she was shot by her lover?"

"An American sniper, who killed himself after Manon. She was trying to bring the Masters' Admiralty down. She very nearly succeeded."

"And we're searching for this traitor to tie up loose ends?" Dimitri asked.

Mateo nodded, clearly convinced that was his mission. After the meeting in Dublin, Cecilia was sure that Manon had *not* been the Domino, but she was sworn to secrecy about the details surrounding the villain through her involvement with the librarians.

So…in addition to animosity, her trinity was also standing on a foundation built on deceit.

Lovely.

Cecilia turned her attention back to the passing hillsides, suddenly sorry she'd mentioned the Domino.

"I'm an inspector for the water reclamation department." Dimitri's comment seemed to come out of the blue, drawing their attention to him. "That's what I do for the government."

It wasn't a lot, but it felt like he was finally opening the door—just a crack—to let them in.

She smiled at him as she said, "Sounds boring."

He chuckled and the car fell silent, each of them lost in their private thoughts.

It took them nearly six hours to get to the Lake District from London. Mateo drove, since, of the three of them, he had the most experience with driving on the left-hand side of the road. The plan had been to take the M1 as far north as Standford Hill, then cut across on the M6 and head north through Liverpool, following the western coast. An accident near Birmingham had traffic backed up, so they took the slightly longer route, staying on the M1 and heading straight through the midlands, passing Leeds, curving west through the Dales.

Her family's property included a beautiful country house on the banks of Ullswater Lake. Once they crossed into Lake District National Park, their speed slowed considerably in concession to the narrow, twisting roads and the tourists clogging the roadways—hikers with walking sticks, families laden down with beach chairs, and other motorists driving slowly so they could enjoy the views.

It was impossible not to notice the natural beauty, and every time life got too stressful, she recalled this place and longed to give it all up and live a simple life here. The Lake District was a soft, rolling landscape of hills and long, narrow lakes. Some of the hillsides were covered by thick forest, others were rocky, the terrain unmarred except for well-worn walking trails.

Ullswater House was perched on the hillside, and the two-story country home was a bright, cheery white against the deep green around it. A sloped, manicured drive spread out in front of it, giving way to wild brush and small trees fifty feet from the edge of the terrace. There was another twenty feet between the edge of the lawn and the shore of the lake. There was a short dock with two kayaks dry-docked in a covered shed near the water.

They glimpsed all that as they drove along the small, winding lane that paralleled the long edge of the lake.

Cecilia put a hand on Mateo's arm, pointing to a driveway on their right. The drive was bracketed by curved stone walls. A painted sign hung from a fluted iron bar.

Ullswater House
Self-catering B and B

"People can rent the whole place and use it for parties. I think there have been some small weddings. The rest of the time, it's a B and B. None of the rooms were booked for tonight, so I've secured the entire place just for us," Cecilia explained as Mateo turned into the drive. Halfway down, there was an iron gate. The gate wasn't tall—she could have stepped over it—but it prevented the car from continuing on.

She hopped out and ran around to the code box. Checking the message on her phone, she keyed in the code and the gates swung open.

"When was the last time you were here?" Dimitri asked.

"I was still in school. When my great-grandfather turned eighty, there was a massive party. Family from all over came."

"All members?"

"Yes. When there are three people in each marriage, families get big fast. That was when James and I got close."

They parked in the circular drive. Trees loomed around the drive, shielding the house from view from the road, though they could hear the leisurely traffic going by. The front door, on the opposite side of the house from the water, wasn't particularly grand. An electronic keypad on the door opened when she put in yet another code.

She opened the door and sunlight spilled out. From the front door, she could see straight through to the back of the house and the panoramic windows there. The floor of the central hall was black and white tile. The walls were painted a pale mint green and the stairs on the right-hand side of the hall were made of pale ash. To the right was a small office, used by the caretaker, the door bearing a sign that said "Staff Only."

"There are six bedrooms upstairs," she said. "Down here there's a kitchen, two parlors, and a sunroom that runs the length of the house. Four of the bedrooms have views of the lake."

"You don't have to play tour guide." Dimitri walked past her, following the black and white flooring to the back of the house. He paused, leaning in doors to check out the kitchen and parlors.

Mateo headed upstairs with his suitcase.

She stood uncertainly for a moment, then followed Dimitri.

He was standing in the long sunroom. Glass double doors linked each of the parlors to the sunroom and let the light fill almost the entire house.

"Lot of windows."

She looked at all the glass. "It's lovely."

He shook his head, then opened the glass French doors, letting the cool breeze washing up from the water flow into the house. Her hair stirred around her face, and when she brushed it away from her eyes, she found Dimitri looking at her.

"He doesn't like me." His grin said he couldn't care less what Mateo thought of him.

"You aren't going out of your way to endear yourself to him."

Dimitri shrugged. "I've never felt the need to be anyone other than who I am."

"I'm not suggesting you pretend to be someone else. But it might help if you stopped accusing him of being a failure."

"I haven't made that accusation."

"You've implied it clearly enough."

They both jumped at the sound of Mateo's voice from the doorway. Cecilia hadn't heard him descend the stairs. Something in Dimitri's face told her he had...and he'd spoken anyway.

"Innocent until proven guilty, Dimitri," Cecilia said softly, hoping her words would penetrate.

"Not in the Ukraine. And not in the Masters' Admiralty."

Mateo stepped into the room, glaring. "If you have a problem with me, now would be a good time to put it all out there on the table. I did not betray the fleet admiral, nor would I ever. And I don't need you to tell me I failed in my duties. I'm aware of that, which is why I am determined to bring the traitor to justice. I won't rest until I do so."

"Or until the week runs out," Dimitri reminded Mateo of the time limit.

"Even after that."

"Well, I suppose you'll have plenty of time, considering you'll be out of work."

Cecilia closed her eyes and attempted to count to ten. She'd reached her limit with this continual game of cat and mouse. Dimitri was being purposely contrary, trying to provoke Mateo, but she couldn't understand why.

Time to change the rules.

"It's clear we can't bridge the gaps between us with words," Cecilia pointed out. "Perhaps it's time to stop trying to do so."

Dimitri's eyes narrowed. "The fleet admiral won't change his mind simply because we're not getting along. We will be expected to marry and live as a trinity."

"We've been instructed to discover the traitor in the guard. I don't intend to disobey that order," Mateo insisted.

Neither of them understood her. It would be much easier if they spoke Italian, but they didn't. So she put it in plain English. "Nor do I. We entered the Masters' Admiralty with the knowledge our partners were not ours to choose. I'm not suggesting we walk away."

"Then what *are* you suggesting?" Mateo asked.

She gave them a sultry smile as she glanced toward the stairs that led to the largest bedroom in the inn. "Sex."

Chapter Five

Dimitri was a master when it came to schooling his features, hiding his emotions. In his line of work, expressions could be as deadly as words. He'd lied to his future spouses about his line of work using semantics.

He did work for the Ukrainian government, but not in the water department. It was more accurate to say he was part of their defense department. He didn't sit behind a desk, pushing papers, as he'd led Cecilia and Mateo to believe.

The truth was…he was a spy.

Recruited out of the military, he became a part of the SBU, the security service of the Ukraine, working as a shadow within the organization to weed out corruption in the Alpha Force. Finding bad guys was his specialty and, while Cecilia may be struggling to determine the reason behind this unorthodox trinity, he understood his mission perfectly.

There was a traitor to the society and Dimitri would find him. And no man, future husband or not, was above suspicion.

"You're joking," Mateo whispered in response to Cecilia's shocking proposition.

"I never joke about sex." She pointed toward the stairs. "The room at the end of the corridor is the largest, the one they use as a honeymoon suite. I think it will suit our purposes best."

Cecilia didn't wait for them to respond. Instead, she started for the stairs. He and Mateo remained in the room for a full minute after she disappeared upstairs.

While having sex with Cecilia would be no hardship—the woman was seriously beautiful—Dimitri wasn't as keen to have Mateo in the bedroom with them.

It wasn't that he had issues with threesome sex, or even sex with just a man. In his line of work, he'd engaged in both in order to discover information.

His hesitance was based on the man, not the act. He didn't trust Mateo, which meant he'd be sleeping with one eye open.

Then he recalled Cecilia's proposition and grinned. They wouldn't be sleeping. "We shouldn't keep our wife waiting."

"We're not married," Mateo pointed out.

He shrugged. "That's never stopped me in the past." Dimitri walked upstairs, Mateo following.

They entered the bedroom together. Cecilia was standing next to the bed, and it was clear she'd been waiting to see if they would take her up on her offer. She smiled, and Dimitri tried not to acknowledge that her happy look had his stomach twisting, his heart beating a bit too hard.

Dimitri didn't fall in love. Never had, never would.

So he would chalk up this unfamiliar response to a woman's smile to lust.

"Take off your clothes," Cecilia commanded, her fingers already undoing the buttons on her own blouse.

Dimitri shook his head as he crossed the room to her, grasping her hands. "No. That's not how this is going to work."

"What do you mean?" she asked, confused.

"I don't follow orders in the bedroom, Cece."

She laughed lightly, though he wasn't sure what she found amusing. Then she reached up and patted his cheek condescendingly. "Oh, Dim. What a pity. Neither do I."

Her words provoked a grin. Cecilia said she never joked about sex, something he understood. For him, it was a means to an end. He had needs, and he found women who would fulfill them...*his* way. Cecilia wouldn't be so easily commanded, and yet, he was looking forward to this more than he cared to admit.

Cecilia tried to escape his grip, so he tightened it.

Mateo stepped next to them, watching their tug-of-war. "Are you certain you want to do this, Cecilia?"

She stopped trying to break free and looked at Mateo. "Yes. I am."

"But we've only just met." Mateo was clearly operating under the assumption all women wanted soft lighting, romance and sweet words rather than sex.

"I suspect none of us are virgins, Mateo. We're facing a lifetime together, and I have no intention of spending it refereeing your pissing contests. If we can't speak civilly enough to get to know each other, perhaps sex will help break the ice, no?"

Mateo frowned.

"Have you been in love with every woman you've taken to your bed?" she asked, taking another tact.

He shook his head.

"Then what's the problem?"

Rather than respond, Mateo reached for the hem of his T-shirt, pulling it over his head in one fluid motion. Cecilia's mouth opened in obvious appreciation.

Dimitri knew he could compete, so that didn't give him pause. What caught him off guard was his own physical attraction to the other man.

Mateo was the stereotypical Spaniard, tall and lean with a stylish haircut that was longer on top and a short, trimmed beard, both dark brown. His high cheekbones drew attention to his black, piercing eyes. Like Dimitri, Mateo obviously appreciated the need to stay in shape for his job. Dimitri imagined the two of them shared similar workout routines.

Despite his earlier hesitance, Mateo showed no reluctance in joining them in bed, evidenced by the erection tenting the front of his gray jeans.

Cecilia attempted to pull free of his grip again, and this time, Dimitri let her. Rather than resume disrobing, she reached over to run her hand down the center of Mateo's bare chest.

"Very nice," she murmured.

Mateo snickered, amused by her obvious ogling. He flexed, tightening his pecs, provoking another "ooo" from Cecilia, his quick wink proving he was making a joke. Dimitri grinned, surprised to discover Mateo had a sense of humor. It had been absent until that moment.

She ran her fingers along his stomach and back up again, stroking his nipples, watching them tighten. Then she turned to Dimitri, her raised eyebrows daring him to take off his shirt as well.

There was no denying she was used to running the show. More the pity for her.

Rather than take off his own shirt, he began to unbutton her blouse. Cecilia didn't put up a fuss or attempt to stop him. Her raised chin proved her confidence wasn't feigned. She knew her worth and wouldn't hide. It made her even more attractive to him.

Once her blouse was open, he slid it off her shoulders. Mateo had stepped behind her and made short work of the hooks on her bra. Between the two of them, they had her topless in seconds.

Dimitri couldn't resist touching her full, firm tits. Using his thumb and forefinger, he pinched her nipple, giving it enough of a squeeze to capture her attention, to cause her to gasp.

She narrowed her eyes briefly at the unexpected twinge of pain, but her flushed cheeks and heavy-lidded eyes told him what he needed to know.

He pinched the other nipple, harder. Mateo stepped closer to her, his chest against her back, letting Cecilia know he was there, ready to protect her. The dark look he gave Dimitri was one of warning.

So they weren't in this together.

That wouldn't work.

Regardless of his feelings for the man, they couldn't bring their disdain for each other into this room, or they risked hurting Cecilia.

Time to recruit Mateo to the cause.

Dimitri slipped down the zipper on Cecilia's skirt. This time, she did protest.

"Your shirt," she insisted.

He ignored her request, pushing her hands away. When they returned once more to stop him, he lifted his gaze to Mateo. "Hold her hands behind her back."

Mateo hesitated, then—to Dimitri's surprise—reached for Cecilia's wrists, clasping them together at the base of her spine.

She flashed Mateo a glare—one of anger, but of arousal, as well. Mateo recognized the look and retained his grip, his attention returning to Dimitri.

"Get on with it," Mateo muttered.

That was when Dimitri realized all three of them were alphas. Cecilia hoped that sex would do the job their words wouldn't, but that seemed highly unlikely, given their dominant personalities.

He tugged her skirt and panties down, delighted when she kicked them—and her shoes—off without further complaint. She was naked, her hands held behind her back in such a way that thrust her breasts forward.

Dimitri bent and sucked one of her turgid nipples into his mouth, tightening the suction until she moaned.

Mateo held her secure with one hand, the free one wrapping around her to toy with the other breast, plumping the flesh, squeezing it firmly.

Cecilia threw her head back, resting it on Mateo's shoulder as they played with her tits. She pressed her legs together, her hips twisting slightly, betraying her arousal.

Dimitri needed more. Kneeling in front of her, he glanced up, waiting until he had her attention.

"Open your legs."

"Take off your clothes." Cecilia wasn't finished trying to get her way.

He gave her a devilish grin, then bit her upper thigh. She tried to pull away from his teeth, the action opening her legs enough that he could place his hands between.

Without preamble, he thrust two fingers inside her soaked pussy. The juices of her arousal allowed him to slide in too easily, so he added a third, wanting her to feel his presence there.

Her hips jerked toward him, an invitation to move. He didn't take it, simply filling her with motionless fingers.

Instead, he took her clit between his teeth, nipping at the sensitive flesh. Dimitri wouldn't give her anything she wanted until she begged.

Cecilia attempted to take matters into her own hands, pushing down on his fingers.

"Hold her still," Dimitri demanded.

Mateo released her breast, using one arm in a vise-like grip around her waist while the other kept her wrists restrained.

Mateo's immediate action took Dimitri aback. It was as if his future husband knew exactly what Dimitri wanted and how to achieve it.

Mateo wasn't obeying him—Dimitri was as certain of that as he was of his name—but then why the instant response?

The answer hit him like a kick to the stomach.

Because Mateo wanted the same thing.

Wanted their woman gasping, out of her mind, begging.

Cecilia's struggles increased. "Take off your clothes. Both of you! Fuck me. *Now.*"

Mateo's chuckle confirmed Dimitri's suspicions, then his words solidified it.

"You're going to have to ask us much nicer than that, *mi cielito.*"

Cecilia stilled for a moment. "Mateo." Her tone was softer, but not yet submissive. If anything, Dimitri could almost see the wheels turning in her beautiful brain, trying to determine how she could get what she wanted without having to ask nicely.

Dimitri decided to add fuel to the flames, taking her clit back into his mouth and sucking hard. Her inner muscles clenched against his fingers, causing him to acknowledge his own discomfort. His jeans weren't particularly tight, but damn if they weren't causing him pain right now. His dick was rock-hard and aching, constricted by the pants.

A quick glance at the tight lines around Mateo's mouth told him he was suffering as well.

"Move your fingers. Fuck me with them."

The more Cecilia demanded, the easier—and harder—it was for Dimitri to refuse. He held them still.

"I'm murdering both of you the second you fall asleep," she threatened.

Mateo laughed. "And here I thought Dimitri was the one I needed to worry about."

Dimitri chuckled, his hot breath tickling Cecilia, who gasped.

"I...God..." she cried. "I think I'm coming."

Dimitri withdrew his fingers, shaking his head with a "tsk."

Cecilia trembled with unslackened need, first in pain and then in full-blown anger. "What are you doing?" Her question was too breathless to pack enough heat.

Dimitri rose from the floor. "Ask nicely."

She snarled, an honest-to-God snarl, that might have been frightening if it didn't turn him on so much. Dimitri reached out and grasped a handful of hair, tightening his fist around her soft tresses and tugging it hard enough that she had to look up into his face.

He expected her capitulation. After all, she was obviously hurting. What he didn't anticipate was the sudden self-satisfied gleam in her eyes. He narrowed his gaze and studied her face in confusion before his eyes shifted to Mateo's.

The other man's pained expression caught him off guard. Then he noticed Mateo was moving, rocking his hips back and forth against Cecilia's ass.

Glancing down, Dimitri realized Cecilia had freed the other man from his jeans and was currently stroking his erection with the same hands he was holding in place behind her back.

She wiggled her ass toward Mateo's dick, and he swallowed loudly.

"Ask nicely, *tesoro*," she whispered to Mateo. "And I'll let you fuck me while Dimitri watches, alone with his hand."

She was a wicked enchantress, and it didn't take a genius to figure out that Mateo was going to give in. After all, it was a way to get what he wanted and make Dimitri suffer.

Cecilia had claimed to want this moment to pull them together, but when faced with not getting her way, she had no issue pitting them against each other.

She was incredible. An enigma. A powerhouse.

Dimitri grinned. "Touché, *koxaha*," he said, adding his own Ukrainian term of endearment to the mix. He'd called her his love, not that she would know that. There were so many words he could have used, yet only that one felt right to him.

"I suggest a truce before we kill each other," Mateo said through gritted teeth.

"No truce." Dimitri had never given in, and he wouldn't start now. However, his actions belied his words as he shrugged off his shirt and shed his pants and shoes.

Cecilia watched him with avid interest, even as she continued to give Mateo a hand job behind her back. Mateo had given up his grip on her wrists, wrapping his arms around her torso so that he could take both of her breasts into his large hands.

Dimitri stroked his hard cock as her eyes devoured him. Cecilia's appetites matched his...and Mateo's. Dragging them to the bedroom had been a spark of genius on her part.

He reached out, running his fingers along her slit. She was still drenched, her pussy so hot, steam should rise from it. He captured Mateo's gaze.

"Tighten your grip. Hold her up."

Mateo followed his direction, though his confusion showed he couldn't read Dimitri's intent. Until Dimitri reached down and lifted her legs, her weight suddenly dependent on the two men holding her.

He dragged her lower body to his.

"Birth control?"

She nodded, and he shifted her into position, driving his cock to the hilt in one hard thrust.

Her legs wrapped around his waist as Mateo kept a strong hold on her upper body, his chest on her back, pressing her upright, sandwiched between them, until her hands could grip Dimitri's shoulders for added support.

Dimitri shifted his hands to her upper thighs, holding her tight to him, his dick fully encased in her tight sheath.

"Need some help?" Mateo asked, even as Dimitri felt the other man's hands on Cecilia's ass.

Mateo lifted her with ease, allowing her to slide up and nearly off Dimitri's cock, before pushing her back down.

Dimitri and Cecilia grunted in unison as Mateo added his strength to theirs, lifting and pushing, lifting and pushing.

It was the hottest fuck of Dimitri's life.

Cecilia was the first to go over, her pussy clenching him so tightly, he saw stars. That was when instinct took hold. Dimitri twisted, walking with her to the bed, following her down to the mattress as he fucked her like a man possessed.

He wasn't sure where Mateo was, but Dimitri didn't care. All that mattered was her. Taking her, claiming her, leaving his mark on her.

She came again, and he was with her, filling her with his come, murmuring more of the sweet words he'd never spoken before. Fortunately, his native tongue took over, the uncensored vows of caring for her, treasuring her as a wife should be, flowing easily in Ukrainian, allowing him to say things he would never utter in a language she understood.

He withdrew slowly, both of them shuddering with the last vestiges of sensation. Dimitri hadn't kissed her yet. None of them had kissed.

Even as he thought that, he moved aside, suddenly aware of Mateo once more. Cecilia slowly sat up, her gaze resting on Mateo, who had shed his pants.

Dimitri was spent, his strength gone. If either of his future partners were sincere in their desire to do him bodily harm, they'd face little resistance.

Or at least he believed that until Mateo circled his finger. "Roll over, *mi cielito*. Put that sexy ass of yours into the air for me. After all that teasing, I want you from behind."

Dimitri pushed himself up, sitting next to Cecilia as she flipped to her stomach, then slowly rose up on her knees. She came up on her hands as well, but Dimitri had found a like-minded lover in Mateo. He understood what the man wanted.

Placing his hand on the back of her head, he applied pressure until she lowered it to the mattress. "Like this," he murmured in her ear.

Mateo ran his hands over her bare ass, the gentle touch provoking a shiver from their lovely lady. Despite what looked like a painful erection, Mateo seemed to be in no hurry to move them beyond this soft exploration.

Then he lifted one hand and slapped her ass, the quick, hard smack leaving a pink mark.

Cecilia tried to rise but Dimitri's hand was still in her hair, and he held her down.

"That was for the teasing." Mateo moved closer, using his hand to drag his cock along her slit. "And this is for us."

Mateo slid inside easily. She was slick with her arousal and Dimitri's come.

They were strangers. And yet, Dimitri was moved by the power of this sight. Of Mateo taking Cecilia.

He was here because he was commanded to be. He hadn't expected to want to be as well.

Mateo was a more patient lover than he was, taking his time, moving slowly. Cecilia seemed to appreciate both approaches, given her soft sighs and sexy squeaks whenever Mateo hit the right spot.

Dimitri wasn't happy with merely observing, so he ran his hand over Cecilia's ass, the back of his fingers rubbing against Mateo's stomach…and lower.

Mateo's gaze slid his direction, but he didn't look bothered. He was curious. And interested. The recognition of that fact jarred Dimitri, reminding him of his need to maintain emotional distance.

His entire life was built on role-playing, sliding into different skin to achieve his goals, to catch the bad guys.

He'd forgotten to do that tonight. Stood too close to the flames. Risked the burn.

Time to withdraw.

Dimitri removed his hand, shifting away to rest his back against the headboard and watch. Retreat was the wisest course of action. This alliance was created to trap a traitor. There was no room for sentiment.

Mateo studied him for a moment longer, his unshielded look of hunger turning to confusion before morphing back to the one he'd flashed at Dimitri all day. Disdain.

Mateo's attention returned to Cecilia, to driving their lover to the brink and beyond again.

Dimitri waited for his racing heart to calm, blaming their hard fucking for the painful pounding in his chest. It didn't subside as Mateo thrust faster, deeper, Cecilia's cries growing louder.

Even as the two of them came together, Dimitri's heart thudded. And that was when he realized, for the first time in his life, he was in over his head.

Chapter Six

"Are you a legacy?" Cecilia asked Mateo as he drove down A75, headed to Stranraer.

After last night, the nonstop tightness in Mateo's shoulders seemed to have evaporated. Weeks on edge, chomping at the bit to get back to the Isle of Man, had taken their toll on him.

With one word, Cecilia had taken all of the anxiety and fears away.

Sex.

His head was still reeling over her suggestion. What was more shocking was the fact that he and Dimitri went along with it…and it worked.

"I am," Mateo replied. "Though I didn't know about the Masters' Admiralty until I was sixteen."

Cecilia gave him a dubious look that he observed from the rearview mirror. For the last few hours of the journey, she'd taken the backseat to allow Dimitri more room to stretch out his long legs. "You never questioned the fact you had three parents before then?"

He drew in a deep breath. He rarely spoke of his parents—only sharing the details of his family's history with his best friend in the Spartan Guard, Derrick

Frederick. Until confiding in Derrick, Mateo hadn't told anyone about his parents' murders and the life-changing revelations that had followed—discovering he had a new father, learning about the Masters' Admiralty.

Mateo wasn't sure he was comfortable talking about it now. Not because of Cecilia. He had a feeling there was nothing he wouldn't tell her over the next week. She was open and interesting and kind. In a lot of ways, she reminded him of his beloved, much-missed mother.

Cecilia was the type of woman he'd share his secrets with, open up his soul to, if he were actually married to her. The fact that once he found the traitor, this trinity would be dissolved…

He shied away from that thought.

Cecilia was the type of woman he could trust, but Dimitri had him hesitating.

He didn't trust the man, despite all that had happened between them last night. For one thing, Dimitri considered him a failure, blamed him for the fleet admiral's death.

And…well…he sensed the man was holding back from them, that he had his own secrets.

"I grew up with my mama and papa. I wasn't aware of my second father until I was sixteen." They passed the turnoff for Castle Kennedy—the gardens on their right and the village to the left. It wasn't far now.

Peripherally, he could see Dimitri studying his face curiously. "Was there a reason they hid the fact you had another father from you?"

Mateo nodded slowly. Very few people knew the truth of his rather prestigious lineage. "My mama and papa were renowned doctors, specialists in their fields. My mother was the world's foremost neurosurgeon."

"Was?" Cecilia asked, leaning forward.

Mateo sighed. "She was died when I was sixteen. She and my papa both died."

Cecilia crossed herself, murmuring a quiet prayer in Italian. "I'm so sorry."

Dimitri remained quiet, but Mateo could see the other man's interest, imagined he was refraining from asking the countless questions his comment had raised.

"After they were gone, my other father came to me. Took me into his home and raised me. He taught me about the Masters' Admiralty...and the Spartan Guard."

Mateo realized he was leaving out a very large part of the story, but there were secrets about his past he'd never shared. Only Kacper and Greta had known the truth about who his second father was, and they'd respected his desire to keep it hidden. Mateo wanted his achievements to be based on his abilities and work ethic, rather than his auspicious ties.

So he took the conversation in a different direction. "Up until I learned about the society, I'd dreamed of becoming a surgeon like Mama and Papa. When my second father told me about the Masters' Admiralty and the fleet admiral, that goal changed, and I dreamed of becoming a Spartan Guard, of protecting our leader, our society."

Cecilia smiled. "It's nice that you managed to achieve your dream. I assure you, working in import and export wasn't what I pictured for myself as a young girl growing up in Milan."

"What did you want to be?" Mateo asked, his curiosity growing when he glanced in the rearview mirror and realized she was blushing.

"A ballerina. I started dance lessons when I was four and continued through school. Unfortunately, my dream became less achievable when I hit a growth spurt at fourteen. Suddenly, I was the tallest in my troupe, amongst the girls *and* the boys. It became difficult for them to balance me during the lifts."

"You should have joined a troupe with taller boys." Cecilia laughed at Dimitri's suggestion. "Yes. Perhaps I should have."

"You are a legacy as well, yes?" Mateo asked Cecilia, recalling her comment about being cousins with James.

She nodded. "*Si.* Raised by my mother, next door to my," she finger-quoted, "aunt and uncle. We all knew the truth of their relationship, of course, but for appearance's sake in our hometown, they maintained a different family dynamic. What about you, Dimitri?"

He didn't look at either of them as he said, "I was not a legacy. I was recruited out of the military."

Mateo debated questioning him further. So far, Dimitri had been very elusive about his background, offering them only tiny pieces without ever filling in the blanks.

"Which branch?" Cecilia asked, clearly unwilling to continue to wait for Dimitri to share more.

Their woman was impatient. Mateo grinned— before pushing that thought away. With this mission, he was actively working to ensure Cecilia and Dimitri would not be his. Allowing himself to get close to them would only make it harder when they discovered the traitor and Mateo held the fleet admiral to his promise to reinstate him to his position as head of the guard.

"*Spetsnaz.*"

Mateo's brows rose. "Special forces." He didn't bother to hide the impressed tone in his voice.

Dimitri nodded, continuing to look outside.

The man had shut down again, had been distant all morning.

No. Mateo recalled Dimitri pulling away last night when they touched. He had been stroking Cecilia's ass, but his fingers had brushed against Mateo as well. The touch, combined with the way Dimitri had looked at him, had inflamed him, made him even harder.

Mateo had never been with another man, but in that moment, as he looked at Dimitri, there had been no denying his desire.

His guard lowered, Mateo had revealed too much. And Dimitri had retreated, pulled away.

While last night had been wonderful, there was no doubt that they couldn't let it happen again. These two people were not meant to be his. His destiny lay with the guard.

And with that, the tension was back, Mateo's shoulders and neck stiff with a new anxiety lying beside the previous worry. He no longer sought to merely find the traitor. Now, he also had to resist these two people until they succeeded in their task and could walk away from each other.

Apparently, he wasn't the only one to sense the return of the heaviness that seemed to blanket them. Cecilia leaned back, her gaze turning to the scenery outside.

Dimitri was silent as well, clearly willing both of them to keep their questions regarding his past and his life to themselves.

Stranraer sat at the bottom of Loch Ryan, which was actually connected to the Irish Sea, creating a long, narrow bay that cut down into the western coast of Scotland. Once prosperous, the small port was no longer as important as it had been. Just up the road from the village of Stranraer was the ferry post, where large ships moved people, cars, and cargo across the Irish Sea to Belfast.

Stranraer wasn't big, but it wasn't so small that every stranger was noticed. That meant members of the Spartan Guard could hop on a small shipping boat, head north out of Loch Ryan with all the other ocean traffic, and then make a U-turn and go south to the Isle of Man.

Mateo stayed on the main road as it went through the village, changing from what was commonly called the "London Road" to a narrow high street. Cecilia craned her neck as she looked around. The buildings huddled close to the street, remnants of a time when the roads had been plenty wide enough for two horse-drawn carts to pass, but once they were widened to allow cars, the front doors opened up practically into the road.

Houses, businesses and pubs were painted white or gray with a smattering of bright pastels in their midst. A pink B and B with a black door looked almost aggressively cheerful.

Feeling a bit like a tour guide, Mateo pointed to a pub as they passed it. It had a small front garden that had been walled off and optimistically turned into a beer garden, though the weather rarely made drinking outside a good prospect.

"That's where we used to come and drink." He pointed to the Custom House pub with one hand, keeping the other on the wheel. "It gets some tourists, so it was a good place to blend in."

"Last stop before Ireland." Cecilia read the slogan that had been painted onto the low retaining wall around the beer garden in front.

Mateo nodded. "The ferries that leave from here go to Belfast. Lots of families take their cars on the ferry, and some stop here in Stranraer before either getting on the ferry or before heading off into Scotland for their holidays."

On the far side of Stranraer, the high street once more became a fairly respectable two-lane road, but the wear was evident in the crumbling shoulder and salt- and time-worn surface.

The landscape was windswept and devoid of trees. Structures were stone with small windows to help weather the storms that blew in from Ireland. Five minutes outside the town of Stranraer, they reached the corner of a stone wall that paralleled the road going one way and, going the other, marched up a small rise to crest a hill before continuing on down the other side to the rocky beach.

Mateo was unaware of his white-knuckled grip until Dimitri spoke. "You're tense. Why?"

Mateo flexed his fingers on the wheel and ignored the question. "We're here. The wall surrounds Craigencross Farm."

"Farm?" Cecilia asked.

"It's been owned by the Masters' Admiralty for a hundred years or more, but originally it was a working farm. That was part of how it was hidden. Plus, that kept them self-sufficient in the early days."

There was a break in the wall, and Mateo turned right, stopping in front of the gates. He pulled on the parking brake and hopped out, flipping up the protective plastic covering that was supposed to keep the metal from rusting, and dialed in the code. The gates swung out—a security measure that meant it would be hard for a car to ram them to force them open—as he jumped back into the driver's seat.

"It would have been simpler to give me the code and let me get out." Dimitri didn't hide the challenge in his words.

"But then you would have the code."

"You don't trust me."

"I don't know you. You're not Spartan Guard."

"Stop." Cecilia gestured as she spoke, seeming more Italian when she did so. "It is not the time for this."

When the gates were fully open, Mateo put the car in gear. He drove slowly, knowing that the camera mounted on the wall would have a visual of the front seats—showing that he'd brought at least one stranger to Craigencross.

He knew what should be happening. When a car pulled up to the gate, an alarm went off. The guard assigned to check the cameras would run for the control room, and if it was a delivery or a known visitor, they would let them in.

Mateo had cut past that by entering the code. That meant the guard looking at the monitors was probably alerting the others. The watch commander would join him and they'd assess the situation.

From the gate, the grounds were a wide, windblown expanse of seagrass covering a small rise. On the left of the drive was a weathered-stone grain barn. On the right were stables that had been turned into garages for vehicles since the salt air wasn't kind on cars.

They crested the hill. From here, there was a panoramic view of the sea—gray, wind-ruffled water, a sky that was also gray but a dozen shades lighter, a brighter patch marking the sun's position beyond the obscuring cloud cover.

In the middle of that view sat Craigencross House. Mateo smiled despite himself. It wasn't exactly home, but it was a place he knew well. A place where he'd been happy and fulfilled.

A breath later, the tension slammed down on him again, heavy as a lead shirt. He wasn't here to talk to the reserves or train new recruits. He was here to find a traitor.

Craigencross House was huge—only one story tall in deference to the location, but long. There were evenly spaced windows and two identical front doors, each a third of a way along the building. The drive swung wide to the right before curving sharply to parallel the front of the building before looping back, creating a large oval. The center of the drive was wild and overgrown with bushes and seagrass. Another security measure. There were cameras hidden in there, as well as a mechanical spike-strip launcher that could be shot out, destroying the tires of a fleeing vehicle. He'd wanted a remote-controlled automatic weapon of some sort, but the salty sea air made that problematic.

Mateo parked in front of the first door. "Stay in the car."

He climbed out, pocketing the key fob as he did so. He kept his face up so the camera above the door would get a clear look at him, and made sure his expression was calm.

That calm cracked slightly when he heard the car doors open and close behind him, then the crunch of gravel under Dimitri's and Cecilia's shoes.

He turned, not bothering to hide his annoyance.

Dimitri didn't crack a smile. "Last night should have proven to you that none of us excels at following orders."

Before he could reply, one of the front doors swung open.

"Sir." Roshanak Geertje was short and compact, radiating the sort of power that spoke of a martial artist. That's exactly what she was, and she taught Tae Kwon Do in nearby Leswalt once a week.

"Roshanak," Mateo said in greeting. He stepped forward and she moved out of the way. When Dimitri and Cecilia moved to follow, Roshanak stepped into the doorway.

It was rare to bring people not associated with the Spartan Guard to the training facility. Roshanak glanced his way, frowning. Knowing her, she was wondering if this action was part of the training and she was questioning the proper protocol.

"Who are you and why are you here?" she asked in accented English. Roshanak was the reserve guard from Ottoman.

Cecilia looked over Roshanak—Cecilia was at least a head taller—and raised both eyebrows at Mateo. Dimitri was staring at Roshanak, and Mateo got the strangest sense that he was assessing her as a threat.

"We're his—" Cecilia started to speak, but Mateo cut her off.

"They're here with me, to help me investigate."

Roshanak turned her head slightly, not actually taking her gaze off Cecilia and Dimitri. "Yes, sir. If I may ask, sir, investigate?"

He didn't want to tell one person at a time. He didn't want to scare the reserve guards. Not that they needed protection—they were all more than capable— but even the most stalwart of guards would react strongly to learning there was a traitor in their midst.

"Let them in. Tell watch command I want to speak to all of you. In the gym, in ten minutes."

Roshanak seemed to consider his command. That was a good thing. The guards were not mindless soldiers who followed orders blindly. It was one of the reasons each guard was from a different territory, and the head of the Spartan Guard was elected. There was an equality among them, a sense of autonomy that made sure each guard assessed every situation and threat individually.

And yet there was a traitor.

If she'd been a member of the active guard and not a reserve, Roshanak might not have obeyed. As it was, she hesitated long enough that he knew she was seriously considering her best course of action, and then she swung the door wide, letting Cecilia and Dimitri enter.

Rather than walk away, Roshanak plucked a phone from her pocket and tapped the screen a few times.

"I'm going to put them in the parlor." Mateo motioned for his trinity to follow him. The small foyer let out onto a long hall that ran the length of the building. Identical solid wood doors lined each side at irregular intervals.

Dimitri grunted in what sounded like approval.

Mateo led them two doors to the left, and into a small parlor. There weren't any public rooms in Craigencross House, but this one was rarely used, and because of that, there was nothing of interest. A small, old TV sat in the corner. Mismatched armchairs were gathered around a cold fireplace and three rolled rugs were propped in another corner. A desk sat under the narrow window that had a less than inspiring view of the driveway.

"Very welcoming," Cecilia said coldly.

Mateo shot her a glance.

"You're not telling them we're your trinity," she accused.

Mateo made sure no emotion showed on his face. He wouldn't tell the reserve guard because if he did that, they'd know he was leaving the guard. He had no intention of doing that, so he wouldn't tell the reserves.

Just as he wouldn't tell Cecilia and Dimitri that if he found the traitor, he was leaving the trinity.

"Stay here. I have to talk to the, uh, guards who are here." He stumbled over the words, not wanting to say "the reserves."

Dimitri stepped in front of the door, preventing his exit. "Why are the guards here and not at Triskelion Castle? That might be why the fleet admiral died. If you have them here and not with him."

Mateo ground his teeth, stepping around Dimitri. He was in no mood to resume this game, listening as Dimitri criticized everything he did.

"I'm guessing these are the reserve guards." Cecilia sounded nonchalant. "There's always eighteen guards. Two from each territory. Nine of them are on the Isle of Man, and the rest, the reserves or junior members, are here, at the training facility."

Mateo swiveled on his heel. "How do you know that?"

Cecilia flicked her fingers in the air. "It is not a secret. It's just not well-known. I told you I like our history. It's my hobby."

Dimitri smirked at Mateo but spoke to Cecilia. "What else do you know about the guard?"

"Just the basic things. The ages of the guards are twenty-five to forty. At forty, they age out and are placed in trinities. I heard once that the guard trains for six weeks with Russian special forces in Siberia. Is that true?"

"Russia," Dimitri muttered, the sound of the word clearly tasting bad on his lips.

Mateo fought the urge to leap across the room to slap a hand over her mouth. Or maybe kiss her to shut her up. She was right, the structure of the Spartan Guard wasn't exactly a secret, but it wasn't common knowledge either. The admirals of each territory knew the details, since they were responsible for nominating individuals to join the guard. The actual selection of new members was left to the fleet admiral and the head of the guard.

Him.

It was very possible he'd helped select someone who was a traitor and a murderer.

"Stay here," he muttered. "I have to go talk to my people." Mateo walked to the door, and just as he was closing it behind him, he heard Cecilia say, "Aren't *we* your people now?"

Mierda.

He closed the door on his trinity.

Chapter Seven

Dimitri counted to two hundred in Mandarin. He didn't know the language well, so having to concentrate on the task kept him focused and calm. While he slouched against the wall and counted, Cecilia paced around the room, touching the weathered pictures of the Irish Sea and various ships and boats that hung on the walls.

When he reached two hundred, Dimitri straightened. "We're going."

Cecilia's brows rose, and she put a hand on her hip. "Going where?"

"To look around. Come."

"We should wait here for Mateo."

Dimitri snorted. "You don't want to wait. But if you want to pretend to be the obedient wife…"

Cecilia bared her teeth, and when Dimitri opened the door, she was right behind him.

Dobre. He didn't want to leave her alone, for her own safety, though he wouldn't tell her that.

He didn't expect to get far; with strangers in their house, the guard would be tense, but it was also possible that everyone in residence would be focused on whatever lies Mateo was telling them. He had no doubt Mateo was lying, if only about who he and Cecilia were.

The long hallway of doors presented many opportunities for discovery, and just as many opportunities to walk in on the assembled guard—and Mateo—who wouldn't take kindly to their failure to wait like sheep.

Dimitri started with the door across the hall. It opened to reveal a large, comfortable sitting room, with a huge TV mounted on one wall. Three narrow windows offered a view of the sea and a small dock. A sweatshirt was draped over a chair by the door, and a half-empty cup of tea sat on a low table. He closed the door.

The next door revealed a small bedroom, almost like a monk's cell, with a single bed, chest of drawers and sink. There were night clothes draped over the footboard, and a scattering of personal items on top of the dresser.

"Oops," Cecilia said as he closed the door. "Maybe we shouldn't do this."

"Why?" Dimitri opened the next door.

"Because they live here. If someone walked into my house and—"

She stopped speaking as she caught sight of what was in the next room.

The floors and walls were white tile, giving it an almost institutional feel. It was about the same size as the sitting room, and the wall closest to the door had a long counter that ran all the way to the lone window. The others had been bricked over to protect the massive server towers.

Dimitri smirked at Cecilia, who rolled her eyes then pushed past him into the room.

"Mateo said we had to come here to check the records." She stopped in the aisle between the counter—which had four computer terminals—and the black server towers.

Dimitri closed the door behind him. "This looks like a good place to start."

Cecilia hesitated for only a moment before pulling a stool out from under the counter and seating herself at one of the computers.

Dimitri slipped behind the first row of servers, examining them.

The closed-in windows had been fitted with fans and filtration systems that pumped in cool air while filtering out any salt or particulates. It was a good setup.

The door slammed open.

There was a barrage of angry Castilian. Dimitri leaned back to look around the end of one row to see Mateo, chest heaving, yelling at Cecilia in his native tongue.

Her eyes narrowed and she rose, oh so slowly, from her stool. She took a deep breath then cursed him out in Italian, complete with a rude hand gesture or two. Dimitri backpedaled so he could take in the show. He knew bits of both Castilian and Italian, but not enough to keep up with two pissed-off native speakers.

Mateo must have caught sight of him, because he whirled, pointing at Dimitri and biting off a few words. Cecilia grabbed Mateo's face, his lips squishing up like a fish's, and forced him to look at her while she continued to hiss at him.

Dimitri laughed.

They both stopped and turned on him with predatory malice.

Dimitri propped his shoulder against one of the vertical server supports. "You both make good points. But perhaps we should do what we've come here to do.

I assume these servers are part of a closed system linked with whatever is on the Isle of Man?"

Mateo scowled and it was obvious he didn't want to answer.

Dimitri merely held his gaze.

Finally, he gave him a short, angry nod.

"How do we get in?"

"I should do this alone."

"No." Dimitri went and sat down at the computer beside Cecilia's. "The fleet admiral himself said we're meant to help you."

Mateo leaned over, his shoulder hitting Dimitri's chest, and typed in a password. The screen clicked on. He turned and did the same for Cecilia.

"I'm trusting you with the safety of my guard," Mateo said quietly. "We keep everything in here— personnel files, medical history, work logs, incident reports..." Mateo's mouth was pinched, a line between his brows.

Dimitri turned to his computer. He felt for the other man, but he had a job to do. "We'll start with the day the fleet admiral was killed."

An hour later, Cecilia looked up from the document she was scanning online, made a note on the pad of paper Mateo had brought her, and then swiveled in her chair. "Mateo, it says in your file that you were elected as head three years ago."

"That's correct," Mateo said. "The head is elected by all other members, including the nine reserve members. Each person gets one vote."

"I always assumed the fleet admiral selected the head of the guard."

Mateo smiled at her. "I'm surprised you didn't know that. You seem to know everything else about the Spartan Guard."

Cecilia shot Mateo a dirty look, but it held no nastiness. Dimitri was amused by their banter, though confused by the relevance of this information.

"Was there some point to this line of conversation, Cece?"

He'd noticed this morning she had stopped giving him hell for the nickname. Dimitri was starting to think she liked it.

Glancing back at the computer, she pointed to whatever it was that had caught her attention. "It says that you were elected head of the guard in a two-man race against Derrick Frederick."

"So?" Mateo asked.

"Was Derrick angry that you won?"

Mateo chuckled. "No. Derrick is my best friend. He didn't even want to win."

"Then why would he run?"

"It looked better that way. It's good to have an actual election."

"What is required to run?" Dimitri asked.

"Anyone is eligible, though usually the reserve officers don't run. Why would they?"

Dimitri frowned. "Why did only you and this Derrick run?"

Mateo shook his head. "We're concentrating on the wrong thing. Cecilia, get out of my file. We need to focus."

Cecilia made another rude gesture at Mateo, but put her hand on her mouse and started clicking. She flipped to a different page on her notepad. "There were six guards on duty when Kacper was shot. So they're the suspects."

"Not necessarily," Dimitri said.

Mateo talked over the top of him. "Yes. We caught the drone operator, but the timing of the shot was too precise. Someone had to be feeding the operator information. Had to tell him when Kacper was out on the balcony. The windows in the castle are all bulletproof glass."

"And that was the first day Kacper had ever sat out there?" Dimitri asked.

Mateo shook his head impatiently. "No. He wasn't well and the fresh air helped him."

"If it was a habit, a predictable habit, then why are you so sure it was someone who was on the balcony with him?"

"I told you already. The timing."

Dimitri raised his eyebrows. "And what if—"

"Enough, Dimitri." Mateo's jaw muscles flexed. "I know each of the guards. Someone I trust betrayed me! Betrayed the Masters' Admiralty."

Dimitri looked at Mateo and his stomach knotted with tension. Mateo was dismissing anything that didn't agree with his personal narrative of what had happened.

Cecilia flipped a page. "There were three people who regularly did errands, which included picking up the fleet admiral's prescriptions. You, Nikolas, and Marie."

Mateo rubbed his forehead. "Three times a week, one guard was assigned to go to the market, pharmacy, and laundry."

"You don't do your own laundry?" Dimitri asked.

"You do?" Cecilia's voice was mockingly shocked.

Dimitri smirked at her. "Of course, I do. *You* don't, do you?"

"Of course not, I'm far too bourgeoisie." Cecilia tossed her hair.

Mateo ignored them. "The volume of laundry is high. Clothes, linens. We use the same service the hotels in Douglas use."

"And only one of you ever went on the errands?"

Mateo's jaw muscle twitched. "Sometimes other guards not on duty would ride in, so they could do their own errands."

"They'd be in the car with you and with whatever you picked up. Including the medicine."

"*Mierda*," Mateo snarled. "Yes."

Cecilia checked her screen. "I only see one person listed as going to do the errands."

Mateo looked like he was about to curse again, then snapped his teeth together, eyes flicking side to side as he thought. "Exit logs. Anytime someone enters or exits the compound, there's a log. We can match up the times the driver left with the exit logs to see if anyone went with them. There are cameras too. We can check the cameras to confirm who was in the car."

Cecilia flipped to a fresh sheet of paper. "How do we access that?"

"I'll find it and read you the names."

Dimitri leaned back just enough to see Mateo's screen, watching what he did. Quietly, he mirrored Mateo's navigation and opened up the log for himself. As Mateo cross-referenced, Dimitri followed along, making sure Mateo didn't leave anyone out.

It took nearly another hour to go through the log, and then cross reference each entry with the camera stills that were recorded every time a gate opened.

Cecilia's paper was a mess of names and lines. She ripped the sheet off, then carefully transcribed it into a tidy list.

She read over it. "Here is what we know. The people who went into town were you, Nikolas, and Marie, who were supposed to go. Almost every other guard went with you at one point over the course of the six months prior to Kacper's death, but the people who went the most were Derrick and Charlotta. We know he'd been given the tainted medicine for a year. Perhaps we should go farther back."

"Charlotta," Mateo said quietly, his attention captured by that name. "She's from Kalmar."

Cecilia's brows rose. "Like the new fleet admiral."

Silence, heavy with what hadn't been said, hung in the air.

Dimitri put his elbow on the counter, bumping it against the corner of his screen, which angled it slightly away from Cecilia and Mateo. He straightened and rubbed his elbow as if it had been an accident. "You're implying that Charlotta and Eric conspired to kill the former fleet admiral so Eric would be made fleet admiral."

Cecilia frowned. "If that was true, they would have had to plan to kill the other admirals, and know how the admirals would vote..." She paused, then shook her head. "That's a lot of unknown factors."

"And one hell of a conspiracy theory," Dimitri muttered.

Mateo didn't look at them as he said, "I don't know Charlotta as well as I know some of the others. She was a reserve member until last year, when Staffan turned forty and retired from the guard to get married."

"She's only been serving on the Isle of Man for a year?" Dimitri clicked open Charlotta's file and Derrick's. He scanned both as the other two debated the likelihood of a conspiracy.

"Derrick Frederick." Dimitri spoke loud enough to draw Cecilia and Mateo's attention. "He graduated from the University of Oxford with a degree in political science. He passed his A-levels in history and chemistry."

Dimitri waited for their reaction.

"Chemistry?" Cecilia asked. "Maybe he was altering the pills himself. We were assuming whoever it was had to be picking up the altered pills and switching them in transit, but what if—"

Mateo crossed his arms. "It's not Derrick."

"How can you be so sure?" Cecilia asked. "You said the traitor had to be on the balcony when Kacper was shot, but Charlotta wasn't."

Mateo shook his head. "Maybe I was wrong. Maybe they didn't have to be there."

"You said before they must have been." Dimitri kept his voice mild.

"Perhaps I was wrong." Mateo bit off each word. "Derrick wouldn't do this. He's a legacy. He's loyal to the Masters' Admiralty."

"And the other guards aren't?"

"Trust me, it's not Derrick. He was in the room with me when we hunted down Manon. If he'd been a part of this, he wouldn't have helped us as much as he did."

Dimitri rubbed his jaw, rough with stubble. He hadn't taken the time to shave this morning, which meant he'd be sporting a full beard by bedtime. "Describe what happened in the room the night Manon was killed."

Mateo took them through the events, describing who was in the hotel room and where. Derrick had helped Mateo bind Manon to a chair with zip ties, then he'd been the one to bind the sniper's hands behind his back.

"What do you know about the sniper?" Dimitri asked.

"Griffin Rutherford, an American. He was the one who killed the territory admirals." Mateo then told them about Manon's raving, how she bragged about being the Domino. "And then Griffin broke free and grabbed the gun, shooting—"

"Wait," Dimitri interrupted. "What do you mean he broke free?"

"He broke the ties," Mateo said.

"How?"

Mateo slammed his hand down on the table, clearly tired of the fifth degree. "He lifted his arms and pulled hard."

"Who secured Griffin in place?"

Mateo bared his teeth. "I told you. Derrick. But there are ways to snap the ties. You could position them so the catch is against a hard surface or..." Mateo sighed. "It's difficult, but possible. We underestimated him, which was a mistake."

"And then?" Dimitri prompted. "After he was free?"

"Griffin grabbed Derrick's gun, shooting Manon and then himself."

Dimitri pushed up, then casually stretched, using that movement to cover that he was preparing himself.

"If it wasn't Derrick, then the next most logical suspect is—"

"Charlotta," Mateo said.

"—you," Dimitri finished.

Mateo stiffened. "Me. You think I did this." It wasn't precisely a question.

"I'm saying that you were the one who semi-regularly picked up the prescription and delivered it to the fleet admiral's private residence. You were on the balcony. You have access and control."

"It wasn't me," Mateo snarled.

Cecilia rose. "We know it wasn't. But Mateo...I think whoever *did* do it, whoever this traitor is, they're trying to frame you."

After that, things got very awkward. They gathered their notes, shut down the computers and left Craigencross House without encountering anyone else. Dimitri wasn't sure what story Mateo had told the guard, but after that meeting, they were left alone.

They got three rooms in the pink B&B they'd passed when they drove into Stranraer. It was midweek, so the place was practically empty, the innkeeper informing them there was only one other room occupied for the evening as he handed Mateo the keys.

They grabbed dinner at the Custom House, the meal a quiet affair. Cecilia made several attempts at conversation, but neither he nor Dimitri bothered to add much, so eventually she stopped trying.

The tension of the day had continued to grow until they'd reached the boiling point. Again.

"It's clear we've hit yet another impasse," Cecilia remarked as they entered the inn. The foyer was small, simply decorated, containing a check-in desk that was unmanned at this hour of night. Mateo reached into his pocket, intent on handing each of them a room key. He was surprised when Cecilia took all three from him.

"Come on."

"Where are we going?" Mateo asked as Dimitri stood by the front door, his arms crossed, his mood dark, angry.

"To my bedroom."

Mateo clearly wanted to refuse, but Cecilia didn't give either of them a chance to respond before turning on her heel and heading upstairs with all the keys.

As they'd done last night, neither Mateo nor Dimitri moved. Dimitri had been the first to follow Cecilia the previous evening, but now…he couldn't. His legs wouldn't move as he searched for a way out. He looked over his shoulder and considered sleeping in the car.

Mateo must have read his intent. "Dimitri."

"This is a mistake," Dimitri said at last.

Mateo nodded as he sighed. "It is." Then he walked to the foot of the stairs, turning before climbing the first one. "Are you coming?"

Chapter Eight

Cecilia sat on the edge of the bed, gripping her knees tightly as a way of hiding the fact they were trembling. She wanted to chalk up the shaking to anger—hers was currently off the charts—but the practical side of her knew it was nerves.

Last night had been the most intense, most incredible night of her life. She'd been placed in a trinity with two men. She'd taken that as a bonus, understanding that there was very little that sex couldn't cure for the male species.

Cecilia enjoyed sex. She always had. More than that, she'd learned very early on that it could be used as a…well, for lack of a better term, weapon.

She was perfectly aware of other people's perceptions of her. Her mother had often admired her confidence, while trying to temper her arrogance with advice like sometimes it's better to be kind than right, words of wisdom Cecilia could never quite wrap her head around.

And her work colleagues called her The Barracuda behind her back, none of them realizing she not only knew about the nickname, but that she loved it. It meant she was smart and powerful, submissive to no one.

Until Mateo and Dimitri.

Last night, she had actually wanted to hand the reins to them, wanted to hand herself over into their very capable hands and follow their lead. She'd fought hard against the temptation because that wasn't a position she ever put herself in. She always claimed the higher ground, making certain things moved according to her will.

To do otherwise would make her vulnerable.

Neither man appeared, so she stood up. They would come. They had no choice. She had their room keys.

If they wanted to fight her about what was going to happen, she was prepared to go to battle, because she hadn't been wrong to suggest sex last night. She hadn't imagined the closeness between them. It may have been brief, but it had been there. All of them had peeked out from behind their walls for a moment, and it had been glorious.

Until they learned to work together, to open up and come together as a true trinity—in every sense of the word—they would have to steal those moments of closeness in bed.

Sex.

For them, right now, it created a loosely tied knot. It wasn't enough, but she'd take it.

Cecilia took off her clothes, stripping down until she was naked. The last piece of clothing had hit the floor when she heard steps on the stairs, the creaking of a floorboard just outside her door.

She'd left it ajar, only an inch, so they'd know which room she'd claimed for them.

The door slid open slowly, Mateo the first to enter.

His eyes widened when he saw her standing naked beside the bed.

Dimitri walked in behind him, closing the door with a quiet snick before throwing the lock. The damn unshakable man gave nothing away with his expression as his gaze took in her nudity.

Government paper pusher, my ass. Cecilia was certain he was lying about his career. She had no idea why, but she would get to the bottom of it soon. So far, Dimitri had worked hard to hold them at bay, but this relationship wouldn't work as long as they were all keeping secrets.

Then she considered her association with the librarians. Yes, it was a secret, but it wasn't one that negatively impacted her trinity, so it would remain secret.

Neither man approached the bed, their eyes taking in her nude form from head to toe. She let them look their fill for a quiet moment, then she climbed into the center of the bed, lying on her back.

At the last second, she decided to tempt her alpha males even more by lifting her arms, placing her hands palms up on the pillow beneath her. The ultimate pose of surrender.

Dimitri moved first, and she worked hard to hide her smile. It was a smug one that he'd no doubt take exception to.

He noticed it anyway. "Be careful, Cece. You don't want to grow too sure of yourself."

She laughed off his warning heedlessly. "You can leave if you don't want to be here, Dimitri. The keys to the other rooms are there on the nightstand." She gestured to the small table by the bed with a quick lift of her chin.

He didn't bother to look in that direction. His eyes locked on her. "Open your legs."

She considered his request—no, command—for a moment, calculating which course to take. Last night, she'd challenged them every step of the way, refusing to bend to their will.

But she couldn't deny that she'd wanted to.

Wanted to put herself wholly in their hands.

Just the thought of doing so frightened her as much as it aroused.

Dimitri walked to the bottom of the bed, his arms crossed, making sure she could see the impatience on his face.

Slowly, she parted her thighs, her gaze moving from Dimitri's face to Mateo's as he came to stand next to him. Because her pride was tweaked, she decided to take away some of the control she'd just given them by running her fingers along her slit.

Dimitri's eyes narrowed when she pushed three fingers into her own pussy, while running her thumb over her clit.

"Stop," Dimitri demanded.

She ignored him, her breath growing shallow as she got more and more turned on. Cecilia liked orgasms. A lot.

However, it wasn't unusual for her to put in seventy, eighty hours a week at work, spending lots of time on the road, which left precious little for dating or lovers. As such, she'd gotten very good at finding her own pleasure.

Dimitri and Mateo had strung her along last night, withholding her orgasm until it had become almost painful. Tonight, she'd take the edge off first. Then they could issue their wicked, delicious torture.

Her eyes had just drifted closed, her pleasure building quickly, when she felt the mattress at her feet give under a man's weight. As she opened her eyes, she found Dimitri coming over her, caging her beneath him.

He gripped her wrist, pulling her fingers away from her pussy. She struggled to break free, but she'd learned the hard way that both of her men were much stronger than she. She wouldn't find freedom until they gave it to her.

The Cecilia she'd always been would have eviscerated any former lover for such heavy-handed tactics, but this woman—their Cece—seemed to blossom under their dominance.

Dimitri glanced to the side and Cecilia saw Mateo had moved next to them. She had no idea what sort of telepathy they were using, but it had become apparent that they were able to communicate their desires without words.

That idea struck her as strange, considering the men couldn't speak outside of the bedroom without pissing off each other.

Whatever Mateo saw in Dimitri's eyes had him stripping off his clothes. Dimitri held her tightly to the mattress as their lover disrobed.

Dimitri's gaze drifted lower, to her lips, and she licked them. Neither man had kissed her yet, and she longed for it.

"Kiss me," she whispered.

Dimitri's expression told her he wanted to, but he didn't move. She couldn't tell if it was another power play on his part, a way to deny her what she wanted until she begged, or if there was something else holding him back.

They stared at each other for a long minute, the pull between them growing tighter, even as they didn't move closer. The spell was broken when Mateo placed his hand on Dimitri's shoulder.

Dimitri pushed away from her, taking Mateo's place beside the bed as her other lover took over.

Mateo was naked, erect, and very ready for the next part.

After the prolonged foreplay of the previous evening, Cecilia nearly sighed with relief, grateful that they were simply getting down to business this time.

She'd spent the majority of the day fluctuating between annoyed and aroused. The hours had taken their toll, physically and emotionally. She needed some sort of release or she was bound to blow.

Cecilia lifted her legs, wrapping her ankles around his waist, so she could draw him closer.

Mateo locked his bent knees in place, her attempts to budge him failing.

"Come inside me," she said, managing to soften her demand as she spoke it.

He shook his head. "No, *mi cielito*. Not yet."

"What does that mean? *Mi cielito*?" Dimitri asked, drawing their attention to him. Like Mateo, he'd shed his clothing, standing next to them, naked and very erect.

"Sweetheart," she and Mateo said in unison.

"*Mi cielito*," Dimitri repeated, the Spanish sounding too harsh in his Ukrainian accent to be a term of endearment.

Mateo moved to her right side, pulling her closer to him so there was room for Dimitri on her left.

Tucked between them, Cecilia relished the warmth, the sense of being completely surrounded. This was, by far, the most intimate she'd felt with them, despite all they had done.

After they'd reached completion last night, Mateo and Dimitri had both retired to other rooms, leaving her alone in the bed.

At the time, she'd been too sated and lost in post-orgasmic bliss to care, but now that she was here with them, she realized they'd deprived her of something just as magical as the pleasure that had been so intense she'd thought she'd spontaneously combust.

Mateo's hand gently stroked the hills and valley of her breasts, his fingers caressing, adoring.

Dimitri ventured lower, toying with her clit, alternating between applying pressure and pinching the sensitive nub.

Her lovers were so different, yet both had a way of weaving a web of pleasure so passionate, she wanted to get lost in it.

She lay on her back between them, both men on their sides, facing her, facing each other.

Cecilia considered everything that had happened at Craigencross House. They'd gone into the training facility looking for a traitor. What they'd discovered there seemed to put them further away from achieving that goal rather than closer.

Mateo was dismissing any suspect he didn't agree with, while Dimitri had moved away from accusing their lover of failing in his duties, to accusing him of being the villain himself.

Both men were blind, reacting instinctually rather than looking at the facts with an unemotional, intellectual eye. There was no place for "gut feelings" in an investigation of this sort. It was why the librarians were vital to this search.

Cecilia didn't know who the traitor could be, but it was plain to see that whoever it was, they were framing Mateo for the crime. Everything had been put into place too neatly, too perfectly.

As such, Cecilia believed their task had grown more important. Because they weren't just searching for a traitor. They were fighting to clear Mateo's name.

"You aren't the traitor," she whispered. Her assertion, coming in the midst of their foreplay, obviously caught them both off guard, their hands stilling.

"No. I'm not," Mateo said, his brow creased in confusion.

Cecilia's gaze turned to Dimitri. "He's not the traitor."

Their lover didn't reply, not with words, a gesture or even an expression. His features were so emotionless, he could have been carved from stone.

"Say it, Dimitri," she demanded, though her voice was soft, little more than a whisper.

Dimitri scowled. "Cece—" he started.

"You don't have to believe it. Not yet. But you have to say it aloud. Now."

Dimitri looked at Mateo. "We barely know each other."

She reached up and cupped Dimitri's face, drawing his attention back to her. "And yet we're going to be married. You're going to give Mateo and me a gift tonight."

Dimitri's jaw tightened as he clenched his teeth. "What gift?"

"A leap of faith. He's not a traitor. Say it."

"He's not a traitor." The four words came out too easily, too smoothly. Dimitri was an accomplished liar, but he'd given her the words she'd asked for.

"You'll say that again to us one day. And the next time, you will believe it," she assured him, even as his mask fell slightly, revealing his doubts.

"Now," she said, her gaze moving from Dimitri to Mateo. "Kiss."

Mateo started to lean down to her, but she placed her fingers on his lips, halting him.

"Not me. Each other."

Mateo reared back. "Cecilia, I don't—"

His refusal was cut off when Dimitri gripped the back of Mateo's neck, pulling him forward to place a hard kiss on his lips.

The entire action—from grab to kiss—lasted mere seconds, but the impact shook Cecilia to the core.

"I want the same gift," Dimitri demanded.

"What do you mean?" Mateo asked, clearly flustered by the unexpected kiss.

"A leap of faith. My intentions are honorable."

Mateo frowned. "What intentions?"

"Say it back to me."

"Your intentions are honorable."

Cecilia sucked in a deep breath. Mateo was as smooth a liar as Dimitri. And then, Mateo sealed that leap of faith in the same way—grasping Dimitri by the neck and giving him a kiss as well.

Cecilia noticed this kiss lasted longer and—God have mercy—included tongue. The temperature in the room spiked.

Watching her lovers kiss was the ultimate turn-on. She took advantage of their distraction, reaching down to resume her earlier masturbating. She had managed one quick stroke of her clit before Dimitri's iron-clad grip encircled her wrist.

Both men were looking at her with dark, hungry, predatory eyes. She shivered in response.

"Be careful, Cece."

It was the same warning Dimitri had issued a few minutes earlier.

"Of?"

"You're playing with fire."

She pondered that. It was apparent he wasn't referring to their bedroom play. Was he referring to her request for trust? She was perfectly aware that trust wasn't something that could be offered blindly, yet that was what she had done.

Because, while they were still oblivious, she had seen the obvious.

This trinity wasn't a mistake, wasn't a punishment, wasn't falling apart.

They were hers. And she was...theirs.

"I'm not afraid of fire," she said, dropping her own mask, letting both of them see her fully, revealing her hopes, her fears, her desires.

Dimitri pulled back a few inches as he studied her face. He even shook his head a couple of times, just a slight movement, a tiny attempt at denial.

"We're all going to burn," he said at last, just before he bent his head and kissed her. His lips were just as rough, just as wicked as his fingers. He took her mouth hard, his tongue pushing in to stake a claim.

That kiss was powerful enough it should have blocked out everything else around them, but Mateo was not happy to merely observe. The mattress shifted and his hands tugged her thighs apart as he bent down to kiss a much more intimate place. Like Dimitri, his tongue conquered, stroking her clit several times before he dipped it inside her empty, needy pussy.

She gasped, attempting to turn her head away from Dimitri. She was suffocating on pleasure, everything coming at her too fast. It was too overwhelming.

"Please," she said, but Dimitri didn't give way. He gripped her face in his large, calloused hand and reclaimed her lips, stealing even more air from her lungs.

"Ours," he barked when he finally moved away to give them a chance to breathe. "You're *ours*."

She nodded, barely restraining from pointing out how obvious and unnecessary that comment was.

Be kind, not right.

Cecilia took her mother's words to heart. "Always," she said instead.

Dimitri moved to the side, allowing Mateo to come over her body. Her legs were open, ready to welcome him inside.

He slid in without pause, without hesitation, burying himself fully, deeply.

Dimitri knelt next to them as Mateo took her. Both of them were nearly at the brink when Dimitri reached between them, stroking her clit before leaning closer to bite Mateo's shoulder.

Mateo jerked in obvious unexpected pain. The sudden thickening of his cock inside her told Cecilia that Mateo had liked the sting.

"Pull out of her," Dimitri commanded.

Mateo narrowed his eyes, but did so.

Cecilia hissed, her body trembling, unsated.

Dimitri shoved two fingers inside. She was soaking wet, slick with her arousal. "That's right, *koxaha*. Coat my fingers. Make them nice and wet, so I can put them in our Mateo's ass."

Cecilia's pussy tightened.

"Dimitri—" Mateo began.

"Just my fingers," Dimitri interjected, not bothering to let Mateo finish. "This time."

Mateo remained still as Dimitri stroked in and out of her, pushing her to the edge once again. She lifted her hips, trying to get there before he withdrew, but Dimitri was too astute, too in tune with her body.

How could he learn that so quickly?

He pulled his fingers free, leaving her unsatisfied, aching.

"Please," she repeated. Last night, they'd told her they would have her begging. It had taken them only twenty-four hours to achieve that goal.

Mateo, however, shared her pain and, bless him, was ready to put them both out of their misery.

He slid back inside her, intent on fucking them to completion, but Dimitri placed his hand on Mateo's back.

"Wait."

Mateo was buried to the hilt, but stilled. Cecilia attempted to wiggle her hips, Dimitri's demands be damned.

"Cece," he warned. "Stop now. Or you won't come tonight at all."

She froze briefly, torn, trying to decide if she should call him on his bluff and risk it or—fuck—obey.

She was still mentally debating with herself when Dimitri said, "Good girl." He'd mistaken her stillness for compliance. Cecilia possessed enough pride that his praise, the words making her feel like a child, almost had her thrusting her hips upward.

That idea was wiped away when Mateo hissed. Dimitri had moved behind him, pushing Mateo lower, his upper body flush with hers, chest to breasts. She tried to look over his shoulder to see what Dimitri was doing, but Mateo had other ideas.

"Distract me," he murmured, his lips against hers.

Their first kiss.

A distraction.

She didn't care. Cecilia wrapped her arms around his neck as he pressed his lips to hers. The touch was hot, but brief.

Mateo pulled away with a gasp, and she knew Dimitri had made his move.

"Fuck," Mateo murmured.

"I can't see. Tell me what he's doing," Cecilia demanded.

Dimitri chuckled at her request. "Dirty girl."

"I don't...this isn't..." Mateo was struggling to speak. "His fingers are in my ass. Two of them. It's fucking tight, stretching me."

"Does it hurt?" she asked.

He nodded, then hastened to add, "But I want it. The sting feels…"

She lifted her head, placing a quick kiss on his jaw. "Your descriptive skills need work."

Dimitri reached between Mateo's legs, finding the place where they were still connected, Mateo's cock filling her.

Dimitri ran the tip of one finger around the base of Mateo's cock and the rim of her vagina before sliding lower. He pressed inside her ass one knuckle deep and wiggled.

"It feels like that. And you'll get your turn soon enough." His finger was gone in an instant, and she was sorry it wasn't her turn *now*.

"Fuck our lady, Mateo," Dimitri said. "You take care of her while I take care of you."

Mateo moved slowly at first, almost gingerly. Cecilia assumed he was trying to become accustomed to the stretch, the burn of Dimitri's fingers pumping in and out of his ass, the rhythm matching that of Mateo's thrusts into her.

He adjusted quickly. Mateo lifted her legs, placing her knees over his shoulders, the position allowing him to press in deeper.

She wasn't sure who was determining the pace. Given the speed and force, she suspected it was Dimitri. The man fucked like his life depended on it.

"Take her harder," Dimitri demanded.

Mateo shook his head, even as he obeyed the order. "Can't. Hold. Off. Too…"

Three thrusts later and he came, filling her as he grunted out the intensity of his feelings. "Fuck. God! *Yes*. Hurts so fucking good."

He'd asked Cecilia to distract him, but she'd been the one distracted, so in awe of Mateo's face, his responses. Belatedly, she realized he'd gone ahead without her.

Reaching down, she stroked her clit, anxious to catch up. God knew it wouldn't take much.

Dimitri, as always, took the control out of her hands.

"Grab her hands, Mateo. Hold them beside her head. And don't let her touch herself. I'll be right back."

She gasped, shocked by his unexpected departure.

"Mateo—" she started.

He lifted his hips, his softening cock sliding out. He shook his head. "Don't try to sweettalk me, Cece. It won't work."

Since when did *he* call her Cece?

And since when did she start liking that silly nickname?

The sound of running water told her Dimitri had gone to the bathroom to wash his hands. She wasn't sure what that meant for her. It wasn't really his hands she was interested in at the moment.

What she needed was someone between her legs, pounding hard.

When he returned to the room, Mateo resumed his previous position on her right.

Dimitri reached for her waist, drawing her toward him. "Facedown," he demanded.

She started to turn, but he took over, using his strength to put her in the position he wanted. Her legs hung over the edge of the bed, her bare feet hitting the chilly floor. She only had a second to assimilate before Dimitri bent over her, tugging her legs open.

"You want to come, *koxaha*?"

She nodded.

"No. Say it. Ask for it."

She gritted her teeth.

"Sweet, stubborn girl," he cooed as he ran his fingertips along her slit. "Always taking the hard way."

She tried to push closer to his hand, foolishly thinking she could get his fingers inside her somehow.

He gave her a quick, sharp slap as a warning.

Mateo had been quietly watching them, but he moved closer, running his fingers through her hair. She lifted her head to look at him, surprised to see such a serious look on his face.

"Leap of faith, *mi cielito.*"

"What?" she asked, perplexed by his words until he explained.

"We won't hurt you."

She blinked, trying to hide the tears his words provoked. Cecilia had asked them to take a chance, to trust, to leap.

She turned around, looking at Dimitri over her shoulder. Mateo's words had affected him as well.

"We won't hurt you," Dimitri repeated.

Every last vestige of fear and confusion and anxiety melted away. "Take me, Dimitri. Hard. Please. God…please. I need—"

Cecilia's plea was cut off when he slammed into her.

She clenched the duvet in her fists, pushing back on every inward swing of his hips. He took her the way she wanted, needed.

She came within a dozen strokes, but he didn't stop, didn't acknowledge the first orgasm…or the second.

Over and over, he pounded deeply, and as he did so, he rained a litany of Ukrainian words. She didn't understand the meaning, but there was no mistaking the tone, the tenor.

She responded in Italian. Like him, she needed her native language to be able to express everything written inside her.

This wasn't love. She was too pragmatic to believe anyone could fall so fast. But there was no denying that was where this was headed.

Her heart could love these men.

They wouldn't hurt her.

Chapter Nine

Cashtal Ny Tree Cassyn—literal translation, The Castle of Three Legs—was on the north shore of the Isle of Man, on roughly the opposite side from Douglas, the capital city. The castle, called Triskelion Castle in English, despite that not being an exact translation of the Manx name, was actually a fortified manor house. Like many such houses in various parts of Europe where landed lords had controlled the countryside,

Triskelion Castle was not just a single building, but an estate with land, multiple residences, and a working farm.

From the deck of the small ship, Dimitri couldn't see the wall that surrounded the grounds. They'd decided last night, somewhere in the wee hours, that their next logical move in the investigation was a trip to the Isle of Man. That revelation came after two hours of cuddling and pillow talk.

Dimitri still couldn't quite believe—or maybe understand was a better word—all that had happened in Cecilia's bedroom. One moment, he'd felt like he'd had a grip on himself, on his mission, the next, she was stealing his room key and he was following Mateo upstairs.

As they approached the shore and the small, sheltered docks used to access the estate by sea, all he could see was the castle.

It rose above the cliff, piercing the gray, cloudy sky. The weather was calm enough that they'd been able to make the crossing by sea in a power boat rather than something with sails. Dimitri was not knowledgeable about ocean travel—something he would have to rectify. He could swim and do some basic scuba, but Kiev was far from the Black Sea, and there hadn't been a reason to learn how to pilot—or was it captain?—a ship in open water like this. The Black Sea was large but calm, compared to the Irish Sea, linked as it was to the wild Atlantic.

Cecilia clung to his leg and prayed for death in Italian.

The lovely, take-charge powerhouse of a woman was terribly seasick.

Dimitri looked back to where Mateo—a knit cap covering his hair and ears to protect them from the cold air—stood at the wheel of the boat. Dimitri was standing in the center of the small seating area, bent knees braced on the bench. Cecilia lay on the bench, clinging to his leg, her hair plastered to her face with salt spray. She was bundled in a black jacket that bore the logo of the Spartan Guard. Her own jacket had been a casualty of her first bout of seasickness and had been tossed overboard.

Mateo throttled back the engine, slowing as they approached the Isle of Man. The slower speed made the boat rock more as it was caught in the choppy, wind-driven waves.

Cecilia started to pray to the Blessed Virgin in Latin. Mateo's lips twitched as he fought a smile. Dimitri's gaze locked with his, and the amusement he saw there was a match for his own. Not that they enjoyed their future wife's suffering, but instead enjoyed her thoroughly Italian way of expressing that suffering.

They both grinned, in unison of expression and thought. What they'd done last night. The way they'd touched each other...that was fresh in his mind. Dimitri's body felt both languid and replete and ready for more. The unspoken desire to touch Mateo again made the shared amusement almost painfully intimate.

Dimitri faked a stumble as they hit a wave and used it as an excuse to look away, his smile fading. It was a mistake to get too close to Mateo.

Mateo skillfully navigated them between the large sailboats moored at the several short docks that stuck out into the water from the base of the cliff Triskelion Castle sat atop. Dimitri pried Cecilia's hands from his leg and stepped out onto the prow of the boat, jumping onto the dock when they were close enough. Dimitri caught the line Mateo tossed him and looped it around a piling.

"I'll secure us, if you can get her off," Mateo said.

Dimitri nodded, waiting for Mateo to jump onto the dock, and then he climbed back into the boat, gathering Cecilia in his arms.

Mateo had finished securing the boat using a proper nautical knot by the time Dimitri stepped carefully onto the gently swaying dock, Cecilia moaning piteously.

Without waiting for Mateo, Dimitri carried her to the narrow, coarse sand beach, setting her on a sea-spray coated rock at the base of the cliff.

"Breathe. Put your feet flat on the ground. Hold yourself still. Feel the earth." He hadn't dealt with much seasickness, but he'd helped his share of those who were airsick, especially after night-flight helicopter rides, which were difficult on the inner ear.

Mateo stepped up beside him. His head was tipped up, scanning the cliff. He shifted his weight from foot to foot.

He was anxious to get to the castle. A switchback path had been carved into the cliff face, and Dimitri could all but feel Mateo's desire to race up the slick stone incline.

"Hold her," Dimitri murmured. "I'm not feeling so well myself."

Mateo's attention immediately snapped to them, and he crouched by Cecilia, putting one hand on her forehead and one on the back of her head, holding it steady.

"Mmmm," she murmured. "That helps."

Dimitri felt fine. He'd used Cecilia's sickness as an excuse to keep Mateo from going up there without him.

If only watching them together didn't make him feel so…

He pushed away the feeling. Refusing to acknowledge it. To name it.

Dimitri did his own scan of the cliff. It took him a moment, but he spotted multiple cameras. As at Craigencross Farm, the Spartan Guard would know they were here.

Perhaps the fleet admiral would know as well.

After ten minutes, Cecilia seemed to feel better, so they started up. By the time they reached the top, she was almost back to herself, though she looked rather pathetic. It was a look he hadn't seen from her before, and the need to protect her was gnawing at him.

They were met at the top of the cliff by a clean-cut man with pale blond hair and patrician features. He had a sort of refined air that was slightly at odds with his heavily muscled arms, which strained at the sleeves of his crisp white dress shirt. Again, the clothing was at odds with the weapon strapped across his chest, the muzzle of the semiautomatic rifle visible over one shoulder.

Dimitri stiffened. He recognized this man from his file.

Derrick Frederick.

"Sir," Derrick greeted Mateo. His gaze, however, was on Dimitri and Cecilia.

Dimitri had to give the guard credit—he was splitting his attention between both of them, though Dimitri was clearly the bigger threat. It was what he would have done—suspect everyone, especially if they didn't look suspicious.

Cecilia, who was clinging to Dimitri's left arm, stomped forward. "Coffee. I need it."

Derrick blinked. "I beg your pardon?" His accent was clipped upper-class British.

"Coffee." Cecilia's snarl was impressive. "Give it to me, or I will kill you."

Derrick blinked again, then looked at Mateo. "Is she aware that I have a gun?"

"She was sick during the crossing," Mateo said.

"Ah."

"And she's Italian."

"Oh. Well yes, that explains it. I'm sure we can get you a nice cup of tea—"

Cecilia snarled again.

"Coffee!" Derrick's eyes widened in mock alarm. "Coffee. Please excuse my mistake. And accept my apologies, but I cannot let you go any farther until you state your business."

"They're here with me," Mateo said. "They're helping to investigate the traitor."

Derrick blinked. "There *is* a traitor? I know you suspected, but..." His gaze shot back to Dimitri and Cecilia, reassessing. Dimitri could almost hear the guard trying to guess who they were—knights, security officers, intelligence specialists?

Cecilia shot Mateo a disgusted look, straightened her shoulders and said, "We're his trinity. Our binding ceremony will happen here on the isle at the end of the week."

Mateo's mouth all but disappeared as he pressed his lips together.

Derrick's stiff posture relaxed in shock as he turned to Mateo. "The fleet admiral is forcing you out?"

"No."

"No?" Cecilia asked. "What do you mean, 'no'?"

That was a very good question.

"Cecilia, I misspoke. I'm only—only trying to explain that we have a task." Mateo looked to Derrick. "And a deadline."

Derrick nodded. "I need your full names."

"Cecilia St. John."

"Dimitri Bondar."

Derrick put one hand to his ear, cuff near his mouth, and repeated their names. A moment later Derrick nodded, and then beckoned them to follow him.

Derrick led them to the front door of the castle. Dimitri knew there had to be other ways in, and he'd been somewhat hoping they'd go to the Spartan Guard's residence, which was an entirely separate building not far from the castle.

It was not easy to impress or awe Dimitri, but there was something about this place that always made him pause. Made him feel like he was part of something bigger than himself. Triskelion Castle looked more like a chateau or a cathedral than a medieval castle. It was three stories, with a steep roofline, arched gothic windows, and elaborately carved stonework. It had been the headquarters for the Masters' Admiralty since 1440, and it was because of the Masters' Admiralty that this small island was only a British Crown dependency, with a level of autonomy.

As Derrick opened the tall, narrow wooden front door mounted in a pointed archway, Dimitri caught sight of other guards on the roof. They were half-hidden by a parapet and the angle he was looking from, but they were there, guns—such a rarity anywhere in the UK—in their hands.

Beyond the door was a narrow foyer that ran deep into the building. Polished wooden floors, oil paintings, and oriental rugs gave the impression of old money, generational wealth.

Derrick gestured them through a narrow doorway, into a small waiting room that contained two couches, a low table in between with a photobook set on it, and a sideboard with a self-service drink station.

Cecilia made a noise of distress when she saw the single-serve coffee maker, but went to it nonetheless.

Derrick followed them in, and once the door was closed, he went to Mateo. They clasped hands, smiling grimly at one another.

"Tell me what's going on," Derrick demanded. "There's a traitor?"

Dimitri held his tongue as Mateo quickly outlined his reasons for thinking there was a traitor. Despite the evidence that indicated Derrick was as much a suspect as any of the other guards, Mateo persisted in trusting the man.

Derrick nodded, a frown causing lines to bracket his mouth. "And the fleet admiral wants you to find the traitor as…one last duty before you get married?"

Mateo nodded stiffly.

Derrick shook his head. "I'm sorry, my friend."

"Yes, because marrying us is such a terrible fate," Cecilia all but purred.

"I assure you I meant no offense."

"Yet, I am offended."

Derrick looked helplessly at Mateo, who had closed his eyes and was rubbing his forehead. "Derrick," he said finally. "Where is Charlotta?"

Derrick, who'd slumped slightly, stiffened where he sat. "She's doing a perimeter check of the farm."

"The farm?" Dimitri asked. Most of the land owned by the fleet admiral was used as part of a working farm that raised sheep to produce Manx wool. As far as Dimitri knew, it was kept entirely separate from the Masters' Admiralty.

"We don't patrol the farm," Mateo said. "Doing so would raise suspicion. Did the fleet admiral—"

"It was my idea," Derrick said. "We told the farm manager that the owner had hired a firm to install new security for both the castle and the farm, and that we'd have people looking around."

"The farm manager doesn't know?" Dimitri asked.

"No," Mateo answered, but he was looking at Derrick. "The farm manager, and everyone who works on the farm, is native Manx. They're part of the community on the island. It helps keep us integrated, while at the same time affording us privacy. The people who work on the farm know the owner of Triskelion is an eccentric who likes his privacy, and they respect that. Most of the people have worked for the farm for generations."

"Why didn't we look at them?" Cecilia demanded. "One of them could be the traitor."

Derrick frowned. "I hate to say it, but she has a point."

Mateo negated the idea instantly. "No one from the farm ever came in contact with Kacper's medicine. That had to be someone inside the castle."

"It still might be worth looking into. Do you want me to look at that angle?" Derrick asked.

Dimitri leaned against the wall, studying the body language and nonverbals between Mateo and Derrick.

"If you already have someone there, yes. With Kacper's death and my absence from the isle for a few weeks, it appears the guard has gotten sloppy with protocol and following the chain of command. It stops here."

Derrick pushed up from the couch. He started to make a fist, then forced his fingers to straighten. "Yes, sir."

Mateo sighed. "I need to talk to Charlotta. When will she be back?"

Derrick checked his watch. "She's on duty for the next four hours."

"I won't pull her off duty. I'll wait until she's back."

"Then we'll talk to her," Derrick said.

Mateo shook his head. "I'll talk to her. I'm going to go check in with the other Spartan Guard and do a perimeter walk." He looked at Cecilia and Dimitri. "Will you two be okay here for an hour?"

"Do you mean will we stay here?" Cecilia snapped.

"Yes."

Mateo opened his mouth, but didn't speak. He shook his head and then walked out with Derrick.

Dimitri waited fifteen minutes and then gave Cecilia a quick kiss on the forehead, promising to return with a good cup of coffee as soon as possible. While the seasickness had waned, it had taken its toll, and he convinced her to lie down for a little while.

He walked quietly to the staircase that would lead to the private residence upstairs. He had been here just a couple weeks earlier, so he knew exactly where he was going. His visit had come late in the evening, the number of guards privy to his arrival limited to just a few. Mateo had still been in England at the time.

Knocking on the door, he was bade to enter.

He walked into the fleet admiral's suite, moving cautiously.

The place was a bit of a mess—remnants of what he assumed had been the previous fleet admiral's furniture were shoved against the walls, leaving most of the open-planned living area bare. There was a wall of glass at one end, which opened out onto a deck that overlooked the sea. The patio where Kacper had been when shot with the fatal dose of activating poison.

The muzzle of a gun pressed against Dimitri's skull, just behind his left ear.

Eric Ericsson's voice was almost cheerful as he said, "Hello, Dimitri."

Dimitri slowly raised his hands. "Hello, Fleet Admiral."

"Any weapons?"

"No, sir."

"You're supposed to say 'my body is a weapon'."

Despite the imminent danger, Dimitri snorted. "I'd rather be shot."

"Lift your shirt."

Dimitri yanked up the hem of his shirt to mid-chest, showing that there was no weapon tucked into his pants. Then bent and pulled up each pant leg, revealing nothing strapped there.

The gun pulled back from his head. Dimitri turned and watched as Eric walked over to a large blank desk positioned so the person seated behind it had a clear view of both the door and the glass wall. If he had to guess, Dimitri would say the desk was probably reinforced with bulletproof material that would allow Eric to take shelter behind it in the middle of a firefight.

He sat, then looked at Dimitri, face serious. "Is he our man?"

Dimitri had expected the question, had struggled to figure out how to reply. In the end, nothing had come.

"I don't know."

Silence followed his response, so Dimitri added, "I don't think he is."

"You know what to do if he is." Eric opened a drawer and pulled out a knife. He checked the blade then slid it into a black sheath with a belt clip. He held out the knife, hilt first.

Dimitri accepted the blade. "Yes, sir. Kill him."

Chapter Ten

Mateo returned from his perimeter check, frustration closing in on him. The trip to Stranraer and to the isle had yielded no conclusive results. Despite his suspicions, he had no proof that Charlotta was the one who'd betrayed the guard and Kacper.

Three days down and he was no closer to catching the traitor.

Failing to bring the killer to justice was wearing heavily on his conscience. He'd been hired to protect Kacper, but to him, his role as head of the guard was more than just a job. He had genuinely cared about Kacper. The man and his wife, Greta, had taken him under their wings, treating him like a son rather than just a bodyguard.

He walked down the corridor, intent on heading to the larger guest room he was sharing with Dimitri and Cecilia, his own small room in the guard house not big enough for the three of them. Word of his impending marriage had spread like wildfire after Cecilia announced she and Dimitri were part of his trinity. As such, they'd been given a nicer room to prepare for their upcoming nuptials.

Halfway there, Marie contacted him through the walkie-talkie, claiming Dimitri was taking Cecilia to Douglas for medicine and to find a room at an inn where she could rest for a few hours.

Mateo didn't understand their desire for a room, considering they'd been given one here. He assumed the decision had been Dimitri's. It sounded like something the paranoid, trust-no-one man would do. Then Mateo considered asking Marie to tell them to wait. The idea of leaving the grounds and losing himself in his lovers for a few hours was very tempting.

He resisted, telling her to give them a car. He needed to focus on the investigation and put some distance between himself, Dimitri and Cecilia.

Since the trip to the guest room was pointless, he left the castle again, heading for the Spartan Guard house, the barracks-style building nearby that he shared with the other guards. Mateo was feeling alone and confused, he needed someone to talk to. With Dimitri and Cecilia gone, he decided to seek Derrick out.

It was obvious Dimitri was unhappy with Mateo for sharing the details about their investigation with his friend. Mateo wasn't sure how to convince Dimitri—a man who seemed to trust no one—that Derrick wasn't their guy.

He'd known Derrick since the beginning of his time with the Spartan Guards, the two of them recruited at the same time. They'd roomed together, trained together.

Mateo had grown up an only child, never knowing what it was like to have a brother...until Derrick.

He knocked on the door, but the room was empty. Of course, Derrick was guarding the back gate until dinnertime. He wouldn't return for hours. Mateo's anxiety was running rampant, making it difficult for him to think, to reason.

He turned the knob, shaking his head when he found the door unlocked. Derrick was Dimitri's polar opposite in the trust department. He'd never locked his bedroom door in his life, proclaiming he had nothing worth stealing, and he was willing to share what he did have with his Spartan Guard brothers.

Mateo entered the room, glancing around at the sparsely furnished space. Derrick claimed he preferred simplicity when it came to decorating his room because it meant there was less to clean up.

The room contained only a bed, made tightly with hospital corners, a dresser—devoid of anything on its gleaming surface—a straight-backed chair, and a desk.

Everything in the room was spotless. The only personal item hung on the wall over the desk. Mateo walked over to the photograph, grinning as he saw the image of him and Derrick hamming it up for the camera, arms draped around each other's shoulders, laughing.

They'd both just been initiated into the Spartan Guard and the picture was snapped near the end of the night, after a great deal of celebrating and too many shots of tequila.

The photograph showed two young men on the cusp of living their dream. The world was theirs for the taking. Or so they believed.

That night was one of the happiest of his life. Laughter had died along with his parents, but the night of that initiation he'd found a way to feel joy again, thanks to Derrick…and tequila.

He recalled last night, and how he'd felt true, unbridled happiness in Dimitri and Cecilia's arms.

Unlike the night with Derrick, Mateo's joy with Dimitri and Cecilia wasn't going to last. His place was here with the guard and his best friend.

His future lie on the Isle of Man.

Not in a trinity with a beautiful, intelligent Italian woman and a gruff, sexy Ukrainian.

It was time to finish the mission and walk away.

Before it was too late.

As he closed the door to Derrick's bedroom, a nagging voice in the back of his head whispered, *It's already too late.*

"I know he's an ass, but shouldn't we wait for Mateo?" Cecilia asked.

Dimitri clicked the unlock button for the car. "No."

Cecilia climbed into the passenger seat. "No? Just no?"

Dimitri glanced out the windshield at the member of the guard who'd given him the keys. Marie watched them with cool, dark eyes, hands on her hips.

"You know there is a room in the castle waiting for us. On the second floor. And unlike last night's bed, the one in there is large enough to fit three comfortably."

Dimitri didn't speak again until they'd driven out the gates. "We're not going anywhere to rest," he told her once they were safely away from Triskelion Castle.

Cecilia regarded him shrewdly. "I knew you were lying."

"No, you didn't."

"Yes, I did."

Dimitri snorted, her sassy retort making him feel better about the lies he'd told to borrow the car and get them off the castle grounds. He'd told Marie that they were going to Douglas to get Cecilia something for her lingering sickness and to check into a hotel where she could rest. Marie had spoken into her headset, and either Mateo had believed them, or hadn't responded while he was off doing whatever it was he was doing.

He was probably telling Derrick everything, the fool.

Dimitri headed uphill toward the center of the island. Once they'd dipped behind a small rise and were no longer in line of sight from the castle, he pulled over, stopped the car and got out. Cecilia opened her door and peered at him as he lay on the ground and scooted under the engine block.

"What are you doing?"

"Disabling the GPS."

"Ah. Then we're really not going to a hotel."

"No. We've got something else we need to do."

Leaving the castle, Mateo decided it was time to approach his number-one suspect. He found Charlotta standing near a fencerow, studying a broken board, and braced himself before approaching her.

He hadn't shared all his reasons for suspecting Charlotta with Dimitri and Cecilia. For one thing, he wasn't sure how he could explain their relationship—if he could call it that.

The best description for it was a one-night stand. He'd succumbed in a moment of weakness, given in to her kindness. It had been a mistake.

For him, it had been a physical affair, a night of connecting with another human being at a time when he couldn't face being alone.

It had meant much more than that to Charlotta.

They had been friends before that night, or so he'd thought. He hadn't realized her feelings had run much deeper. If he had, he never would have gone to her bed.

He should have come clean with Dimitri and Cecilia, but he didn't know how to explain his actions without telling them why he'd done what he had.

"Mateo?" Charlotta turned and saw him. Her expression was wary, curious. "Where have you been?"

"London," he said as he approached her. "There were loose ends to attend to after Kacper's death."

"Murder," she corrected.

He nodded. "Yes. Murder." Mateo leaned against the fence, absentmindedly looking at the sheep as they grazed in the field. "It looks like there have been changes here since my short time away."

"There was a lot to deal with after Kacper was killed. We've been busy. There are questions we need answers to. How the drone operator knew Kacper would be on the balcony. How he got onto the property. How the tainted medicine was brought into the castle."

"I've been conducting a similar investigation."

"How?" She bit the word off. "You haven't been here."

He'd become accustomed to her resentment over the past year. For several months after their unwise night together, she'd pursued him with a fervor, insistent that they should continue the affair. Charlotta had created some dream future for them, certain they could work together as a couple until they aged out of the guard, at which point, they could ask the fleet admiral to place them in a trinity together.

She was a good member of the Spartan Guard because she was driven, intense, with a laser focus on every objective, every detail. Those were admirable things in a work colleague. They were frightening when placed in a romantic mindset.

Charlotta had set her sights on him, making their future lives together her top priority. It had taken him months—and in the end, some fairly hurtful words—to convince her their affair had been a mistake and that it would be the height of unprofessionalism to enter into a real relationship. When she professed her love, he was forced to tell her he didn't return her feelings.

Her jilted-lover persona was as terrifying as her woman-in-love one had been. Derrick, privy to the entire affair, had warned him Charlotta was not the type to forgive and forget.

It was those words that kept playing in his head as he considered Cecilia's belief that someone was trying to frame him.

Charlotta had changed in the last year, grown more distant from the guard, more aggressive and argumentative. Not just with him, but with everyone.

He'd overheard her making a disparaging remark to another guard about Kacper's desire to take his breakfast in his bedroom instead of his office. Charlotta had been of the belief that the fleet admiral should step down due to his declining health.

Mateo had pulled her aside once the other guard was out of earshot and told her in no uncertain terms that the fleet admiral's ability to continue in his role was not hers to pass judgment on. Her only job was to ensure that he was protected.

She had apologized for her comments and he'd forgotten about the entire conversation.

What if Charlotta had expressed her desire for a healthy, strong fleet admiral to Manon?

What if Manon had viewed that opinion as a way to sway Charlotta to her cause?

Did Mateo believe that Charlotta could predict the future leadership of the Masters' Admiralty? No. He didn't. But he couldn't deny that Charlotta was probably quite pleased by the current turn of events.

"My investigation is ongoing. Until I have proof of wrongdoing, I'm not going to discuss it."

Charlotta narrowed her eyes, but said nothing.

"I want to talk to you about the security detail in regards to the new fleet admiral."

Charlotta smiled, but there was no happiness in the expression. "I don't think that's necessary."

"Excuse me?"

"Word travels fast. You're about to be married, which means the position of head of the guard is no longer yours. Eric Ericsson is not your concern."

"I am still the head of guard until the end of the week."

Charlotta shrugged as if unconcerned. "Mere days. And then we can elect a new head."

"And who do you think that will be?"

This time, her grin was genuine as she shrugged. "All I know is it won't be you."

Dimitri spread the paper map of the island on the hood of the car. It was safer to use paper than in-car or app-based maps. The fleet admiral, whose past meant he, like Dimitri, knew how to operate with an abundance of caution, had given it to him.

Right after Dimitri had reaffirmed his promise to kill Mateo if he was the traitor.

The thought made Dimitri sick. With the ease of practice, he pushed the emotions aside and focused on the task at hand.

"What are the dots?" Cecilia asked quietly. She seemed to have picked up on his mood.

There were four black dots on the map. Three were on the north side of the island, not more than a mile or two from the border of the Triskelion property. The last was on the south side of the island, not far from Douglas.

"They're places Manon, the murdered fleet admiral's other wife, might have met with her lover."

Cecilia took a steadying breath. "And we're going to investigate?"

"Yes."

"Why us?"

"Because there's a traitor in the Spartan Guard." It wasn't a lie, but it wasn't the full truth. Dimitri knew how to keep secrets. He wouldn't tell her that the fleet admiral had been escaping the guards, roaming the island, doing an investigation of his own, and had identified these four locations—each of which was a holiday home, a property rented by people who vacationed on Isle of Man to enjoy the pastoral beauty of the island.

"I thought Manon left the isle, and that was part of the problem—Mateo didn't tell anyone because he was protecting their privacy."

"Yes." He studied the map, folded it small, and returned it to his back pocket. "But that kind of betrayal and loyalty takes years to build. Not months." He opened her door for her.

She waited until he climbed in and started the car before saying, "You think Manon and her lover—the American sniper—were secretly meeting somewhere on the Isle of Man."

"Yes."

"Right under the Spartan Guard's nose? Her husband's nose?"

"Exactly."

Dimitri knew what drove people—or at least the less noble aspects of human nature. From what he'd learned of Manon, what Mateo had recounted about what she'd said when confronted, he suspected meeting with her lover near to Triskelion was part of the appeal. The very nearness would satiate her desire to undermine and repudiate her spouse, the fleet admiral.

That was why, of the four locations the Viking had identified, he chose the one that he suspected would have a view of Triskelion Castle.

He merged onto the winding country road, bringing them almost into Douglas before turning east, and then north, backtracking, but staying on the winding road that hugged the east coast of the island.

They stopped in Laxey, Dimitri racing into a pharmacy to get some seasickness pills and a bottle of water for Cecilia, whose queasy stomach hadn't appreciated the scenic drive.

After some cursing in Italian and the application of damp paper towels to the back of her neck, Cecilia was ready to go. Needing to take care of her helped pull Dimitri out of his grim frame of mind, and when they turned inland, taking A14 up to the high center of the island, passing Tholt-e-Will Plantation and neighboring Tholt y Will Glen, he was chuckling at Cecilia's running commentary on how much she hated the countryside.

"In Singapore, there are parks. Beaches. That is nature. This is...rustic." She spat the last word, then took a sip from the bottle of water.

"I think British people all secretly want to be farmers."

"*Sono deficienti.*"

"They *are* morons," he agreed.

He caught sight of the small sign reading "Testraw Treen Self-Catering Cottage" and turned into the gravel driveway.

The cottage sat atop a small rise and had a panoramic view of the northwest shore of the isle, including the distant and distinct pointed rooflines of Triskelion Castle.

The flaw in the plan was if the cottage was currently occupied. Dimitri had planned for that, deciding he'd pretend to be maintenance or from some vague government office come to inspect something like the gas line.

There was no car in the drive, and after looking in the windows of the single-story white house with a gray roof, he was betting it was currently empty. No lights were on, no clutter visible anywhere.

"How are we going to get in? Do you know how to pick a lock? Or break one of these?" Cecilia gestured to the dial-code lockbox by the front door, partially hidden by a wall basket of pink flowers.

"Window," he said. He started around the house, checking to see if any had been left off the latch. He made it back to the front door without finding any— only to see that the door was now open.

He tensed, reaching for the knife the Viking had given him, which was tucked into his pants at the small of his back and hidden by his shirt.

Cecilia stuck her head out, grinning. "The code was the year the cottage was built." She pointed to a plaque on the wall, which read "Testraw Treen Cottage. 1740."

Dimitri snorted and followed his fiancée inside.

Mateo left Charlotta, uncertain what could be gained by engaging her in further conversation. He was more convinced than ever that she was the traitor.

She'd had everything to gain by joining forces with Manon—getting rid of Kacper, framing him, then grabbing the promotion. The admirals naming a fleet admiral from her territory might have been merely icing on the cake.

Or maybe she's figured out the possible results, and gambled on them making the decision to make Eric fleet admiral.

If that was true, was Eric in on it? Was he the Domino?

Dammit, he'd been spending too much time with Dimitri. He was suspicious of everyone.

Since Dimitri and Cecilia had gone into Douglas, he went to rest in his own room in the barracks. He hadn't gotten much sleep lately.

He unlocked it and walked in, sinking down on the bed. Looking around, he realized he and Derrick had a great deal in common. Both of them lived a monk's style of existence, only surrounding themselves with the necessary furniture and skipping the special touches that might make the place feel homey.

That had never bothered him, or even occurred to him, in the past few years, but after spending the last three days with Cecilia and Dimitri, he was reminded of his parents, of the home they'd shared, how warm and inviting it had always been.

He could see himself living in a place like that with Cecilia, could imagine her delight in decorating their home, in picking out the colors and theme of a nursery for their baby.

What surprised Mateo was discovering it wasn't that hard to picture himself with Dimitri, setting up a crib and moving the same heavy dresser this way or that until Cecilia was satisfied with its placement.

There were too many things wrong with those images, but Mateo let them come anyway. He'd spent nearly half his life fighting memories. He thought that made him stronger, better able to do his job.

He wasn't sure that was true.

Walking to the small stack of books placed on the edge of his desk, he pulled out an old medical journal he'd kept that had belonged to his mother. Enough dust floated from the cover to make him cough. It had been years since he'd touched the thing.

Opening the hard cover, he flipped through the pages until he found what he was seeking—an old photograph. It was taken just a few weeks before his parents were murdered. His *futbol* team had won a big match against their cross-city rivals, and his mom and dad had rushed over to congratulate him for his key role in the win. The mother of a teammate had snapped the picture of the three of them. Mama's hand rested on his cheek affectionately, while Papa had his arm slung around Mateo's shoulders. All of them were smiling widely.

Mateo swallowed deeply, his throat thick with unshed tears. His chest ached as he acknowledged how much he missed them.

Then he flipped farther in the book and pulled out the second picture.

This one was newer, but it evoked the same painful response. He was standing next to his second father, the two of them posing for the photograph right after Mateo's initiation into the Masters' Admiralty. Neither of them smiled, their faces more serious, but that didn't mean there wasn't love. It was simply more guarded, less open.

Mateo ran his finger over the face of the admiral of Castile, and let the first tear slide.

He hadn't had time to mourn the death of his father. He'd been too wrapped up in the investigation surrounding the Domino and the murder of the fleet admiral.

The Domino hadn't merely taken their society's leader. The villain had also stolen the lives of a knight and two admirals…one of whom had walked into his parents' house on the darkest day of his life and given him a new home.

He rubbed his eyes and swallowed down the rest of the tears. There was no time to shed them. He was determined to discover the traitor in the guard, desperate for retribution and perhaps even some sort of closure.

"Bernard."

Mateo jerked at the unexpected voice, standing too close to him. He dropped the two photos he was holding.

The fleet admiral bent down to help him retrieve them, picking up the one of his parents and glancing at it. The man's eyes narrowed slightly, but he made no remark. Mateo took it from him as they straightened, with a quick word of thanks. He tucked both photographs back into the book and closed it.

"I didn't hear you come in, sir." Mateo kicked himself for admitting as much. He was already on shaky ground with his new boss. It wouldn't help him to point out his shortcomings when it came to people sneaking up on him.

Eric's gaze was hard, his face stern when he said, "I think it's time you and I have a talk."

Dimitri and Cecilia checked the cottage, which was clearly meant to be charming and rustic. In places, the plaster had been chipped away to show the original stone of the walls and timeworn beams crossed the ceiling.

Cecilia sniffed. "Ideally, buildings like this are restored, not left to look so...vulgar."

He finished reading through the guest book, which was on a table by the door. There was nothing in there of use. "In Ukraine, people have homes that look like this because they do not have the money to fix them or find better. Perhaps we should market to British tourists."

Cecilia started opening cupboards in the kitchen. "Dimitri?"

"Yes, Cece?"

"Do you think…do you *truly* think Mateo is the traitor?"

"No."

The lie rolled easily off his tongue, and he frowned.

Was it a lie?

He'd told the fleet admiral he didn't *think* it was Mateo, not that it *wasn't* Mateo. He had to be careful. Make sure what he said was based on fact, not on Dimitri's own hope that it wasn't the other man.

Cecilia sighed then flipped open a small folder set prominently on the counter. She read quietly, flipping a few pages, while he checked the undersides of furniture and pried at the baseboard in the small sitting room. It was routine to check. He was hoping for some sort of drop point, a hidden place Manon and the sniper could have left each other notes, or where she might have hidden records she didn't dare keep at Triskelion Castle.

"There are stables," Cecilia said, reading from the book. "You can rent horses and keep them in the stables while you visit. How is this a holiday if you have to care for livestock?"

Stables that weren't always used would make a safer drop point than anywhere in the house. "Smart, *koxaha*."

"You keep calling me that. What does mean?"

"Sweetheart," he lied, hoping his clever woman didn't decide to attempt to learn Ukrainian anytime soon. If she did, she'd soon discover his feelings for her had grown into genuine affection.

"And of course it was smart." She followed him out the back door, and across a large garden of abundant flowers and herbs. The smells—rosemary, lavender, the spice of thyme mingled with the floral scents of a dozen different kinds of flowers—reminded him of his grandmother's house.

The stable was clean and seemed newer than the house. There were two stalls on opposite sides of the aisle from one another, a tack room, and an open space where bales of hay were stacked. A lean cat opened its eyes when they walked in. Dimitri stopped to pet her, praising her in Ukrainian.

Cecilia joined him and tried to pet the cat, who hissed. "The cat likes you."

"I am very likeable."

"Ha!"

"You like it when I pet you," he crooned.

She narrowed her eyes, but he didn't miss the obvious desire he saw in them.

Dimitri was tempted to toss her onto one of the hay bales to show her just how easily he could make her purr. However, doing so without Mateo felt wrong, so he dismissed the idea.

It was easier for his head to let go of the image than his cock, which had grown thick at just the mere thought of getting inside dear Cecilia.

Cecilia went to check one of the stalls, while Dimitri continued petting the cat and looked around. The tops of the exposed beams would be a good option, as would inside or behind the hay bales.

Finding nothing of interest in the stalls, Cecilia opened the door to the tack room, which was about the size of the stall beside it. She flipped on the light, then grabbed a packet of laminated pages off the wall, an instructional booklet similar to what she'd read in the house.

Dimitri thanked the cat for allowing him to pet her, then walked to the tack room, hoping for a stool or mounting block he could use to check the beams.

"There's a page for each horse you can rent. Apparently, it's very relaxing to go for 'scenic trail rides.'" She snorted, as if that very idea was ridiculous.

Dimitri slipped past her, reaching for the small mounting block, which would make the perfect step stool. The walls of the tack room were lined with tidily hung equipment. Bridles and harnesses on one wall, half a dozen saddles on posts sticking straight out of the wall opposite the door. Riding boots in various sizes were neatly lined on shelves. In one corner were pegs hung with miscellaneous items—long lead ropes, hand crops, and even a coiled long whip. There were framed photos of people on horses, horses posed outside the stables, and a few of what he guessed were the views from the scenic trail rides.

Dimitri turned to leave, hauling the mounting block with him. Then stopped. Something he'd just seen was out of place.

He set the block down and turned in a slow circle.

"Dimitri?" Cecilia asked.

He held up a hand to silence her. She made an irritated noise but didn't speak.

He walked slowly around the room twice. He could feel Cecilia watching him.

Once he was sure, he stopped at the coiled whip, lifting it off the peg. It was beautiful, a work of art more than a tool. He shook it out. Five feet of braided black leather, with a large pommel end. Gold leather was worked into the braiding on the stiff handle and pommel, and a small decorative medallion hung from the wrist strap.

He snapped it, the crack loud in the small tack room. Cecilia sucked in air and took a step back.

"Are you afraid?" he asked softly.

"No." She was lying. She scooted to the side, so her back was to the open door.

"This is not a horse whip," he said.

"Then—then what is it?" she asked.

"This is meant for people."

Cecilia took a quick step back, out of the tack room, and grabbed the doorknob, clearly preparing to close him inside.

Dimitri dropped the whip, holding his hands up. "Cece, stop. I will not hurt you. I promised, remember?"

She hesitated. The fact that she did meant she trusted him.

She shouldn't.

"The whip is soft leather. Maybe deerskin. It's not a tool to be used on horses."

"You said that. What do you mean it's for people?"

"This is a custom-made BDSM whip." He stepped to the wall of bridles, fishing out a small one that had been hidden behind the others. "This is too small for a horse. Look at it. It's meant for a person."

Cecilia joined him. "You think this is a holiday home for people who enjoy that kind of sex?"

"It's possible, though there was nothing in the house that would support this being a sex retreat." He handed her the bridle, then picked up the whip, turning over the small tag so she could see it.

"Is that a Masters' Admiralty symbol?" she asked.

"Close, but no." The circular symbol was sectioned into three parts by curved lines. "This is the symbol for BDSM." In the center of each section was a set of initials.

Cecilia bent closer. "M.K. G.R. A.R." She looked up at him, her eyes wide. "The American sniper's name was Griffin Rutherford."

"M.K." He rubbed his thumb over the tag. It was well-made, sterling silver. The whip, the bridle, they were both very expensive pieces, hidden in plain sight amid the other tack. "Manon Kujakski."

Then Cecilia asked the question still left unanswered by the whip. "But…who is A.R.?"

Chapter Eleven

"Have you made any progress in your investigation?" Eric asked him.

Mateo shook his head as they walked from the Spartan Guard residences back to the castle. The air smelled like saltwater, and was so familiar it made his stomach ache. This place had been his home for so long. He couldn't lose it.

As far as the traitor, all he had at the moment were suspicions without proof. Until he had concrete evidence that would allow him to name Charlotta as the traitor, he would have to remain silent.

"You realize time is running out." Eric mounted the steps to the second floor where the guest rooms were.

"Yes, sir. I do. I need more time. One week is not long enough to launch a prop—"

"You have one week, Bernard. Be thankful you have that much."

Mateo sucked in a deep breath, trying to remain calm. His nerves were frazzled, his emotions running too close to the surface.

"Do you truly intend to uphold your end of the bargain?" Mateo's tone was too belligerent to be considered anything less than rude.

It wasn't lost on the fleet admiral, whose eyes narrowed. This man was not Kacper, who had a quiet sort of command. He'd been frail toward the end, but strong. Eric was…he was a different kind of strong.

He was a force to be reckoned with, a man who could probably protect his guards better than they could him. Something about that rubbed against the grain.

Mateo was good at his job. He'd spent years training for, then serving in the Spartan Guard, protecting the position Eric now held.

Rather than call him out, Eric simply said, "Don't insult me by questioning my word. *If* you give me the traitor's name. *If* you have enough proof to make me believe it."

"If I do, you'll dissolve my trinity? And I will resume my place as head of the guard?"

Eric nodded—but that response was overshadowed by a gasp from the open doorway.

Mateo saw Cecilia standing there, pain in her eyes. Dimitri stood behind her, his expression reflecting pure murder.

"You're searching for the traitor so that you can get your job back?" Cecilia's words were tight. "So that you can leave us?"

Mateo hated the thickness in her voice that betrayed the tears she was fighting to hold in.

"Cecilia." He stepped around Eric, walking over to her. "Cece."

She erupted in anger. "Don't you dare call me that!"

Before he could reach her, she spun around and darted away from him, down the corridor toward the guest room they'd been given.

He looked at Dimitri. "I thought you were getting a room in Douglas."

"You were misled. Apparently we all were." Dimitri flashed an unreadable look over his shoulder at the fleet admiral, then he followed Cecilia.

Mateo didn't spare Eric another glance. He didn't have time. His chest was tight, his heart racing.

He'd hurt her. Hurt *them.*

That same stupid voice that had warned him it was too late was now telling him to go after them.

He rushed toward the guest room, but pulled up short outside the closed door. No doubt they'd locked it to keep him out.

Mateo stood rooted to the floor, fighting for some answer, some reason he could give for deceiving them, for sleeping with them while actively working against their union.

There was none.

He'd been wrong.

Which meant there was only one course of action left to him.

He reached for the doorknob. If it was locked, he'd piss them off further by using his master key rather than knocking, but he couldn't give them the option to refuse him entrance.

Mateo was surprised when it turned with ease. They hadn't locked him out.

Stepping inside, his stomach roiled with nervousness and guilt as he saw Cecilia and Dimitri sitting on the edge of the bed, holding hands. Neither of them was speaking or looking at each other. Rather, they were facing him, as if they'd been awaiting his arrival.

"Mateo," Dimitri said, gesturing to the chair by the bed.

He would have preferred to stand, but he joined them, taking the seat. "I need to—"

"When did you find out we were being placed in a trinity?" Cecilia asked, cutting off his apology.

"A few minutes before the two of you. The admiral of England told me."

She looked much calmer than she had a few minutes earlier in the hallway. He was constantly amazed by her strength and intelligence. "And he offered you a deal. Find the traitor and the trinity is dissolved?"

He started to nod, but stopped. "I asked to be given the chance to do the investigation and keep my job."

"Why weren't we told?" She was determined to chisel away until she got all the answers she needed.

"That was the fleet admiral's decision. I suspect that condition was put in place because he didn't expect me to succeed. Not in the allotted time frame."

"Which was one week?"

Mateo sighed and nodded. "The date of our binding ceremony remains if we don't produce the name of the traitor in the Spartan Guard before that."

"And if we do give the fleet admiral a name?"

"I keep my job as head of the guard."

"What happens to us?"

Mateo didn't have a clue. Eric had been promised the trinity would be dissolved, but he didn't know if that meant they would all go their separate ways, or if another third would be partnered with Dimitri and Cecilia.

Mateo wished he didn't hate the idea so much of the two of them living out those damn fantasies he'd had of a home and nursery with someone else.

He lifted one shoulder. "I don't know."

Dimitri had been silent during Cecilia's questioning, his eyes hard and dark.

"You don't know?" Cecilia asked quietly through gritted teeth.

Her tone suggested she didn't believe Mateo. And why should she? For the past few days, Dimitri and Cecilia had thought the three of them were not only searching for a traitor, but building the foundation for their futures…together. Now, they knew he'd been doing the opposite—actively working to escape the trinity.

"I'm sorry," he said, his chest burning, his head pounding. "I'm so sorry."

Cecilia rose from the bed, walking to the foot of it, grasping the post. Her back was turned to him. It appeared she'd asked all her questions and his apology would never be enough.

Mateo stood slowly, his gaze on Dimitri. He half expected the other man to throw a punch. He almost wished he would.

"I'll spend tonight in my own bed."

"No," Dimitri said, not rising from the bed. It was the first word he'd spoken since inviting him to sit down.

Cecilia turned around to face him. "What?"

Dimitri looked at her, offered her a smile that revealed his true affection for her. Mateo had seen that look only when they'd been in bed together, only when they were in the throes of passion, when he thought neither Mateo nor Cecilia would notice.

This time, he didn't try to hide his feelings for her. "He's staying with us, Cece."

She narrowed her eyes, clearly ready to argue that assertion, but Dimitri raised one finger to silence her.

"We have four days left to deliver a traitor to the fleet admiral. If we fail to do that, the three of us will be bound together for life. We will do tonight as we've done before when our words failed us. We will use our bodies to communicate, to say what we cannot."

Cecilia had been the one to initiate that bizarre though effective way of forging a relationship, but it didn't appear that she had any expectation of sex succeeding tonight.

"You can use that if you wish." Dimitri gestured toward the corner of the room just behind Mateo's left shoulder. He turned to look, his eyes widening at the sight of the wicked-looking whip propped there.

"Where did you get that?" Mateo asked, walking over to it.

"A vacation home near here."

Mateo didn't bother to look at them as he picked up the whip to examine it. "I thought you were going to Douglas."

Dimitri had followed him across the room. "We lied."

Mateo glanced over at Dimitri, his lips parted to tell them they should have waited for him, but he stopped himself, considered what they were saying.

They'd escaped the castle...and him. Perhaps they weren't disappointed by his attempt to leave the trinity. Perhaps they didn't care if he was there or not.

What if their true anger lay in their fears of being parted from each other?

"We were given one week to root out the traitor. I thought it would be expedient if we split up." Dimitri's response made sense.

The whip did not.

"This is part of the investigation?"

Dimitri nodded. "It is. Look at it."

Mateo studied the braided cord, taking in the elegance, the obvious expense.

"You know what it is," Dimitri murmured.

Mateo nodded, even though Dimitri didn't ask a question. He was no stranger to BDSM. Something told him Dimitri wasn't either.

A small tag-like medallion dangled from the end. Mateo sucked in a deep breath when he saw the initials. "Manon. Griffin."

"Yes," Dimitri said, pointing to the other set of initials. "But who is A.R.?"

Mateo thought about it, ran through their list of suspects, then shrugged. "I have no idea. How did you get this in here?"

"I carried it through the front door. When Cecilia and I arrived, we came here first, thinking to find you in our room."

"No one noticed you carrying it in?" Mateo asked.

"Only Marie, the guard at the front. She looked equally terrified and impressed, but her behavior was normal, not suspicious."

Mateo recalled his one and only night in Charlotta's bed. It had been very vanilla, almost chaste, and he'd come away with the impression her sexual experience had been limited. He'd indulged in no more than missionary with her, something in the somewhat rigid way she held herself, telling him that was all she would be comfortable with.

Cecilia left her post by the bed, walking over to join them. She lifted the braided part of the whip, studying it.

Then she looked at Mateo, as she swung the braid slowly.

He shook his head, giving her a slight grin. "I'm more sorry than I can say, Cecilia. But I'm not that sorry."

The joke worked. Thank God.

Cecilia giggled and Dimitri grinned.

Cecilia was the first to sober up, and Mateo could tell she regretted her momentary lapse when she said, "This isn't funny. I'm still angry with you."

"I know. And you should be. I hope you'll believe me when I say I wanted you and Dimitri to know exactly what we were working for right from the beginning."

"To end our trinity," she said softly.

He nodded. Mateo wanted to reach out to her, to pull her into his arms. He wanted it more than he should. More than was wise.

"I'll spend tonight in my own room," he repeated.

Cecilia shook her head. "No. You won't."

She spoke with confidence, even though she feared spending another night in Mateo's arms—and Dimitri's—would only lead to certain heartbreak for her if they uncovered the turncoat in time. Then she realized her broken heart was imminent regardless.

She was a St. John, a family known for their intellect as well as their passion. Her family tree was overflowing with brilliant minds in the fields of science, mathematics, and history. Yet when it came to matters of the heart, they led with emotion rather than reason.

"Cece," Mateo whispered. She heard the same regretful longing in his voice. He wanted to be here. He wanted to leave.

She raised her arms, wrapping them around his shoulders, pulling him toward her for a kiss. Mateo didn't resist. Not even a little.

His lips were gentle at first, a continuation of the apology he'd spoken. This one was delivered with his mouth and tongue, soft caresses of remorse.

166

She didn't want that right now. While Mateo was suffering from guilt, she was still furious...at him and at the situation. This was not the way the Masters' Admiralty worked. Trinities were formed to strengthen the society, and they were made to last.

Cecilia would find this new fleet admiral tomorrow and set him straight on that. But for tonight...

Tonight, she would show Mateo what happened to a husband who lied to his wife. She was a forgiving person...after a time. Later, she would find a way to put the anger and hurt behind her.

This was not later.

She broke the union of their lips, glancing at Dimitri. As always, his head was the hardest to get inside. She suspected he was also angry about Mateo's deceit, but she couldn't tell if he was upset or perhaps even a little bit relieved to know there was an out.

She took Mateo's hand, then reached for Dimitri's, intent on leading them to the bed.

Dimitri resisted her pull, his eyes lingering on the whip. "No whip?" He didn't wait for a reply from either of them before following Cecilia's lead. "Pity," he murmured.

She prayed to God he was joking because if he wasn't, she'd turn over every stone on the Isle of Man to find the traitor herself.

Dimitri chuckled, and she realized she must have given away her fear of the nasty-looking "sex toy," though nothing about the thing looked playful.

"Fear not, sweet Cece," Dimitri said, releasing her hand so he could wrap his arms around her from behind. Whispering in her ear, he said, "There are plenty of other delicious ways Mateo and I can punish you."

She tried to break free of his grip, intent on turning around to set him straight, but he anticipated her response and tightened his hold.

"I'm not the one in need of punishment tonight," she reminded him.

"That is true," Dimitri murmured.

Mateo stood before them, facing them, clearly considering that. After a few moments, he sighed and lifted his arms, his palms up in surrender.

"Do your worst," Mateo said at last.

"Take off your clothes," Cecilia demanded.

Mateo responded without hesitation, shedding his shirt, pants, shoes and boxers with quick, quiet efficiency. His guilt clearly wasn't impacting his arousal. Cecilia ogled his thick, hard cock for a little longer than was probably polite. Then she realized both men were watching her.

Dimitri's arms slackened. "Why merely look, Cece? When you can touch. Taste."

She slid free and sank to her knees before Mateo. It was hard to disagree with something that made so much sense.

Cecilia wrapped her hand around the base of Mateo's cock, sliding her closed palm from root to tip, then back down again.

Mateo sucked in a loud breath that he expelled as she finished her first two strokes.

She used just her hand at first, loving the chance to look up at Mateo's face, to see the pleasure there, to hear his low moans. When he drew his fingers through her hair, gripping it to pull her mouth closer, she resisted.

He looked down, his gaze curious, then determined.

Mateo pulled harder. Cecilia's pussy clenched at the strength, the force. She loved the slight sting in her scalp and the power of his unspoken demand.

At first, their dominance in the bedroom unnerved her, but there was something about the image of that whip, the way Dimitri talked of delicious punishment, and Mateo's hands in her hair that had her longing to do something completely out of character.

Submit.

This time, Cecilia responded to Mateo's desires, parting her lips and sucking the head of his cock into her mouth.

Mateo hissed when she used her teeth to tease him, clenching down until she knew she'd skirted the line between play and pain.

His fingers tightened and he tugged her mouth off of him, tilting her face upwards.

"Bad girl," he said in a dark, sexy voice.

This wasn't turning out according to her plan. Cecilia had decided to push Mateo right to the edge of his climax before pulling away. She'd intended to ask Dimitri to hold their lover's hands behind his back the way they'd done with her, to keep him from finding pleasure on his own.

Withholding his climax, keeping him on edge for hours, had seemed like a suitable punishment before Mateo had taken the reins away from her. Now it was she who was hurting, impatient and ready to do whatever it took to get him inside her.

Before she could act on her own desires, Dimitri reached beneath her arms and pulled her from the floor.

"As much as I love seeing your mouth on our lover, Cece, I think he likes it too much. Perhaps it would be better to save that for another time."

Mateo's gaze darkened. "Dimitri." His tone was laced with warning. Mateo had wanted the blow job. Badly.

"Lay in the center of the bed," Dimitri said.

This time Mateo *did* hesitate. It appeared his guilt wasn't enough to counteract the dominant man struggling to take control.

"Now," Dimitri added, when Mateo didn't respond.

Funny how that single word pushed Mateo over the edge.

The wrong edge.

Mateo crossed his arms, his stance one of outright defiance, which was an amazing feat considering he was completely nude and sporting an impressive erection. "I don't take orders in the bedroom, Dimitri."

Dimitri didn't move, didn't respond with words, but Cecilia felt the tension between her lovers hovering, thick in the air, and she suddenly understood. Dimitri *had* been hurt by their discovery.

Like her, he was angry to have been deceived by someone they'd started to feel a genuine connection with.

No, it was more than that. Cecilia had begun to care for Mateo, had opened her heart and mind to the idea that they'd be spending a lifetime together.

Until that moment, she'd questioned Dimitri's feelings. Not anymore.

"I will," she said softly, a sudden wave of desperation washing through her. If their time was limited, she would be selfish. She would take everything she wanted from them and live with the heartache. Better that, than suffer regret over wasting even a few precious days with them.

"Cecilia," Mateo whispered.

"Cece," she corrected. "To you, to Dimitri, I'm Cece. And I'm yours. Whether for the rest of our lives or only for a few more days, I am yours."

Dimitri reached for her, gripping her hair in his hand, ponytail style, before tugging it, turning her face toward him.

His strong pull had the desired effect and a softly whispered "yes" escaped as her eyes drifted shut. The intensity, the pain, sent electric currents shimmering along her skin, down to her pussy.

Her nipples budded tightly and she suffered a need so powerful it hurt.

Dimitri didn't slacken his hold. Instead, he used it to pull her toward him, not stopping until her breasts brushed against his chest and she was forced to open her eyes, finding he'd bent slightly, their lips mere inches apart.

She tried to move closer, intent on kissing him, but Dimitri held her away.

"Look at me," he demanded, when her eyelids began to slide shut again. They flew open at his command.

"Only in the bedroom."

She frowned, confused. "What?"

"I accept the gift of your submission, but I only want it in the bedroom. Away from here, I want your sass, your intelligence, your take-charge-and-no-prisoners attitude. Do you understand?"

She grinned and rolled her eyes at him. "Dim, you were always only getting this woman in bed. If you think for one second I'd let you or Mateo boss me around—"

Dimitri kissed her into silence, robbing her the opportunity to finish setting him straight.

When he released her, he relinquished his grip on her hair as well and stepped away, looking at Mateo.

She turned to face him. While he shared that same undeniable need to be in power, Mateo wielded feathers, rather than whips. He cupped her face between his large hands, a sexy, endearing grin emerging even as his eyes bespoke wonder.

"I don't deserve you."

"You're right. You don't. But in all fairness, neither of you do." She let the tease land before laughing lightly.

"Careful, *koxaha*. I'm itching to punish someone for tonight's revelations. If it cannot be Mateo…"

"Punish how?" she whispered, perfectly aware the breathlessness of her question revealed her desire, rather than fear.

"Take off her clothing, Mateo. Undress our wi— woman."

Dimitri's quick correction wasn't lost on any of them. If they succeeded in their investigation, there was a good chance Cecilia would never be their wife. She felt the loss of it profoundly.

Mateo unbuttoned her blouse, taking his time, stroking each uncovered bit of skin with his hands or his tongue. Dimitri stood next to them, still as stone, watching the unveiling…and the adoration Mateo lavished on her.

Hours could have passed, for all Cecilia knew or cared, by the time Mateo had her completely naked. Her skin was flushed, her body feverish, and every intelligent thought she might have managed fled. She was a vessel for pleasure—hers and theirs—nothing more.

It didn't need to be more because what she felt in that moment was everything.

Mateo kissed her one last time, then stepped aside, both men flanking her, clearing her path to the bed.

"Lay down, sweet Cece," Dimitri crooned. "On your hands and knees. Let's see how sincere your offer to submit to us truly is."

She didn't move. Rather, her gaze shifted to where the wicked-looking whip rested in the corner of the room. She recalled the loud cracking sound Dimitri had produced with it in the tack room, the expert way he'd handled it.

Dimitri reached for her earlobe, tugging it in a playful way that felt too silly for the serious man. "Not the whip. Never the whip. I can read your expressions, can recognize the difference between fear and desire. You do not have to be afraid of me."

"Or me," Mateo added.

She knew that. Had known it without needing the reassurance.

It was then she had to admit her hesitance was based on something more. "I don't know how to…"

Dimitri grinned, and even though she hadn't voiced her concern aloud, he knew what was truly bothering her. "Submission will be hard for you. I doubt you'll be able to shut that beautiful mind of yours down enough to fully master it. It means Mateo and I will have our work cut out for us. Get on the bed. Hands and knees."

Before she could move into position, Mateo climbed on the bed, lying on his back. "Come. Over me."

Having him below her made it easier for her to obey. Dimitri was right. She would be a challenge. And the clever man was wise to tell her so because it made her sound powerful in her own right, not passive or weak.

She climbed over Mateo, placing her hands by his shoulders, her knees resting next to his hips. His erection was too tempting, so she started to lower herself onto him.

Mateo's grip was unrelenting as he held her away, shaking his head. "Do only as you're told."

"You know you want what I'm offering as much as I do," her voice sultry, seductive.

A loud slap punctuated by a serious sting assaulted her bare ass.

"*Cazzo!*" She glared at Dimitri over her shoulder.

"Not yet, *koxaha*, but soon."

That was the second time today Dimitri had known the meaning of her Italian, and while it probably wasn't difficult to figure out what she was saying when put into context, something told her he had more than a passing knowledge of the language. Tomorrow she would ask for more specifics regarding his so-called government job.

Dimitri spanked her again, three quick slaps that weren't as hard as the first, but when put together in quick, successive motion added to the soreness in her ass. "You're thinking too much," he warned.

Cecilia tried to move away, but Mateo's grip on her waist was unyielding.

"I changed my m—oh!"

Her words were abruptly cut off when Dimitri followed up his spanking with something much more to her liking. The tip of his index finger stroked her clit, rubbing it in that lovely way that never failed to make her body hum.

She stopped resisting, arching her back to invite more.

Dimitri ignored her desire and added half a dozen more spanks to her already tender ass.

"So warm," Dimitri said, following the spanking with a gentle caress that left her panting, the warring sensations of pain and pleasure putting her in an unfamiliar idyllic state, one where she was mindless, powerless, yet peaceful.

Dimitri's hand vanished, but she didn't have time to wonder where he'd gone because Mateo took over the sensual torture, grasping her breasts, squeezing the flesh.

Using his fingers, he pinched her nipples, increasing the pressure until she cried out. Then he kissed away the hurt before teasing the sensitive tips with his tongue. She sighed, but the feeling was short-lived once again when Mateo brought his teeth into the play. The soft strokes of his tongue turned to a bite, as he constantly turned his head left to right and back again, giving both of her breasts the same study in contrasting sensations.

It was brutal. It was bliss.

Once again, she tried to lower herself on Mateo, her pussy agonizingly empty. This time, it was Dimitri who stopped her. The mattress sank under his weight as she turned to look at him. While Mateo distracted her, Dimitri had undressed.

More than that, he held something in his hands.

"Where did you get that?" she asked.

Dimitri gave her a sexy grin. "The pharmacy in Douglas. When we stopped for motion-sickness medicine."

He uncapped the tube of lubrication. His position next to her lifted ass indicated his intentions well enough. She shivered before the first touch of cold lube hit her anus.

Dimitri slowly rubbed it around just the rim, teasing her. Cecilia's head dropped as she tried to still her breathing.

Mateo ran a hand through her hair, tugging until her eyes met his.

"You know what we want?"

She nodded.

"You know you can refuse?"

Cecilia considered that. She'd never taken a man into her ass. Her experience with anal play consisted of the fingers of a previous lover and a small butt plug she'd bought for herself on a whim, but had enjoyed.

Neither man moved until she nodded again. "I know I can. But I won't."

Dimitri remained silent as he pressed the tip of the tube to her back hole and squeezed a generous amount of the cold lube inside. He followed that up with his finger, sliding it in slowly. Just one finger and she already felt full, stretched. How would she be able to accept his hard cock? Neither Dimitri nor Mateo were small men…anywhere.

He added a second finger, and she hissed at the initial sharp prick. Dimitri didn't stop, but he also didn't rush. He gave her time to accept his invasion in incremental degrees, somehow seeming to know when she'd acclimated to it.

The third finger robbed her of breath entirely. Mateo tightened his grip in her hair—she'd forgotten he was still holding it—and it distracted her briefly. He pulled her face down to his, kissing her passionately, deeply.

By the time the two of them came up for air, Dimitri had buried three fingers deep in her ass, stroking them slowly in and out in the same way he'd fuck her with his cock.

Any semblance of pain was gone, replaced with a primal need that had her ready to claw them to pieces if they didn't take her now.

Mateo had the benefit of seeing her face, so he recognized the change.

"Now, *mi cielito*," he murmured softly. "Lower yourself onto me. Take me inside you."

Dimitri didn't remove his fingers as Cecilia obeyed Mateo's gentle demand. She would take the time to analyze what was happening to her later. Right now, she couldn't put words to the feelings—physically or emotionally.

That was surprising by itself, but the true shock of it lay in the fact she didn't care.

"I'm yours," she whispered, once she'd taken Mateo in fully.

She saw the sadness in his eyes even as he smiled at her words.

He's leaving us.

The thought came in, unbidden, unwanted. She'd managed to forget that for several blissful minutes, but now it was back.

It vanished when Mateo said, "And I'm yours, Cece."

If it was a lie, she'd take it, and gladly.

Dimitri's fingers slid away and the shifting of the mattress told her he'd moved directly behind her. The front of his thighs brushed the back of hers, and then she felt his knuckles against her still tender bottom as he directed the head of his cock toward her ass.

She wasn't aware she was holding her breath until Mateo whispered, "Breathe."

Dimitri had prepared her well. At some point, he coated his cock with the lube and, while there was no denying the pinch as he pressed in, there was no pain.

Mateo held still until Dimitri was completely inside her.

Two men. Two lovers.

Cecilia had considered herself an experienced woman until that moment. Now she couldn't imagine a life without these two men in her bed, taking her like this, night after night.

She was surrounded, possessed, claimed.

And she never wanted to be free again.

Somehow, Mateo and Dimitri knew exactly what to do, moving in tandem with a rhythm that felt natural, practiced. While her lovers found it difficult to form a bond away from the bedroom, there was no denying they'd found their common ground here.

She gasped when they increased the speed. Whatever grip the two of them had held on their control appeared to have slipped.

Thank God.

She urged them on, begging for them to take her harder, faster. They granted her every wish, every command, and suddenly she understood there was no dominance, no submission here.

Only pleasure and desire and…

Love.

Cecilia went over twice, coming with loud cries, but they didn't follow, didn't give up this heaven they'd created together.

Suddenly, it felt as if she'd left her body, as if she were floating above them. In a lucid moment, she would also try to analyze that.

Right now…

Cecilia came again, and this time they were with her. Mateo grunted as he pressed in deep one last time, calling her *mi cielito, mi alma*, and then…*mi vida*.

His heaven, his soul.

His life.

Dimitri was only a dozen heartbeats behind them, and his climax appeared just as powerful, as overwhelming.

His hands tightened on her hips as he jerked inside roughly, filling her.

"Cece… My Cece."

It was all he seemed capable of saying. It was enough when coupled with the soft kisses he pressed against the back of her head, the slow, gentle way he withdrew, as if now she were suddenly made of glass.

They shifted on the mattress, Dimitri taking her left, Mateo her right. Each of them grasped the hand nearest them as they lay on their backs, panting for air, grinning like lovesick fools.

There were so many similarities between her lovers when they were here, like this.

She prayed that someday soon this camaraderie, this ability to work together would follow them into the daylight, into the investigation. They were good together. Cecilia knew they could discover the traitor if they would put aside their distrust and their secrets.

Discover the traitor.

To do so would spell the end of this.

Of them.

Chapter Twelve

Mateo slipped from the bedroom silently, leaving Dimitri and Cecilia naked and wrapped in each other's arms.

He needed a few moments away from them to sort out the million different emotions pummeling him. He was being torn in half as he acknowledged his deepest desires ran in opposite directions.

Four days ago, he wanted nothing more than to root out the traitor in his guard and resume his position, finishing his career as he'd always intended.

Tonight, a bigger, more powerful desire overshadowed that dream.

Cecilia's sweet offer of submission had taken his breath away. The trust she'd bestowed on him, even after discovering his deceit, was more than he deserved.

Yet he wanted to be a man worthy of her love.

And Dimitri's.

That feeling was the harder one to sort out. His instincts told him Dimitri was holding something back, and he knew—*knew*—that the man didn't truly trust him.

But when they were in the bedroom together, he felt a kinship with the other man like nothing he'd ever felt before. Like they were cut of the same cloth, two soldiers fighting for the same cause. If only Mateo could figure out what that cause was. And why they couldn't maintain that same closeness when they weren't in bed.

It was time one of them took the first step in that direction.

Mateo traversed two corridors before realizing where he was headed. The decision hadn't been made consciously, but somewhere deep inside, he knew what he needed to do.

He would be the first to open a door.

God willing, they wouldn't slam it in his face.

Eric turned sideways to slide behind the elegant love seat, then grabbed the edge of a wall-sized canvas painting, opening it like a door. It swung on silent, hidden hinges, revealing the entrance to the small hall beyond.

He'd discovered this hidden tunnel on the first day at the castle, nearly had a fucking heart attack that it existed and didn't have some sort of biometric scanner required to open it, and he'd questioned the Spartan Guard about it. Looking back on it, his questioning might have looked more like him yelling and asking if they were all imbecilic.

Years ago, when the fleet admiral's private quarters were upgraded to include electricity and modern plumbing, the remodeling had necessitated cutting off an old staircase. The result was a low-ceiling hallway above the Great Hall that would have, at one time, served as a servant's hall. Now it was an access point for plumbing and electrical maintenance, and an emergency exit. For those reasons, it had been covered over with the painting, but not totally sealed off from the inside.

He stepped over the two-foot lintel and into the dark hallway, pulling the painting back into place as he did. It was a shitty emergency exit because his predecessor had used it not only for tradesmen's access, but storage.

In near perfect darkness, Eric skirted around a chair and several small trunks. The wall was just under a meter wide, and crammed with items the previous fleet admiral and his wives had wanted out of the way, but close on hand. He'd been through every box, looking for anything the traitorous Manon might have left, but they were mostly linens, old clothing, holiday decorations and extra chairs that matched the dining room set.

Eventually he'd get rid of it all, but for now he'd memorized exactly where to step so that he could navigate the hall in darkness.

He told himself it was only because he didn't have time, not because some part of him couldn't bear the thought of throwing away the memorabilia of a marriage.

Eric had a coil of rope over his shoulder. He held it close to his side as he stepped over and around the clutter so it wouldn't catch on anything. At the far end of the hall was a heavy exterior door that let out onto the ramparts behind the low, sculpted upper edge of the outer walls. A long fire ladder was kept in a box just inside the exterior door. Clearly the plan was that if there was a fire, and for whatever reason no other exit was possible, the fleet admiral could escape through this hall, and use the fire ladder to scale the wall to safety.

He hitched the rope higher on his shoulder. Whenever he went out this way, he brought his own rope and scaled down the wall. It wasn't that he didn't trust the fire ladder…

Actually, that was exactly it. He didn't trust the fire ladder.

Or the Spartan Guard.

Eric skirted around yet another chair, took a sideways step—

And plummeted through the floor.

Mateo walked through the castle, steps quickening. Dimitri and Cecilia had stolen his heart, and all he'd given them in return was deceit. He wanted to offer them something real.

While their futures were so uncertain, Mateo wanted to share his past with them. It was all he had to offer. Something he'd always given parts of to those closest to him, while withholding other bits.

He wanted to share it all with them, so he walked silently through the corridor, intent on heading to his bedchamber in the barracks to retrieve the photos of his family. They'd been tucked away in that medical journal for years, rarely looked at.

Today, he would take them out…and leave them out. Maybe even frame them. It was something people did when they were in true families. They kept memories visible, present.

He wasn't sure what Dimitri and Cecilia would say when he told them about the brutal murders, but he could imagine—Dimitri's quiet simmering anger that the murderer had never been brought to justice, Cecilia's hand on his shoulder, offering comfort.

Mateo had had more time to deal with the loss of his mama and papa. It was the more recent blow he hadn't faced, hadn't taken the time to even acknowledge. To do so would be to admit that he truly was alone in this world.

Or…he had been.

Until…

Eric began to drop through into the cavernous Great Hall below. It was nearly ten meters down to the unforgiving stone. The fall would probably kill him, certainly incapacitate him.

Those thoughts flashed through his head dispassionately as his legs went through the floor. The small carpet that had covered the booby-trap hole fluttered into the darkness.

He thrust his arms out, right arm slapping stone, elbow cracking as it hit, shoulder joint screaming in pain. His left hand grabbed at the air, and managed to catch hold of a dusty chair. It was enough to arrest his movement. He stopped falling, his entire body weight suspended on his right arm and left hand. He was chest-deep, his breathing hard from a combination of effort and shock. He stilled his instinctively kicking legs and slowed his breaths with the ease of long practice and many hours of training. There was a time for panic and a time for assessing.

For a moment he thought he'd be okay. His right arm was flat on the floor, his armpit jabbed against the opening he'd fallen through. His left was stretched out and up, his fingers barely grasping a leg of the chair.

In this position he didn't have the leverage he needed to pull himself up with his right arm, he could put his left arm flat on the floor and haul himself up that way. That assumed his right shoulder didn't fail him. His shoulder and elbow were screaming in pain, as if there were a hot poker stabbing into the joins.

He wasn't willing to bet his life that his right arm was strong enough to support him. But he knew he could do a one-armed pull-up. It was part of his regular workout. If he could hold himself up long enough to wedge the chair into place to then use it as a pull-up bar, he'd be fine.

And he had the rope.

As tempting as it was to swing his legs and use the momentum to make a desperate grab for the spindle or back of the chair, he'd done enough mountain climbing to know how foolish that was. Partitioning his panic into a dark back room in his mind, he tensed his right shoulder, fingers white as he tried to pretend the smooth edge of a well-worn stone was enough of a handhold to keep him from falling to his death. Then he took a deep breath and released the leg of the chair.

The coil of rope slid down his shoulder into his left hand. His right elbow and shoulder screamed at him, and for a moment he felt like his arm was sliding across the floor.

When he figured out who'd done this—because this was no accident—there was going to be hell to pay.

Maybe he'd loosen his control. Maybe he'd let the berserker out.

Eric flipped the coil of rope into the hall. Finding one end by touch, he looped it through the rung of the chair. In theory, he should be able to tie a one-handed surgical knot. In practice, the rope was too thick, and despite its name, it was a whole lot easier with two hands. Every time he reached out to work the rope, his lower body swung, pulling against his right arm and shoulder.

Maybe he'd have Dimitri torture Mateo before killing him.

His wife, Dahlia, would have been horrified that he'd even thought such a thing. She wouldn't have loved the man he'd become after her death.

Eric tugged on the rope, securing a single loose knot.

Then his right arm slipped, he lost his tenuous hold, and the fleet admiral hurtled through the air toward the ground below.

Mateo was nearly at the stairs to the first floor that led to the side door and path that would take him to the barracks when he heard a faint shout. He stopped, listening. The shout came again—and then there was a crash.

He turned in place, gauging where the sound had come from. He wished he had his radio on him but since he wasn't on duty, he wasn't carrying it.

He did have his phone. Pulling it from his pocket, he speed-dialed Derrick.

"Where are you?"

"Mateo?"

"Where are you?"

"I'm…why? What's happened?"

His tone must have given him away. "All guards to the castle. Low-profile search."

"Yes, sir."

Mateo heard Derrick start barking orders, probably into his radio, before he hung up.

The second floor had the bedrooms, a sitting room more private than those on the first floor and, more importantly, one end of the second-floor hall had access to the small interior balcony that overlooked the Great Hall. That was where Mateo headed. He was fairly certain that was where the noise had come from, and even if it hadn't, the balcony was a good vantage point to do a sweep of that room. He'd start there and move on.

On the rare occasions the membership—or at least whatever portion of it they could fit in the Great Hall— gathered at Triskelion Castle, the balcony served as a stage for the fleet admiral to use to address the crowd.

He opened the door and stepped out, looking over the railing to the floor of the Great Hall below. It was dim, but not so dark that he couldn't see a huddled mass of what looked like broken furniture on the floor. That must have been the crashing sound.

He looked up, spotting a darker hole in the ceiling of the Great Hall, near the edge wall, where the ceiling was flat rather than steepled.

The mound on the floor moved. A bit of what looked to be a broken chair tumbled down, clacking on the floor to reveal a blond head.

Mateo's heart stopped. "Admiral!"

The figure twitched. He was alive.

Mateo turned and ran, racing for the main stairs. He would not let another fleet admiral die on his watch.

After all he'd been through, all he'd survived, this is how he was going to die?

Fucking figures.

Eric waited for the blackness to take him.

Nope. He was conscious. And alive.

Someone—who'd been torturing him at the time, so they were in a position to know—had said he was too stubborn to die.

He was alive, which meant he had to deal with what just happened.

Eric didn't want to assess his injuries. With any kind of serious fall, the risk of life-altering injury was high. He'd definitely survived. He was in too much pain to be dead. Even hell couldn't hurt this much. Eric gritted his teeth. Pain was probably a good thing. It meant he still had feeling in his limbs.

"Admiral!"

He recognized the voice. Mateo's accent was thicker than normal.

There was the hollow sound of the large doors to the Great Hall being unlocked, then opened. Damn it all, he was defenseless right now. He'd landed on his side, the chair falling on top of him. He grabbed with one hand for a bit of broken chair, holding it like a club. He hissed as his hand touched it.

He'd grabbed the rope just before he fell, and the skin of both palms was burned from the friction with the rope. It was good nylon climbing rope, so it wasn't as bad as it could have been.

His grip on the makeshift kludge lasted only a minute, then the bit of wood tumbled from his fingers.

Helpless. He hated being helpless.

"Fleet Admiral!"

Eric sagged in relief. It wasn't Mateo who'd opened the door, but Charlotta, the Spartan Guard from his home territory. It was foolish of him to trust her just because she sounded like home. Exceptionally foolish, but right now, he needed to trust someone.

He didn't have a choice. Her footsteps rushed toward him, and damn it but he hated to have his back to the door.

"Gun," he said in his native language. When she didn't respond, he repeated the command in Swedish.

"Sir?" she replied in the same language.

"Get me my gun. Back."

The bits of chair were shifted off of him. Charlotta was kneeling at his side. He blinked—there was either blood or sweat in his eyes—and tried to get a better look at her. Charlotta's mouth was open, her face pinched with distress.

She must have felt him looking because her expression closed down. "You need medical attention."

Behind him, he heard the door open, and footsteps he thought he recognized as Mateo's.

"Gun," he snarled.

Charlotta took the gun from the hidden holster at his back and passed it to him. He felt the cool air when she tugged his shirt up. Another good sign. Eric's hand shook, but the metal felt strangely good against his burned skin. His fingers obeyed, and he was able to hold it.

He'd be able to fire it, too, if needed.

Mateo raced into the Great Hall, his phone in one hand, ready to call the paramedics. For specialized medical care, they usually took the fleet admiral to London or Belfast, as they had with Kacper, but for emergencies, including the odd training injury among the Spartan Guard, they used the local emergency services.

Charlotta had beaten him there. She was kneeling beside the fleet admiral, whose back was to Mateo.

She surged to her feet and raised one hand. "Stop."

Mateo slowed to a fast walk, but skirted the fleet admiral so he wouldn't risk touching him. "Get the backboard and the neck collar. We need to stabilize him until the paramedics get here." He dropped to a squat near the fleet admiral's head. "Fleet Admiral. Eric. Can you hear me? You need to remain still."

Charlotta hadn't moved.

Mateo twisted to glare up at her, putting steel in his words. "Go."

"I'm not leaving him with you," Charlotta said quietly.

Mateo blinked. She shifted her weight, and he noticed she'd swung her on-duty side arm around. Her hand was on it.

Mateo pushed to his feet, angling his body to put himself between her and the fleet admiral.

"What are you doing, Charlotta?"

"Distracting you." The fleet admiral's words were weak, but when Mateo turned, Eric was looking up at him.

And there was a gun pointed at Mateo's chest.

"Fleet Admiral?"

"Stop right there, Mateo."

Mateo froze, partially in shock, partially in response to the gun.

The door burst open, and Derrick, Nikolas and Marie pounded into the room.

Mateo looked up. "Nikolas, get the backboard and C collar from the emergency kit. We need to stabilize him. Marie, call an ambulance, and call ahead to Noble. Then call in Dr. Chandler."

He was the head of the Spartan Guard. His job didn't end just because the fleet admiral was planning to shoot him.

Derrick ran up, started to kneel by Eric, then saw the gun pointed at Mateo. "Bloody hell. What—" He pushed to his feet, looking between Mateo, Charlotta and the fleet admiral.

Charlotta took a half step closer to Eric.

"Stop," Mateo ordered.

She bared her teeth. "I will not let you hurt him again."

"Again?" Derrick yelped. "Wait, what happened? How did he fall? Was it an accident?"

"It wasn't an accident." Eric's voice was stronger now than it had been, though he hadn't moved, remaining on his side. "It was an attempted assassination."

The word made Mateo feel ill. Derrick and Charlotta both turned to stare at him. Charlotta looked at him with cold fury and accusation. And Derrick...

Derrick looked shocked, and then suspicious.

No. Not Derrick, too.

"What happened, Admiral?" Charlotta asked.

"I was leaving the castle via the back hall."

"What are you talking about?" Mateo asked. "What back hall?"

Derrick's shoulders slumped. "Fleet Admiral, it makes it hard to protect you if you keep sneaking out."

Eric only grunted.

"Sneaking out?" Mateo turned to Derrick, focusing on something smaller than the suspicion directed his way. "What is he talking about?"

"The fleet admiral has taken to leaving the castle via alternate routes," Derrick said. "He's been using the rear emergency hall to get out onto the ramparts."

"The one full of boxes? And you didn't stop him?"

"We tried, sir."

"Don't call him that," Charlotta snapped. "Mateo said he's been looking for the traitor, but he hasn't been here to do so. Now he comes back and there's an attempt on the fleet admiral's life."

Mateo's anger overwhelmed his shock, and he faced Charlotta. "Do not accuse me, Charlotta. Not without proof."

"What more proof do I need?" She pointed to where Eric lay on the floor.

"You said he used the back hall. That's where he fell from?"

"Yes." Eric's voice was softer than it had been, and Mateo's stomach clenched.

Ignoring Charlotta's threatening body language, he dropped to one knee. "Fleet Admiral. If you fell through the roof, there's a strong possibility you're severely injured. You need to stay calm and hold very still."

"I was only in free fall the last ten feet or so. I managed to tie a rope to this chair." He indicated the broken bits. Eric sounded worryingly dispassionate and calm. He met Mateo's gaze. "I have no plans to move, unless I need to shoot you."

"Then I will give you no reason to shoot me."

Eric licked his lips. There was blood on his face from a cut to his cheek.

"Did you hit your head?" Mateo asked.

"Get away from him," Charlotta snarled.

Mateo's fingers curled into fists. "You were a reserve guard last year. Remember your place. I am still in charge here. You will not speak to me that way."

"You tried to kill him! Pretending to care now won't change that."

"How could I have tried to kill him? I didn't know he'd been using that hall."

Charlotta snorted. "I'm sure Derrick told you. False ignorance won't help. And where were you? You got here fast."

"I was on the second floor." Mateo rose once more, stepping close enough to Charlotta that he could glare down at her. "You were the first one here. Where were *you*?"

"On guard at the front door. I came as soon as I got the call."

"You want revenge for that night," Mateo said quietly. "That's not a secret. Are you willing to kill the fleet admiral to get it?"

Charlotta turned to Derrick. "Did you tell him about the fleet admiral sneaking out that way?" She jabbed a finger at the ceiling.

Derrick hesitated. "Uh, no. Of course not. Mateo would never…"

Mateo spun on his best friend. "Derrick, what the fuck? You know you didn't tell me."

Derrick sputtered. "I didn't. You're right. I *didn't*. And I know you wouldn't do this. He wouldn't do this." Derrick looked from Eric to Charlotta and back.

It was a weak protest.

The betrayal hit him like a sucker punch to the gut. Derrick—his best friend—thought he was the traitor.

The door opened again, and Nikolas rushed in with the bright yellow backboard under his arm, another guard at his side.

"Back up, all of you," Nikolas ordered.

Nikolas had served during several conflicts in Bosnia and Croatia and had paramedics training. That's why Mateo had sent him to get the medical equipment.

They carefully placed the collar around Eric's neck. Nikolas tugged a gun holster from the back of Eric's pants and held it up. Before Mateo could grab it, Charlotta took it. With one person holding his head steady, Nikolas placed the board against his back, strapped him in place, and rolled him face up.

Eric grunted in pain once or twice during the process, but otherwise didn't move. Just as Nikolas finished, the door opened and Marie ushered in blue-jumpsuit clad paramedics.

Charlotta stooped and plucked the gun from Eric's hands, placing it back in the holster and hiding it and her own gun with her jacket before the medics could see. They raced over, assessed Eric, and then one went to the vehicle for additional strapping. The other started to clear away the remaining bits of broken chair.

"Who speaks Castilian?" Eric asked in that language.

Mateo jerked upon hearing his native language.

There was a chorus of "I do's" from the Spartan Guard.

Moving only his eyes, Eric look around, assessing each of them. He shouldn't have looked powerful— immobilized on the floor, his face creased with pain— yet the big man still looked every inch the Viking they called him. The backboard looked pathetically small, and the medics were going to need help lifting him off the floor.

"I don't have time to deal with this. Once I'm gone, take Mateo to the dungeon. I'll question him when I return."

Everyone but Charlotta sucked in shocked breaths. She nodded.

The paramedics returned and, together with Nikolas and Marie, lifted the backboard, carrying Eric to the ambulance rather than using the stretcher on the bumpy stone floor of the Great Hall.

Once the doors closed behind them, there was a moment of silence.

"Don't fight me," Charlotta said quietly. She took Mateo's arm, and with a little tug made him start walking.

He didn't fight her. He was too shocked, too defeated.

He'd left the bedroom filled with hope for the future. In the course of minutes, that hope had been destroyed. His guard had turned against him. Derrick…

Mateo struggled with his best friend's betrayal. There was no mistaking the suspicion in Derrick's eyes, in the way he'd hesitated to defend him.

However, all of that paled when he considered Dimitri and Cecilia. Would they believe him guilty as well?

Mateo went where she steered him, down a spiral staircase, into the dungeons of Triskelion Castle.

What if they didn't believe him?

That question—that fear—blinded him to everything else that had happened.

An hour ago, he'd been a part of a family—temporary or not.

And now, he was alone once more.

Chapter Thirteen

Dimitri stirred at the sound of a knock on the door. A quick glance told him Mateo was no longer in the bed.

He rose and threw on his jeans before walking across the room.

"Derrick?"

Derrick glanced over his shoulder and, even in the dim light, Dimitri could see the man flushing. "I need to speak to you."

Looking over his shoulder, Dimitri realized Cecilia had awoken as well. She was sitting up, holding the quilt to cover herself.

Dimitri was a jealous man, something he'd never felt the need to temper or control. What was his was his. Cecilia fell into that category.

"Give us a moment," Dimitri said, closing the door in the other man's face. "Cecilia."

She was already out of bed, throwing on the clothes Mateo had stripped off her earlier. He wasn't sure what Derrick wanted, but he feared it had something to do with Mateo's disappearance.

Once Cecilia was covered, Dimitri opened the door again and gestured for Derrick to enter.

The man was frazzled, upset. "I came here right after…right after…"

"After what? Spit it out, man."

"Mateo has been accused of killing the fleet admiral. They've taken him to the dungeons below the castle."

"Manon killed the fleet admiral," Cecilia said. "We know that."

"Not Kacper," Derrick clarified. "Eric Ericsson. Tonight."

Dimitri's blood ran cold. "The fleet admiral is dead?"

Derrick ran a hand through his hair, his expression one of confusion and panic. "No. He's still alive. Or…he was when the paramedics took him."

"An attempt was made on the fleet admiral's life tonight? When? How?" Dimitri asked.

"A stone was moved in a secret corridor only the fleet admiral uses, covered over with a rug. Someone set a booby trap. He fell through the roof of the Great Hall. Hit the floor. I told the other guards that it wasn't Mateo, but they didn't believe me."

"Why do they think Mateo did it?" Dimitri fought hard to remain calm. He knew it was pertinent to get all the details before reacting.

"The timing. He came back, and as soon as he did, this happens. Plus, he was one of the few guards who knew the hall was there and how to access it. The fleet admiral believes… I told them it wasn't him."

There was something in Derrick's demeanor that felt off to Dimitri. To the untrained eye, he appeared to be genuinely concerned for his friend, almost overly upset. Perhaps that was what bothered Dimitri. Derrick was a soldier, a well-trained Spartan Guard. Emotion had no place on the battlefield or in a situation like this.

As if that wasn't enough, he was far too emotional for someone British.

Mateo had been accused and locked up. The situation was perilous, but certainly not at critical mass. Nothing had been done that couldn't be undone.

Unless…

"How badly was the fleet admiral injured? Will he survive?"

Derrick nodded. "He fell from the third floor into the Great Hall. Over ten meters."

"But he's alive."

"Yes," Derrick confirmed.

Dimitri blew out a long, pained breath, considering how lucky Eric was to be alive, as Cecilia crossed herself and murmured a short prayer in Italian.

Derrick started pacing the floor. "How can they believe Mateo would do such a thing? I tried to stop them from taking him. I swear I did."

Dimitri nearly snorted at the man's over-the-top acting. The more he listened and looked, the more he was convinced Derrick had come here specifically to trick them.

Cecilia walked over and placed a comforting arm on Derrick's shoulder. "It's okay. We'll find a way to help Mateo."

Her eyes locked with Dimitri's, and when she narrowed them slightly, revealing her own suspicions, he realized their clever woman had not been fooled by Derrick's act either.

Dimitri's gaze landed on the whip in the corner, behind Derrick, and he spied an opportunity. Pretending to pace, he walked in the direction of the whip, drawing Derrick's attention to it while seeming to be thinking about how they could help Mateo.

Dimitri surreptitiously watched Derrick, catching the sudden widening of the other man's eyes when he spotted the whip. The look changed from surprise to one of genuine confusion, then concern before he shuttered away all emotion.

"Where is Eric now?"

It took Derrick a moment to respond, his concerned friend act faltering in the face of the whip. "Noble's Hospital on the isle. He clearly needs X-rays, and we can't risk moving him to London or Belfast until we see how badly he's hurt."

Derrick's eyes darted toward the whip once more.

Dimitri put his hand on the table, fingers inches from the handle. "Do you like this? I found it." Dimitri smiled. "In the stable of a vacation home on the east side of the castle."

"Why were you there?" Derrick's voice held an edge of strength...and perhaps anger. The worried friend had disappeared, the soldier in place once more.

Dimitri shrugged casually. "Just exploring."

"This afternoon?"

"Yes."

"Mateo wasn't with you."

"No," Dimitri said. "He wasn't. He was here in the castle, conducting his investigation alone."

Cecilia frowned. Dimitri wasn't exactly giving Mateo an alibi. If anything, he was telling Derrick that Mateo had the time to set up the trap if he wished. His actions were calculated. He wanted Derrick to believe that Dimitri also suspected Mateo guilty of the crime.

"Why did the two of you leave the castle without him?" Derrick asked.

"Cecilia wasn't feeling well from the ferry ride to the isle. She needed some air."

"That home isn't exactly on the beaten path. How did you find it?"

Derrick's questions were posed casually, but there was no mistaking his concern.

Dimitri smiled. "We simply got in the car and drove. That was where we wound up."

Cecilia had been silent throughout their conversation, but her anxiety finally won out. "Can we go see Mateo?"

Derrick shook his head. "I don't think that will be possible. Charlotta has taken charge of the situation and she's...well...given her history with Mateo, she is in no mood to be merciful."

"History?" Cecilia inquired.

Dimitri could almost imagine he saw delight on Derrick's face that Cecilia had taken the bait, though he tried to hide it. "They were lovers."

Dimitri had to hand it to her. Cecilia had a better poker face than Derrick.

She simply nodded. "I see. Thank you for coming to tell us, Derrick."

He nodded at her dismissal, though it was apparent he wanted to stay. The man had more questions for them. Dimitri appreciated the way Cecilia removed that option by walking to the bedroom door. "I hope you'll let us know if anything else happens or changes."

"Of course." Derrick left the room slowly, reluctantly.

Cecilia closed the door behind him and leaned on it, the strength she'd maintained in front of Derrick seeping out. Her shoulders fell and her face crumbled.

"What are we going to do? It wasn't Mateo, Dimitri. You must know that."

Dimitri walked over, hating to see her upset. "Do you trust me, Cece?"

She nodded without hesitation. "Of course I do."

His heart felt as if it might burst with joy. An unfamiliar, yet wonderful feeling for him.

"I have a few things I need to do. It could take some time. I need you to pack up all of our things and wait here for me. Will you do that?"

"I want to come with you."

He'd expected that response. "I know. But you have to trust me when I say you can't. Not this time."

Dimitri anticipated her continued insistence, so he was surprised when she relented easily.

"Are you going to help Mateo?"

"Yes."

"Fine. I'll pack and wait here."

"Lock the door behind me. Don't open it for anyone." Dimitri gave her a hard, quick kiss, praying he'd be able to pull off what he had planned. For her sake…and his.

Cecilia had packed their bags in record time even though Dimitri had warned her that he could be gone a while. He hadn't lied. Nearly three hours had passed, and she was about to come out of her skin.

After setting their suitcases by the door, she'd stripped the sheets, then cleaned the room and the bathroom, and still Dimitri hadn't returned.

The screen on her phone lit up. It was James. Again.

She'd turned the ringer on her cell off after his third call because she was afraid of what he might say or ask.

Until she knew what Dimitri had planned in terms of helping Mateo, it was best that she avoid speaking to the husband of the admiral of England. Even if he was her cousin and one of her closest friends.

Too nervous to sit still, she rose from the bed, pacing the length of the room until she stood in front of the whip. She hated the wicked-looking thing. Dimitri said it was a toy, but to her, it looked like a weapon.

With that thought in mind, she picked it up, spinning around to face the large, sparsely decorated room. Flicking it lightly a few times, she was surprised by the weight of it. She tried to recall the way Dimitri had wielded it, the way he'd flicked his arm and wrist to produce the powerful swing and loud crack.

She swung it several times, increasing the speed and motion each time until she managed a weak snapping sound. As she did so, she considered the way the whip made her feel.

In the tack room, she'd felt fear in the face of being struck by it, but holding it, swinging it, put an entirely different perspective on it.

She felt...powerful. She wasn't physically weak, but she couldn't manhandle her lovers, control them, the way they controlled her. With this whip in her hand, they'd do what she wanted.

She flicked the whip again, thinking about those lion tamers who stood, soft and defenseless, in the ring with lions, a whip their only means of command, the creature far stronger and more dangerous than they were.

With the whip, it was she who could command and control her lions. It was a heady feeling, more arousing than her lovers would be comfortable knowing.

That thought made her smile.

After several more attempts at producing a satisfying crack, Cecilia's arm began to ache. She was just about to place the whip on the bed when the door to the room flew open.

She spun around, arm thrown back, ready to bring the whip down to defend herself.

Dimitri pulled up short, his hands flying up protectively. "Easy, *koxaha*. It's just us."

"Us?"

Mateo stepped around Dimitri, his eyes widening when he saw the whip in her raised hand. "*Válgame Dios!*"

Cecilia dropped the whip and raced across the room, throwing herself into Mateo's arms. "They freed you! I knew they'd come to their senses. See that you were innocent."

Mateo gave her a quick squeeze, then disengaged himself from her arms. "No, Cece. Not exactly."

She looked from him to Dimitri. "What did you do?"

"Did you pack?" he asked, ignoring her question.

She nodded.

"Good. There's no time to explain now. We need to leave the castle immediately." Dimitri picked up their bags, gesturing to the whip still in her hand. "You hold on to that. Don't be afraid to swing it if necessary."

His words felt like a joke and she was tempted to laugh. It died, however, when she saw the seriousness on his face.

So the toy *had* become a weapon. She tightened her grip as they stepped into the hallway. The stealthy, wary way Mateo and Dimitri walked through the corridors, taking turns to check around corners, answered her question easily enough.

Somehow Dimitri had helped Mateo escape, and now they needed to flee before someone sounded the alarm.

Fortunately, Mateo knew the castle, the grounds, the placement and schedules of the guards better than anyone.

"We just ran through the emergency protocols when Kacper was killed. The guards will no doubt have moved away from our regular nightly detail to the low-personnel emergency protocol since several of them traveled to the hospital with Eric."

Cecilia wondered if his quiet words were meant to keep her calm or a way for him to think through each of their moves.

"And Marie is…indisposed," Dimitri said.

Cecilia flashed Dimitri an accusing look. "Did you hit a woman?"

Dimitri rolled his eyes, then lifted his shirt to reveal a boot-sized bruise on his left side that had to have cracked a few ribs.

Cecilia gasped.

"I wouldn't call Marie a woman. Ninja is a more fitting term."

Mateo grinned. "I taught her that move."

Cecilia shook her head. "I think it's sweet how proud you are of that, considering she used the move attempting to keep you locked away for a crime you didn't commit."

Mateo pulled up short just as they reached the back door. Cecilia thought he was pausing to take stock before they moved outside. Then she realized he was looking at her.

"What?" she whispered.

"That's twice you've mentioned my innocence. You truly believe—"

She cut him off with a quick kiss. "Never doubt that," she said when they parted.

Mateo smiled, then looked at Dimitri. "What you did in that dungeon—"

"Save it, Mateo. Until later. This isn't the time."

Dimitri's reminder was all he needed. The Spartan Guard reappeared. Mateo lifted one finger as he slowly opened the door an inch or two, peering outside.

He closed it once more, satisfaction on his face. "It's just as I thought. The east gate has been left unguarded. It's little more than a path that leads directly to the cliffs that overlook the coast. Due to lack of use, vines have grown over it, concealing it. Typically, there is a guard stationed here, but because very few people know of its existence anymore, it's considered the least threat in times of true emergency, so we move our guards to more key positions."

Mateo held his left hand up, the back of it to them, signaling for them to hold. He opened the door and peered outside once more, then motioned for them to follow him without looking back.

They walked quietly, considering their haste to cross the narrow patch of grass to the ivy-covered gate. Mateo opened it, freezing when it creaked. In a calmer frame of mind, Cecilia would have recognized the noise wasn't that loud, but given her current state of panic, it sounded like a gunshot piercing the silent night.

Mateo must have been more reasonable because he went ahead and pushed the gate open wide enough for the three of them to pass through. Despite the noise, he closed it behind them.

"I don't want to leave them any way to trace which way we went," he whispered.

"Where now?" she asked.

Dimitri grasped her hand. "This way. I managed to steal a car before I set Mateo free. It's hidden just outside the castle grounds behind some tall bushes."

"Who are you?" Cecilia asked in a hushed voice, not bothering to move despite Dimitri's tugging.

He turned and gave her a mischievous grin that he punctuated with a quick kiss.

"I'm a Ukrainian spy."

Chapter Fourteen

James met her by the door, walking fast enough that he was limping a little. His limp was always worse when he was upset or worried.

Cecilia held up her hands, palms out. "I'm okay, James."

James looked from her to scan the space behind her, as if she would have hidden Mateo in the small stairwell. It was late, but the interior security light above the door they'd used to access the Trinity Old Library was enough for her to see the expression on her cousin's face.

"What the hell is going on?" James demanded. "Arthur got a call that someone tried to kill the fleet admiral. Then ten minutes later, we find out it was Mateo! I try to call you. No answer. I *keep* trying to call you, and you don't answer. Then Arthur gets another call. Mateo has escaped, and you and Dimitri are MIA."

"Mateo didn't do it, James."

He took a halting step back. "Cecilia...my husband is the admiral of England. If you helped Mateo escape...I have to tell him."

"I didn't," she insisted.

"And what about the other one?"

"Dimitri didn't either. He was with me. We got on the ferry to Dublin and didn't find out he'd escaped until we got here."

It was a little scary how good she was getting at lying.

She and Dimitri had bought tickets for the ferry from Douglas to Dublin as walk-on passengers. Mateo had slipped into the camper of an inattentive Irish family returning to Ireland from a camping holiday on the isle. Once the camper was driven aboard, Mateo slipped out and joined the foot passengers.

There would be video evidence—of him getting out of the camper, of him walking off the ferry with all the other foot passengers. Dimitri assured her it would be okay, and that the trick would be for them to stay far enough ahead of their pursuers that, by the time someone went through all that video, they were safely out of Dublin.

"James, please. We need your help. The librarians' help."

James' face creased with worry for her. "Cousin, I know he was supposed to be your third, but—"

"But he didn't do it. He's being set up—"

"I know this must be hard—"

"—which means the real traitor is still out there! And with the fleet admiral injured..." Cecilia raised her brows.

They'd both raised their voices as they interrupted one another. James could, annoyingly, out-shout her, but she could hold her own in an argument through tenacity.

James' eyebrows twitched and his face relaxed into a more customary smile. "Come on."

The librarians were gathered at the same table they'd used before. The chair at the head of the table was pushed out at an angle—the seat James had vacated to come meet her at the door.

Hugo sat beside Josephine, who was talking animatedly, though in a low enough voice Cecilia couldn't hear what she said. Hugo was nodding, even as he blinked in apparent surprise. Nyx was across the table from them, her pale hair pulled back into a bun that should have made her look studious, but instead she seemed like an artist about to take brush to canvas.

"Where's Karl?" Cecilia asked.

James shrugged. "I don't know. He said he was coming, but I haven't been able to get ahold of him since. I filled the others in on the task assigned to your trinity and what's happened in the past twenty-four hours in order to speed things along."

"Excellent." The three at the table looked up when she spoke. There was an awkward silence.

She crossed her arms, knowing it looked defensive but not caring. "Mateo didn't do it. He's being set up, and I need your help to prove it wasn't him."

Hugo looked unconvinced, while Josephine seemed sympathetic. Nyx—as always—appeared unemotional, almost otherworldly.

"Do you have proof he wasn't the traitor in the guard?" Hugo asked.

She shook her head.

"Have you discovered who the true traitor is?" Hugo wasn't purposely being unkind, Cecilia knew that. He was a man of facts, one who found truth in the details, in the things he could see and understand.

"No." The word hurt to speak.

Hugo didn't back down. "Then your assertion that Mateo is innocent is based on…what?"

Cecilia knew her answer would appease none of them, that it wouldn't help her case. "I just know. I've spent the past four days with Mateo. I've gotten to know him. He isn't capable of what he's been accused. He's loyal and honest. He would never betray the fleet admiral or the society."

Nyx sighed. "Cecilia," she said kindly. "There is no shame in falling in love, but to let it blind you to—"

"No," Cecilia interrupted. "My feelings for Mateo aren't playing a part in this."

"Of course, they are, Cecilia," James said gently, calling her out. "But without any evidence to lead us to another suspect, we can't discount Mateo. Especially not when all the proof seems to point to him."

"Not all of it. We found a...well, a sex toy." Cecilia wasn't a prude, but the words seemed vulgar within the hallowed stacks of the Trinity Long Room. She'd stashed the thing in a bag and dropped it by her seat as soon as she'd walked in.

Everyone looked at her. She cleared her throat, then tossed her head back, ready to forge on. They didn't believe her, but she was determined none of them would leave this room until they agreed to help her clear Mateo's name.

"Dimitri had a list of places where Manon might have been meeting with the sniper. When we were on the isle, we investigated them. That's where we found the whip."

"Who gave him the list?" Josephine asked.

"No one. I think he came up with it." However, as soon as she said it, Cecilia questioned that answer.

It didn't help that Josephine smiled as if she knew some secret, but she said nothing else.

"You think she met with the sniper so close to Triskelion Castle?" Hugo asked. "Why take the risk?"

"That might have been part of the enjoyment. Proximity either to the object of her hatred—Kacper— or the danger of discovery are both possible motives for an otherwise risky behavior." Nyx glanced around the table with those unsettling dark eyes as she spoke. Dimitri had suggested the same motives in the stables.

Cecilia opened her tote and pulled out the whip, placing it on the table.

"That's a sex toy?" Josephine asked, her eyes wide with horror behind her thick-framed glasses. She shoved them up on her nose as she leaned closer to examine the whip, her expression equal parts curiosity and terror.

"Yes," Cecilia answered. "According to Dimitri."

Nyx picked it up. "Yes. This is a custom-made piece." She looked at the small metal tag dangling from the handle. "M.K. G.R. A.R."

Cecilia answered Nyx's questioning look. "Manon Kujakski, Griffin Rutherford was the American sniper. Perhaps A.R. is the traitor."

"What about the drone operator? The one who actually shot Kacper."

James shook his head. "No, Lorelei—England's vice admiral—ran his fingerprints through the computer and discovered his name was Bertrand Fenwick." James looked slightly ill. "He died right in front of me. A lot of people died that day."

Cecilia put her hand on her cousin's shoulder. She should have considered what kind of memories talking about all this would bring up for him.

"Well, then it should be simple. Which member of the Spartan Guard has the initials A.R.?" Hugo asked.

"None of them, but maybe they have a nickname?" Cecilia suggested, even though Dimitri and Mateo had discounted that as an option.

The four other librarians shared the same doubtful look her lovers had when she'd posed it.

"Think of it this way," Cecilia said. "If Mateo is the traitor, he's on the run and the fleet admiral is safe. If he's not, once the fleet admiral leaves the hospital, he's going back to the castle with the traitor, and he'll be vulnerable. He's hurt. I'm not willing to risk his life by saying it was Mateo."

There was a moment of silence, then Hugo sat forward. "I was looking into the history of the Isle of Man itself. That led me to asking Josephine—"

"About the history of the Spartan Guard," Josephine interrupted. "There was a time when most of the guard were Manx—from the Isle of Man—and it was a big tradition, kind of like the Swiss Guard at the Vatican. And—"

"And," Hugo cut in, "I started working on tracing the lineages of the families who used to traditionally hold the Spartan Guard positions."

"What connection are you making?" Nyx asked, still holding the whip.

"I'm saying that the Domino—an old enemy— might have been able to tap into old grudges or feelings of displacement within the society."

"So maybe it's not a member of the current Spartan Guard at all," Nyx said.

"No, it had to be someone in the guard. They're the only ones with the access needed." That much had been clear when she, Dimitri and Mateo talked about it.

"Or maybe someone in the Spartan Guard had to work too hard to get there." Hugo's eyes were alight with enthusiasm. "Thinks that by right they should be more important than they are, and the Domino traded in on that. It's like what Nyx said last time about how the disenfranchised are recruited into organizations or cults."

Cecilia sat forward in excitement. "If that's true, then that could explain them trying to frame Mateo. To get his position. Who are the descendants?"

Hugo shook his head. "I don't know."

Josephine frowned. "We're having trouble sorting it out. We're talking hundreds of years, multiple generations."

"Start with Charlotta Nielsen. She's the one who wants Mateo's job." Cecilia paused before adding the other suspect to her list. "And Derrick Frederick."

Even Mateo's trust in his friend had begun to waver.

"Why do you suspect them?" Hugo asked.

Cecilia outlined what had happened with Charlotta and Derrick.

"Then we should be working those angles too. That's what we'd do if we were investigators or assassins." Josephine grinned, and it was a rather bloodthirsty expression.

Even Nyx blinked. "But we're not investigators. We're scholars. There are investigators, spies, and security operatives in the Masters' Admiralty. If that's what we need, we should turn it over to them."

Josephine waved her hand in the air, dismissing that argument.

"I might have another way to find out." Nyx set the whip down, took out her phone, and snapped a picture. "I think I recognize the work on this whip. If I'm right, it's by an American craftsman. I've seen the gold deerskin before."

James frowned. "Arthur went to this sex club in London. Garden something. I could ask him to show them—"

"The Garden," Nyx cut in. "Damon Knight's club. I'm texting a picture to Charlotte Taggart. She might recognize it."

"Who?" James asked.

"She's an American. Not a member of the...what is the American copy called?"

"Trinity Masters," James said quietly.

"She's not one of those, but she's a major player in the scene in Texas. She knows Damon—she and her husband and Damon and some others own McKay Taggart and Knight, a security firm. If we find the whip maker, we might figure out who A.R. is."

"And I'll keep trying to trace the Manx family lines," Josephine said.

Nyx was frowning at her phone, typing occasionally. "What if our two lines of inquiry don't end at the same place?"

They all looked at her.

Cecilia's eye started to twitch. "What do you mean?"

"We're assuming that the traitor is in the Spartan Guard. They may not be."

Cecilia shook her head. "No, like I said, it has to be because—"

"Fine." Nyx picked up the whip and snapped it in the air, with a skill that even Dimitri hadn't shown.

Conversation stopped.

"Okay, then. That's...uh." Josephine shoved her glasses up her nose again. Cecilia noticed they constantly slid down.

"Frightened or aroused?" Nyx asked conversationally.

"I am *so* not answering that question."

"This is not a toy for a casual player." Nyx set the whip down. "It's possible that the traitor in the Spartan Guard is 'A.R.' but it's not likely."

"Why not?"

"First of all, I doubt they would have been able to keep it a secret. This kind of play leaves marks."

"You mean scars," Cecilia said.

"Not from deerskin, but they might enjoy other forms of impact play. A paddle would leave bruises, a cane, welts. But also there would be a paper trail. A history of membership at clubs, regular expenditures on dues, toys, fetish wear. That is, I assume, something that would have come up when the person was vetted."

"Derrick," Cecilia said. "Derrick looked at the whip like he knew about it. Like he'd seen it before."

"So either he knew about Manon's affair or..." Hugo raised his brows.

"Or he could have just been surprised because he thought we were getting married to his best friend and didn't expect to see a whip in our room." Cecilia fought the urge to scrub her hands over her face. It would just mess up her eye makeup, and experience had taught her that she couldn't make her brain go any faster by doing that. "Charlotta is aggressive. I could imagine her enjoying that type of sexual play."

James groaned and put his head in his hands. "Okay, hold on. Let's get organized." His low, rumbling voice pulled their attention. Josephine took out a pen and a pad of paper.

"First, there is definitely a traitor in the Spartan Guard. If we assume it's not Mateo, we potentially leave the fleet admiral, who is hurt, vulnerable to the real traitor."

"The other guards are there," Cecilia added, "but they think it was Mateo, so they won't be looking for another traitor. Might not be as on guard as they should be."

"Agreed." Josephine had a worry line between her eyebrows. She shoved her pen and paper at Hugo, who accepted them and, after a surprised hesitation, took over the act of taking notes. Then, she fished her phone out of a pocket and started typing.

"Secondly, we have a whip that we think belonged to Manon. She was having an affair with Griffin. It's possible there was a third person in their relationship, someone with the initials 'A.R.' This person might be the traitor in the Spartan Guard," James held up a hand when Nyx started to object, "or they may not. They may be totally unconnected to the Domino and the Masters' Admiralty."

Hugo, who had been dutifully writing, snorted. "Not likely."

James continued, "I agree. Third, we have the history of the Spartan Guard itself, the Manx bloodlines. If traced, those may lead to someone who has reason to resent how the current guard is run."

Then Hugo added, "And fourth—actually, fourth and fifth—we have names. Charlotta Nielsen and Derrick Frederick."

James looked pleased. "There are plenty of strings there to tug."

Hugo looked at the list, then around at the people at the table. "Divide and conquer?"

"Yes," James said. "But we're going to be smart. I'm going to call England's vice admiral. Have her look into Derrick. He's from England after all."

"What about Charlotta?" Cecilia knew Mateo thought it was her, and from what he'd said, since she was from the same territory as the fleet admiral, Eric might trust her too much.

What Cecilia hadn't told the librarians was that Mateo and Charlotta had been lovers. There had been no opportunity during their escape from the Isle of Man for her to question him about that relationship. Until she did, she was keeping that piece of information to herself.

James answered her question. "I'll give that to Lorelei too. She could always send one of the security officers to Kalmar."

Hugo looked disappointed. "What are *we* going to investigate?"

"You and Josephine are going to run down the history angle. Nyx, you're going to try to figure out who made that whip."

Nyx nodded. "If that's all, my task is complete. My friend Charlotte suggested we take the whip to Red. It's a club outside of London. Not as exclusive as The Garden, but they have a lot of exhibitions and classes, and the vetting isn't as tight, so if one of our members were to join a club, that's probably the one they'd join."

"That was fast," Josephine said without looking up.

"There are hundreds of paths up the mountain. The only one wasting time is the one who runs around the mountain."

"Hindu proverb?" Cecilia asked, the words vaguely familiar.

"Very good," Nyx said.

"Focus." James' eye appeared to be twitching. "Okay, Nyx, why don't you go to the club?" James said.

"No," Cecilia cut in. "Dimitri and I will go."

Nyx raised a brow, and Cecilia realized she was clutching the whip possessively. "He'll insist on going," she said.

Nyx looked to James. "Do we trust the Spartan Guard to continue to protect the fleet admiral?"

James shook his head. "Maybe Arthur can send some of the knights from England. Or maybe Sophia's brother, Antonio. He's security in Rome."

"I have a better idea." Josephine was still on her phone, smiling a little. "How about we just warn Eric?"

Cecilia's heart stopped. "You...texted the fleet admiral?"

"Mmm-hmm."

"And told him that we suspected Charlotta and Derrick?"

"No. I told him that Mateo told you that *he*, Mateo, suspected them."

"Josephine!"

"What?"

Cecilia looked at the whip, and for a moment seriously considered strangling the Irish woman with it.

"Well, that, uh, sort of takes care of that." James angled his chair so the bulk of his body was between her and Josephine. Cecilia bared her teeth at her cousin.

"How do you know the fleet admiral so well?" Nyx asked. "First names, phone numbers, casual texting?"

"We're friends." Josephine's response was far from satisfying, but before she could expound, her phone pinged.

"Wait." Josephine's smile disappeared. "Eric says he's home from the hospital. Charlotta is with him, but he's going to keep three other guards with him at all times, so he won't be alone with her. He asked for Derrick—keeping his enemies close and all that—and apparently Derrick is gone. He'd scheduled time off prior to the previous fleet admiral's death, planned a trip to England. I think given the circumstances, everyone assumed he wouldn't leave. He did. He's about to board a flight to London."

"Maybe he's gone to help Mateo?" Hugo asked.

"No," Cecilia said. "Mateo's not—" She realized what she was saying and stopped speaking mid-sentence.

Hugo snorted. "I thought you didn't know where he was?"

"I don't." Bad time for her newfound proficiency at lying to fail her.

Nyx sat forward. "Derrick is on a flight to London?"

"Yes," Josephine confirmed.

Nyx looked at Cecilia. "Where the club is."

Cecilia blinked. "You're the one who said that the third owner of the whip wasn't the same as the traitor in the Spartan Guard."

"I only posed the question. We also have to consider Occam's razor."

"We don't have time for this! You're talking in circles." Cecilia almost snarled the words.

"She's a religious scholar. What did you expect?" Hugo joked.

Rather than respond to Josephine, Cecilia pushed to her feet. "I'm going. Dimitri and I will go to this sex club in London and figure out who owned this whip."

She slid out from between the stacks and headed for the door. She wasn't surprised to hear James following her.

Just before she opened the door, letting the Dublin night into the warm intimacy of the closed library, James put a hand on her shoulder, arresting her movement. "It doesn't look good for Mateo."

"He's innocent. I know it."

"You're in love with the man."

She grinned. "I've known him—them—a handful of days. Safer to say I'm in lust with the hope of love." Even as she spoke the words, she knew her feelings were far more engaged than she could admit even to herself.

"Mateo isn't on the run alone, is he?"

Cecilia didn't respond. Wasn't sure how. James was married to the admiral of England. Wouldn't he feel compelled to tell his husband that she had helped the man suspected of attempted murder escape and was now harboring him?

"Fair enough," James said, not waiting for an answer. "Do what you have to do, but if you need help...call me."

"I couldn't put you in a position like that."

"We're family. You will call me. Promise."

She hesitated, and James raised one eyebrow, proving he would find other ways to push the issue until he got what he wanted.

"Fine. I promise to call if things get rough."

James gave her a quick, hard bear hug.

Dimitri and Mateo were waiting for her in a pub just off College Green. It was packed, and she slid between people speaking a dozen different languages. Amid all the tourists, no one noticed or noted a Spaniard and Ukrainian, though Cecilia thought she saw some young women eyeing them.

Her men were good-looking.

Dimitri pulled out the stool they'd saved for her, but Cecilia shook her head. "Let's go."

"What?"

She practically had to shout to be heard. "We need to go. To London."

Mateo frowned. "Why?"

Rather than answer, she pulled the handle of the whip out of her bag just enough so they could see it. "I have a lead."

Dimitri and Mateo shared a look and then, as one, rose and followed her out.

Chapter Fifteen

Dimitri rubbed the grit from his dry eyes, blinking a few times in the dim light in hopes of clearing his vision. He was fucking tired. He, Cecilia and Mateo had only managed to steal a few minutes of restless sleep since escaping the Isle of Man two nights ago.

Last night they'd been in Dublin, though they'd only spent a few hours in their rented hotel room after Cecilia's secret rendezvous with God only knew who, and before the alarm went off at four a.m. so they could catch the early ferry.

Cecilia knew it was the safest route for Mateo— ferry tickets weren't tracked and centralized like plane tickets—so she'd popped a couple of motion-sickness caplets and girded her loins. They'd found a quiet bench near a wall and she'd dozed between them, her head bobbing from his shoulder to Mateo's during the trip.

Dimitri hadn't managed to sleep on the ferry at all, his mind refusing to shut down as he considered his new mission. Unbeknownst to Cecilia and Mateo, he'd driven to Noble's Hospital to talk to Eric after his tumble through the ceiling of the Grand Hall before breaking Mateo out of the dungeon.

Dimitri wasn't sure what had compelled him to make the visit, not even certain what he'd intended to say until he got there. Two of the Spartan Guard had been standing as sentries by the doorway, so he'd lied and said Eric had called and requested a meeting. Then he'd held his breath while Nikolas confirmed it.

Eric had played along, lying to the guard about the meeting, mistakenly thinking Dimitri knew who'd set the booby trap that had almost cost him his life.

Instead, Dimitri stood there and pleaded Mateo's case, boldly asserting the man's innocence. Eric had listened quietly, then given Dimitri one week to find the proof that would clear Mateo's name. Unlike the deal Mateo had been given, that ended in marriage, Dimitri's task wouldn't end as happily. If he failed to prove Mateo wasn't involved, the fleet admiral said the trinity would be dissolved, and Mateo "would rot in that godforsaken dungeon after I drop his ass through the ceiling a few times."

Dimitri chose to believe Eric didn't really mean that, but was speaking out of pain and anger. The man really was lucky to be alive. He was also fairly certain that when Eric gave Dimitri time to prove his future husband's innocence, the fleet admiral didn't intend for Mateo to be with him. Breaking Mateo out wasn't part of the deal, which meant Dimitri had landed himself a very powerful, very dangerous adversary in all of this.

Rumors had circulated about Eric for years after he'd stepped down as admiral of Kalmar. Dimitri had heard stories spanning the spectrum from him being a sheep farmer in Ireland, to his membership in an exclusive BDSM club here in London, to him being a paid-for-hire mercenary. The truth was probably somewhere in the midst of that.

Or all of that.

The bottom line was, Eric wasn't a man to be crossed. And Dimitri had crossed him.

Once the ferry landed in Cardiff, they caught a train to London. It had been a quick trip through Wales and into Paddington Station—only a couple of hours—and while they'd all closed their eyes, Dimitri could tell from the dark circles under his lovers' eyes that they hadn't managed to sleep any better than he had. It was dusk, the dimness of the gray London sky fitting for his almost drunken drowsiness.

Cecilia had her cell out, plugging in the information for Red, the club her connection in Dublin suggested they check out.

"We can grab a taxi to the club," she said through a yawn. "See if Derrick is there."

Dimitri shook his head. "No, *koxaha*. First, I doubt the club is open yet. Second, the only place we are going tonight is to a hotel."

"We don't have time for that," Mateo said sharply, his own exhaustion translating to a short temper.

Dimitri chuckled, wishing Mateo hadn't planted the seed of sex. "There is always time for *that*. But that isn't my plan for tonight. None of us is in the proper frame of mind, or attire, to tackle what you hope at the club. We will check into a hotel, sleep, and tomorrow, we'll make our plan."

Mateo clearly hated the idea, and Dimitri understood why. Mateo had a noose dangling loosely around his neck and until they found the true traitor in the guard, it would continue to tighten. Time was running out.

"What do you mean by attire?" Cecilia asked.

"While it's not uncommon for guests to arrive at a sex club in street clothing, I believe, for our goal, it would be better to truly blend in. We'll need to do some shopping tomorrow."

"Leather and fishnet?" she inquired. Even though exhaustion was written on every inch of her face, Cecilia's curious brain hadn't shut down and there was no denying she was looking forward to their trip to the sex club. Dimitri knew they weren't going there to play, but if the opportunity presented itself, he would enjoy giving her a taste of BDSM.

"Something like that. Come." He took her hand and led her to the street, waving down a taxi. Mateo begrudgingly followed.

Dimitri began to instruct the driver to drop them off at the nearest hotel, but Cecilia spoke over him, louder. "Take us to The Goring, please."

At Dimitri's raised eyebrow, she said, "I've stayed there several times when I've come to London for business. It's lovely."

"And costly," he murmured.

She gave him an inquisitive look, her head tilted as she studied his face. "You're familiar with London."

"I'm familiar with a great many things," he replied with a wink.

Cecilia still looked pensive. "When we get to the hotel, I think we need to have a conversation."

"About?" Dimitri asked.

"Your career."

Dimitri wasn't surprised by her response. He'd been waiting for Mateo and Cecilia to question him about his revelation that he was a spy ever since he'd spoken the words. There hadn't been time before now.

"And," she added, pointing to Mateo, drawing his attention to her, "your affair with Charlotta."

Mateo's eyes widened in surprise. "How did you—"

Cecilia didn't bother letting him voice the entire question. "Derrick told us."

Mateo rubbed his hand over his forehead, then his eyes, no doubt trying to wake up a bit. "I should have told you." His voice was remorseful, defeated.

Cecilia reached over and patted his knee, giving Mateo a very sweet smile. "We've been together less than a week. I hardly think it surprising we haven't had time to delve into each other's pasts."

"But…that wouldn't have been pillow talk. It might have been vital to our investigation."

Dimitri agreed with Mateo. "Why didn't you tell us?"

Mateo shrugged. "I wanted to speak to her first, to see if…" His words drifted away, and Dimitri sensed he was struggling to express himself. Stress, fear, and the lack of sleep seemed to be hitting Mateo harder.

"See if…?" Cecilia prompted.

"If my instincts were correct."

"And were they?"

Mateo nodded a couple of times, then stopped. "I don't know. I'm not sure of anything anymore."

Dimitri understood that sentiment completely. They'd been running nonstop without sleep for over thirty-six hours. The past twenty-four had been spent in travel as they constantly looked over their shoulders.

"We'll figure it out, Mateo," Dimitri said.

Mateo looked at him—really looked—and Dimitri saw pure gratitude in the other man's eyes. "You didn't have to come down there and get me out of that dungeon."

"Yes, I did," Dimitri said. "They had the wrong man locked up."

Cecilia reached out to take Dimitri's hand, her other still resting on Mateo's knee. None of them spoke again, the rest of the taxi ride made in silence.

Cecilia took charge once they arrived at The Goring, securing them a suite that Dimitri suspected cost her a fair penny, and he realized that he didn't know much about her career or life either.

They dropped their bags by the door as they entered the suite, and Cecilia walked over to one of the couches, sinking down.

Dimitri stood before her, shaking his head as he reached down to pull her right back up. "No. Straight to bed. We can have our conversation there."

She didn't resist, grabbing her small suitcase and heading to the bathroom.

Mateo hadn't even bothered to look around the living room when they entered. He was already sitting on the edge of the bed, staring at the wall in front of him, almost zombie-like. "I'm tired."

Dimitri thought that was an understatement. "I know. Get undressed and crawl in. Things will be clearer in the morning after some sleep."

Mateo pulled off his shirt, then shed his jeans and shoes. Dimitri noticed his lover was going commando.

At his questioning glance, Mateo shrugged ruefully. "I'd only left our bed for a minute. Didn't bother putting all my clothes back on."

"Why did you leave the room?" Dimitri wondered what had driven Mateo from the bed, worried he'd misinterpreted how incredible the sex had truly been.

Mateo glanced toward the closed door of the bathroom. "That's an answer Cece should hear too."

Dimitri nodded, then started stripping off his own clothing as Mateo pulled back the sheets and climbed beneath them. He sat with his back against the headboard, pillows propped up behind him.

The door to the bathroom opened and Cecilia came out, dressed in an oversized T-shirt that hung mid-thigh.

She'd washed her face and combed her hair, looking youthful, wholesome. Incredibly beautiful.

She started toward the bed, intent on joining Mateo, but Dimitri caught her, his hand wrapping around her upper arm. "Shirt."

Cecilia tilted her head. "I thought tonight wasn't about *that*." She threw his words in the cab back at him.

"It's not. But you'll never come to our bed with clothing on."

She narrowed her eyes, clearly taking exception at his proclamation. "Oh. Is that right?"

Dimitri grinned and kissed her, hard, pressing his tongue into her mouth. She didn't resist him, despite her annoyance. More than that, she lifted her arms, wrapping them around his neck, making it very simple for him to grip the hem of her shirt and tug it over her head.

She laughed when their kiss ended as the cotton swooshed up. "You fight dirty."

"It's the only way to win in my line of work."

Cecilia turned and climbed onto the mattress, claiming the middle and assuming the same position at Mateo, then patting the empty place next to her. "Nice segue. I think perhaps we should start with a few more details about this Ukrainian spy job of yours. You told us you worked for the water department."

Dimitri sat on the edge of the mattress, facing them. "I could hardly tell you I was a spy, and during one of my earlier investigations, I did pose as an investigator for the water reclamation department. So that wasn't a complete lie."

She crossed her arms. "Semantics."

Dimitri reached out, grasping one of her hands and giving it a squeeze. "In my line of work, it's not wise to walk up to strangers and give them your life story."

"What do you mean when you say you're a spy?" Mateo asked.

"How much do you know about Ukrainian history?" Dimitri asked.

"Only a little bit," Mateo admitted.

Cecilia's response was exactly as he'd expected. "I read a fascinating book about it that started with the time of Herodotus right up to the crisis with Russia."

"My job has less to do with Herodotus and everything to do with Russian dealings. I'm part of the SBU."

"The what?" Mateo asked.

"Security Service of Ukraine," Cecilia answered for him.

Dimitri nodded, pleased by her knowledge of his homeland and his people. While he was attracted to her looks, it was her personality and her brilliant mind that was ensnaring him, capturing and claiming his heart.

"I'm currently working as a shadow within the organization to weed out corruption in the Alpha Force."

Mateo looked at Cecilia, not Dimitri, for the answer to his unspoken question.

"Soldiers who are still loyal to Russia," she explained before turning her gaze back to Dimitri. "It sounds dangerous."

"Some aspects are. Other parts of my job are fairly perfunctory."

"You enjoy it?" she asked.

He did for a long time. However, in the past year or so, he'd begun to lose his passion for it. The politics involved, the secrets, the time spent constantly questioning everyone's motives was exhausting. "I've been thinking lately that it might be time for a change."

"Lately," Mateo murmured, with the first smile Dimitri had seen on his face in hours. "Like the past week."

Dimitri chuckled, but didn't respond. Only the tiny spark of that desire had existed before meeting Cecilia and Mateo. In the last week, it had erupted into a wildfire that told him his place was not with the SBU, but with them. What that meant for his future eluded him, but it certainly didn't frighten him.

"Your turn," Cecilia said. "Charlotta."

"We didn't have a relationship. It was nothing more than a one-night stand. I reached out to her at a time when I was feeling low. We had a few too many drinks and fell into bed together. I didn't realize Charlotta's feelings for me at the time ran deeper than mere friendship. If I had, I never would have taken her to bed. When I tried to explain I didn't feel the same, she was hurt and angry. The friendship gone."

Cecilia frowned. "Derrick made it sound like more."

Mateo's brows furrowed. "What do you mean?"

"It sounded to me as if perhaps it was a longer affair." Cecilia seemed to think back to what Derrick had said. "He said something about your history and the fact that you'd been lovers. I don't know. Perhaps it was his tone more than his actual words."

Dimitri agreed with Cecilia's assessment. Derrick had been playing them that night. He wasn't sure how or why, but everything the man had said—though innocuous enough—felt calculated to him. It was his instincts about the hidden nature of men that had served him well as a spy, had prompted his superiors to ask him to act as a shadow within the organization.

"I'm not sure why he would have done that. Derrick was aware that it was only one night, and that I regretted it. Of course, he did the same thing when..."

Mateo's words faded, and Dimitri thought his lover was finally starting to come to the same suspicions he and Cecilia had in regards to his best friend.

"What is it, Mateo?" Cecilia asked.

"After the fleet admiral fell through the ceiling...Derrick..."

"What?" Dimitri prompted.

"Charlotta asked if Derrick had told me about Eric's secret escape route. He stumbled. He said he hadn't told me—which was the truth—but he said it in such a way that it sounded as if he was lying to protect me."

"Finally. You see."

Mateo looked at Dimitri and nodded slowly. "I think we have to add Derrick to the list of suspects."

Cecilia took Mateo's hand in hers. "Oh, *tesoro*. He was always on the list."

Dimitri chuckled and, then, thankfully Mateo did as well.

"I let our friendship blind me. Derrick was like a brother to me, and yet..." Mateo paused again. The poor man truly was struggling to finish his thoughts tonight. This time, they didn't rush him. "And yet, I feel closer to the two of you after only a few days then I ever did to him. Is that strange?"

Cecilia shook her head. "I feel the same way, *caro*."

"Why did you leave our bed the other night?" Dimitri repeated the question he was still waiting to have answered.

"I wanted to share my past with you."

His response took Dimitri by surprise, confused him. "What do you mean?"

"I was going back to my bedroom to retrieve photographs. Of my parents. I wanted to tell you about them. About what happened to them."

"Happened?" Cecilia asked.

Mateo nodded. "I came home one day after *futbol* practice and found my parents in the dining room. They'd been brutally murdered."

Cecilia gasped. Dimitri's stomach lurched, his chest growing tight, as he considered what Mateo must have seen, felt.

Cecilia reached out for Mateo, cupping his cheek sweetly, and Dimitri saw the tears in her eyes. "I'm so sorry," she whispered.

Mateo swallowed deeply, trying to compose himself. Both Dimitri and Cecilia gave him the time to do so.

When he was ready, he continued with his story. "As I said before, I wasn't aware of the Masters' Admiralty until that night. As the police were searching the house, collecting evidence, my other father arrived."

Cecilia's eyes were sad, but kind. "That must have been quite a shock to you, coming on the heels of your parents' deaths."

Mateo gave them a rueful smile. "It was. But perhaps that was the best time to spring it on me. I mean, after what I'd seen, the shock had left me sufficiently numb to pretty much everything."

"That was truly the first time you'd ever met him?" Cecilia asked.

"Yes. But there was no denying he was who he claimed. He was clearly my biological father. The resemblance between us was unmistakable."

"Why would he stay away all those years?" Dimitri asked.

"He was an important man in the government, as well as the Admiralty. At the time I was born, there had been some threats leveled against him and his trinity, and my parents thought it best to protect me from that danger. It was several years before the threat had passed, and by then, I was a five-year-old boy with two adoring parents.

"The night Mama and Papa were killed, Father took me to his home, and it was there that I saw the countless photo albums—filled with pictures of me at every age—as well as the letters my parents had sent him over the years detailing my day-to-day life, funny things I'd said, awards I'd won. He gave me up to protect me. And when my parents were gone, he gave me a home, a loving one."

"You said he was important in the Masters' Admiralty," Dimitri said.

Mateo nodded. "He was the admiral of Castile."

"But—" Cecilia started, stopping when she realized her words might be painful.

"But," Mateo finished for her, "he's dead now. Killed by the Domino."

Cecilia didn't bother to hide her tears. Instead, she let them fall as she wrapped her arms around Mateo.

He accepted her embrace, and then Dimitri saw the first traces of genuine sorrow on Mateo's face, replacing the numbness that had been there before.

"I haven't had time, a chance to mourn him. Kacper died. Then my father. It's all happened so fast." His voice broke on the last word and his grief came to the surface, spilling out as he tightened his grip on Cecilia.

Dimitri couldn't remain apart, not in the face of such pain. He shifted closer, wrapping both Cecilia and Mateo in his arms, holding them as Mateo slowly fell apart.

They remained that way for a long time, content to simply share that small, warm space until Mateo managed to pull himself back together.

Mateo was the first to move away, rubbing his face to wipe away the tears he'd shed. "I'm tired."

He'd said the same words earlier, and Dimitri had misunderstood how bone-deep that exhaustion was. He had chalked it up to a sleepless night, but now he knew that Mateo had been running on empty for much longer than that.

"Lay down," Cecilia said, gently pushing Mateo to his back on the bed. She followed him, curling up against his chest.

Dimitri sat there for a few moments, looking at them, overwhelmed by the power of his feelings.

He'd fallen in love with them. And it hadn't even taken a week.

Cecilia glanced over her shoulder at him when he didn't move, raising her eyebrows in a silent demand for him to hurry up and take his place beside them.

He lay down behind her, wrapping his arm around her waist, his palm lying flat on Mateo's bare chest.

They lay there long enough that Dimitri thought perhaps Mateo and Cecilia had both fallen asleep.

When Cecilia asked, "Why didn't you become a doctor?" Dimitri realized they were all still awake.

Mateo sighed. "After my parents were killed, and I learned of the threats against my father that prevented him from being a part of my childhood, my goals changed. I realized I wanted to protect those who saved others. A day doesn't pass when I wonder how many lives might have been saved if my parents hadn't been murdered. More than two lives were lost that night. When I learned of the Masters' Admiralty, of its value to the world, I saw my future, and realized I wanted to dedicate my life to protecting their leaders."

"That's a wonderful desire. Selfless. Brave," Cecilia whispered.

Mateo shrugged off her praise, clearly embarrassed by the compliment. Then he continued his story. "Initially, I aspired to become a knight in my territory, to protect my father. It was he who insisted I was destined for greater things, who put my name forward to the fleet admiral for admittance in the Spartan Guard. He was very proud of me when I was accepted. And I can still hear his voice the night I called to tell him I'd been elected head of the guard. It was the only time he'd ever said the words 'I love you' aloud. He wasn't the type to wear his heart on his sleeve or to coddle, but I never doubted his love for me. Not once."

Cecilia lifted her head from his chest. "That's why your job is so important to you. The Spartan Guard isn't a career. It's a calling."

Mateo considered that, then said, "But I failed. Kacper. My father. Mama and Papa. Eric. Everyone."

"Mateo," Cecilia whispered. "No."

Mateo's grief slowly disappeared, morphing into a determination so powerful, Dimitri felt its presence in the room like a tangible being. "I will find the traitor, will make him pay for what he's done. It's too late to change what's passed, but I will not stop until justice is served for those who have died."

"Your cause is mine now, Mateo. I swear it," Dimitri pledged.

"So do I," Cecilia vowed.

The room fell silent for a moment as those words, their promises, sank in. Dimitri sensed the heaviness pressing down on Mateo. He understood it because he was coming to learn they were kindred spirits, the same type of men under the skin.

Dimitri propped himself up on his elbow. "Tomorrow, we'll go to Red. We'll get the answers we're seeking."

"How?"

There was time enough to make their plans in the morning, when clearer heads prevailed. For tonight, they'd prepare for just one aspect.

"Simple. We'll go to the club to play. I have the perfect roles in mind for each of us."

Mateo grinned, and Dimitri's heart lightened to see it.

"I'm sure you do," Mateo murmured. "Am I to assume you'll be taking the lead, dominating our dear Cece?"

Dimitri laughed. "What do you think?"

"Why is it always assumed that I'll submit?" Cecilia asked. "I think I should be the Dominatrix and you two can be my slave boys."

Dimitri reached out and tugged down the sheet, pinching one of her nipples sharply. "That's a dream you'll have to enjoy in your fantasies alone. I'll be the Dom tomorrow…and every other night."

She glared and opened her mouth, clearly intent on lodging her complaints. He pinched her other nipple.

"Perhaps we should practice," Dimitri purred, bending close and taking one of her earlobes between his teeth, nipping at it.

"You don't need to practice," Cecilia said haughtily. "You've got that 'lord of the manor' act down perfectly."

"Oh, the practice wouldn't be for me. But for you." Dimitri looked over at Mateo. "And him."

"I'm not submitting," Mateo said.

"We need to cover all the bases. I will feel out the other Doms, Cece can communicate with the other female subs, which means you can converse with the male submissives."

Mateo shook his head, but Dimitri didn't intend to budge on this. This was one reason why he'd suggested they practice. They needed the distraction after the revelations of the evening. But more than that, submitting didn't come natural to Cecilia or Mateo.

"Think about it, Mateo. You'll understand I'm right."

"Then you play the male sub. I'll be the Dom," Mateo countered.

"Have you ever been to a sex club?"

Dimitri could tell from Mateo's face he hadn't, so he continued, "Dominating a woman in the bedroom is one thing, but there are rules, standards of play, expectations for behavior in these clubs. I can guide both of you through those if I'm the Dom."

Mateo didn't reply. Dimitri respected his lover's hesitance. Submission would rub against the grain. Giving up control would never come easily to him. Now that Dimitri knew about Mateo's tragic background, he understood why.

"I will only do what is necessary to keep up appearances. I will not humiliate you, Mateo."

Cecilia ran her finger along Dimitri's chest. "Am I going to get the same promise?"

Dimitri shook his head, giving her a sexy smile. "No."

"That hardly seems fa—"

Her words stopped sharply when Dimitri gripped both her wrists in his hands and pulled her upright and then off the bed.

"Kneel."

Cecilia's spine stiffened in anger, but it only fueled Dimitri's blood, his lust for her submission.

"Now, Cece."

She did as he asked.

Chapter Sixteen

For a sex club with an ominous one-word name, Red was a bit of a disappointment as far as first impressions went. Nyx had said it was outside London and she was right. Red wasn't in the bustling, cosmopolitan city of London; rather, to the east, on the edge of what was considered greater incorporated London. The small concrete office building was situated in a commercial area not far from the M25 motorway between two sleepy little villages that were predominantly inhabited by commuters. The sign on the front of the building listed businesses that included solicitors, a dentist, and an estate agent.

The very last name on the sign said only "Red – Lower Level."

There were no residential streets around them, and since it was well past business hours, the small parking lot should have been deserted. Instead, it was packed with vehicles. They'd had to park on the street, two wheels on the footpath.

They stood three abreast on the wide walkway up to the front door. Tall glass windows on either side showed a miniscule foyer with three uncomfortable-looking chairs and one sad potted tree.

"I feel ridiculous," Mateo grumbled.

"You look good," Cecilia assured him, stroking his bare arm.

"And cold."

"Cecilia gets to complain about the cold before you do. She's wearing less than you are." Dimitri hadn't stopped looking around, assessing, since they got out of the car.

Cecilia struck a pose. They'd gone to a High Street store that catered to disenfranchised teenagers with disposable income to get their outfits. She was wearing black fishnet stockings and a miniskirt made entirely out of black tulle. That was paired with a red and black plaid bra that was a size too small, resulting in more than ample cleavage, and a black tube top that was nothing more than a twenty-centimeter-wide band of stretchy fabric. Her arms and midriff were bare, her shoulders covered only by thin red bra straps, her legs by the fishnet stockings. She had on black boots—for safety. Dimitri had wanted her in something they could run in if the situation got dangerous—and she wore thick leather cuffs buckled on each wrist.

Mateo, in comparison, was naked from the waist up, except for wrist cuffs that were a match to her own. The faux leather pants he wore were too short—the store hadn't had anything long enough for someone his height—but that was hidden because he'd stuffed the ends of the pants into the tops of his black boots. It gave him a fetish-commando look that she liked.

On her other side was Dimitri. He too wore faux leather pants—the same pair Mateo had purchased—but unlike them, he wore a black button-down shirt. It was a sort of formal kink that she also liked. He had the whip, which he'd coiled and attached to his belt with a small strap that reminded her of a luggage tag.

If not for Dimitri looking around like he was expecting trouble, and Mateo radiating tension, she would have been looking forward to this. She'd never been to a sex club before. She couldn't imagine a better way to visit than with two such delectable men by her side.

"Pardon us." The speaker was behind them, their voice vaguely apologetic in a very British way.

Dimitri snaked an arm around Cecilia's waist and pulled her to him, turning them so they were no longer blocking the path to the door of the office building. Mateo stepped to the side too.

The speaker was a middle-aged British man, with pale blond hair. He wore a three-piece suit and a tie. Cecilia winced in embarrassment, at least until she saw that he held a leash.

"Thank you." He walked up to the door, his companion trailing behind him.

The companion was a middle-aged woman in a black slip dress. She was barefoot and wearing a bright red collar with the other end of the leash attached to the ring in the center.

The couple opened the door, went into the small foyer, and then pressed the button for the lift.

"We're at the right place." Mateo folded his arms over his bare chest.

"Let's go." Cecilia started forward, but Dimitri tightened his arm, arresting her forward motion.

"You two are my subs when we go in there," he growled. "That means I give the orders."

"Then why don't you order us to go in?" she asked.

"How do you think that's going to go for you?" Mateo asked Dimitri, grinning at Cecilia's smart-ass question.

"Keep it up, Cece, and there will be a spanking."

Cecilia turned to look at him over her shoulder. "If you want me to spank you, Dim, all you have to do is ask." She patted Dimitri's cheek.

His eyes seemed to glitter with need—and just enough menace to have her shifting her weight from foot to foot.

"Come," Dimitri ordered.

Mateo nodded and went first, opening the door for them.

They crowded into the small lift and pressed the button for the basement level. The lift lurched a bit as it started down. She tried to calm herself. This was probably going to be very disappointing. Certainly the outside had not been promising. Still, she felt sexy if not sophisticated in her outfit, and the presence of her men, so close to her that she could feel the heat of their bodies, was making her think all kinds of kinky things.

The doors opened—and Cecilia let out a little moan of delight.

The plain office building above them was the perfect cover for this delectable den of iniquity.

Red was massive, occupying the entire basement level of the building. The club was open, with evenly spaced concrete support columns and furniture dividing the single larger space into different areas.

The floor was concrete that had been stained dark and varnished so it gleamed. Red light was everywhere, so though the space was brightly lit, it was oddly dim. The walls were a pale color—probably white, though it was hard to tell with the colored bulbs—and painted with images of naked men and women in bondage.

Cecilia would have stayed in the elevator—not because she didn't want to exit, but because she was too busy looking around—if Dimitri hadn't put a hand on her ass and given her a little push.

"Check in, please."

They turned to find a small table set up in an alcove to the right of the elevator. A woman in black fishnet gloves and a long red dress motioned them over. "IDs."

They shared a glance, but then Dimitri reached into his pocket and pulled out their passports. They'd debated bringing them, but Dimitri hadn't wanted to leave them in the car.

The woman glanced at each, then handed them back. "Sign the waiver. Make sure you know the rules. The club Doms will be happy to escort you out if you can't mind your manners."

Cecilia blinked as she was handed a clipboard. She eagerly started to read it, skipping the boring parts about liability in favor of the juicy bits with club rules.

No penetrative sex.

No exposing the vagina, penis, or female nipples. Socks and tape are allowed.

Socks and tape? What did that mean?

Mateo cleared his throat. She glanced over to see him handing his clipboard back. She scrawled something illegible at the bottom and then passed hers back.

"Go, go." The woman shooed them with a flick of her fingers. "Off you go then."

Cecilia spun on a heel and looked around the club again, this time focusing on the people. Not far from where they stood were a few wooden benches encircling a man who stood with his arms stretched up over his head. He was bound in place with rope that stretched from his upraised hands to a chain that dangled down from the ceiling. His companion—no, that wasn't right—his Domme circled around him, her nails scraping over his bare skin. He wore loose shorts, and the front was visibly tented.

As she watched, the Domme took what looked like a black athletic sock and reached into his shorts. The man moaned, tipping his head back, his teeth bared in what was either pleasure or pain. A second later, the Domme carefully removed his shorts. His cock was now encased in the black sock thing, which technically hid it from view, but in practice didn't do more than help to bring attention to his erection.

A woman walked between Cecilia and the scene. She was naked except for a black thong and two X's of black tape over her nipples.

"That is what socks and tape means," she murmured.

"What was that?" Mateo leaned close, his hand sliding over the bare skin of her lower back.

"Hands to yourself, sub." Dimitri took Mateo's upper arm in one hand, Cecilia's wrist in the other, and led them away from the check-in table. Cecilia looked around as they walked, but Dimitri was moving too fast for her to see more than a wild impression of nakedness. It was loud—there was electronic music playing in the background, plus the murmur of voices and the thwack and slap of hands, crops, and paddles hitting flesh.

Dimitri found a vacant chair—a blood-red wing-back chair that was up against the wall—in a spot that was quieter than the rest of the club. He took a seat, then pointed at the ground. "Kneel."

Cecilia looked at Mateo, whose jaw muscle was standing out. She put a hand on his arm and then dropped to her knees. Mateo followed suit.

Dimitri leaned forward. "Mateo. Strategy."

Mateo hated having his back to the room—it made him twitchy that he couldn't see if someone came at him. He hated that he was weaponless. He hated these fake leather pants that were making his balls sweat.

But he didn't hate kneeling in front of Dimitri. Which was the surprising part.

"Would Derrick be here as a Dom or a sub?" Dimitri asked.

"I have no idea," Mateo said.

"He's your best friend. You know. Take an educated guess."

Mateo replied without hesitation. "Sub. He'd be a sub." He wasn't sure how he was so certain, but there was something about Derrick that told Mateo his strengths lie only in following orders, not giving them.

"What about Charlotta?" Dimitri asked.

"Oh, that girl's a Domme for sure," Cecilia interjected, though Mateo wasn't so certain about that assessment. He didn't bother to correct her. After all, Charlotta wasn't here tonight. She was on the Isle of Man. It was Derrick who was on the loose.

"Then we play that angle. I don't want to use them, but if we need a last resort, do you have the photos?"

Mateo nodded. They'd taken a stack of photos of all the current Spartan Guards from Stranraer, the idea being they'd look them over on the boat, but that was before Cecilia's bout of seasickness. Derrick and Charlotta's pictures were amongst them. Flashing pictures to people in a BDSM club was probably certain to fail, given how many members prized their secrecy.

"Do we just go up to people and ask if they knew them?" Cecilia asked.

"No." Dimitri stood. "We're going to watch the scenes and use them as an opportunity to start asking questions. Only use the pictures if they do not recognize the names."

"Why do we say we're asking about them?" Cecilia asked.

243

"Say that we enjoyed them."

"No, say we 'scened' with them. That's how they'd say it in English," Mateo corrected. He was still on his knees, neck craned to look up at Dimitri.

Dimitri bent, cupped Mateo's head, and kissed him.

Then Dimitri led them over to a scene in progress not far from the red chair. Per their plan, Cecilia knelt close to another female sub, Dimitri took a seat on a small bench within arm's reach of her, and Mateo leaned against the closest support column.

The scene featured a female sub straddling a wooden carpentry horse. Her arms were stretched overhead, and she was naked except for two red nipple pasties with tassels and a matching thong. She was balanced on the balls of her feet, her calf muscles tensed and hard. She whimpered into the bit-gag in her mouth and then relaxed her legs, her bodyweight coming down on her crotch.

"Ouch." Cecilia winced and leaned toward Dimitri. He nudged her with his knee, pushing her toward the sub kneeling beside her.

Cecilia shot one glance over her shoulder at him, then turned to the other woman, bending her head close to be heard over the music.

"Hello."

The dark-haired sub smiled, looked at her Dom, who nodded permission, then replied to Cecilia. "Hi."

Mateo forced himself to be patient, to pretend to be paying attention to the scene, but really keeping an eye on, and protecting, Dimitri and Cecilia.

His patience paid off. The Dom of the dark-haired woman Cecilia was talking to leaned over to talk to Dimitri. Mateo took a half step forward, straining to hear.

"It appears our ladies have made friends."

"Yes. It does." Dimitri deliberately thickened his accent. Another part of their strategy—Mateo would do the same. He could always fall back on pretending he didn't understand as a way to exit a useless conversation.

"Do you come here often? I don't think I've seen you before."

"No." Dimitri looked around. "We came here only once. Now we are wanting to find someone."

"Oh?"

"Two someones. A woman Domme named Char...Charlotta, I think." He pretended to consider. "A man. A submissive. Named Derrick or Dominic."

"Derrick?"

Inside, Mateo went cold. He'd hoped against all hope it was Charlotta.

Dimitri smiled and nodded. "Yes, yes, that was his name."

"I saw him, but I believe he's in a private scene."

"He's here, tonight? Private?" Dimitri looked around the club.

"Yes, back near the bathrooms. There are a few private rooms, though they're not much, and the club Doms monitor them."

Dimitri's expression hadn't flickered with anything more than mild interest. He was playing the part perfectly.

Mateo's mind raced, trying to think five moves ahead, when Dimitri said, "Ah, so they are not for..."

"No." The other man smiled ruefully. "Intercourse, even in the private rooms, is forbidden."

"Pity."

Dimitri leaned forward and stroked Cecilia's hair, then sat back. Impatience bit at Mateo but he forced himself to wait. Dimitri was the Dom. It was up to him to decide when the three of them moved.

Finally, Dimitri stood, then reached down and tangled his fingers in Cecilia's hair, giving it a light tug. She stood, swaying a little. Dimitri nodded to the other Dom, then led Cecilia and Mateo away.

"Derrick," Cecilia said. "The woman I was talking to recognized his name."

Mateo's jaw muscle jumped as he clenched his teeth. "I know. The Dom did too."

"I'm sorry, Mateo. I know this must be hard—"

"No time," Dimitri said. "He's here."

"This way." Mateo was in the lead as they wove through the crowd toward the far reaches of the club. What he'd thought was just a patch of shadow was, in fact, the entrance to a hallway. There were bathrooms on one side, and two doors bearing "private" placards. Mateo grabbed the first door and threw it open.

The room beyond was Spartan, with bare walls and floor. Instead of recessed lighting, there were wall sconces with red bulbs in them.

Mateo slammed the door and lunged for the second knob.

"Stop." Dimitri caught his hand.

"Let go, Dimitri."

"Step back. I will take the lead."

"You may be playing the Dom right now, but I don't take orders from you."

Cecilia slid between them, putting her hands on Mateo's arm, pushing him back. Dimitri slipped in behind her, taking point at the door. "Derrick is your friend. That makes this hard."

Dimitri tested the door to the second room. This one was locked. He dug into his pocket as Cecilia murmured to Mateo in a calm voice. When Dimitri pulled out lock picks, Mateo bit back the urge to demand that they just throw themselves against the door until it burst open.

It wasn't a complicated lock and Dimitri had it open in less than a minute. Tucking the picks into his pocket once more, he stepped to the side, motioned for Mateo and Cecilia to get clear, and then opened it.

This room was much like the other—a bare concrete box. But this room wasn't empty.

For a moment, Mateo thought they had the wrong person. The man standing in the center of the room, arms raised and held in place by chains, ankles spread and locked to a meter-long spreader bar, didn't look like Derrick at first glance. He had Derrick's coloring, but seemed slighter and shorter than the man he'd called best friend for so many years.

There was a gag obscuring the lower half of his face, and his hair was mussed, falling over his eyes. He wore a pair of red leather briefs but was otherwise naked, his skin crosshatched by welts and bruises. There was a thick metal collar around his neck, with a large box resting on his clavicle.

The sound of the door opening was obscured by the crack of a whip. As they watched, the room's other occupant, a statuesque Dominatrix, twirled the short whip around herself in a figure eight motion before flicking it. The small motion caused the tail of the red whip to lash against the man's right thigh. A line appeared, first white then angry red.

He threw his head back, eyes squeezed closed, and Mateo got a good look at his face. It was Derrick.

He cursed in Castilian and turned away.

Dimitri unfastened the loop that held the whip at his side, letting it unfurl onto the floor. Then he stepped into the room.

The Dominatrix looked up, her eyes cold.

"We need to speak to your sub. Alone."

She examined him from head to toe, gaze lingering on the whip in his hand.

It was clear Dimitri expected some resistance—after all, no good top would leave a vulnerable sub with strangers.

At that moment, Derrick's head dipped forward and he opened his eyes. He caught sight of Dimitri standing inside the room, Cecilia and Mateo framed in the doorway.

He started to babble into the gag. His chest muscles flexed as he pulled at his bonds.

The Dominatrix looked from Derrick to Dimitri. She smiled, though it was more of a perfunctory curving of lips, then walked out of the room, brushing past Mateo who was rooted in place, staring at Derrick.

"Derrick." Mateo spoke the man's name in a dark voice laced with menace. Mateo knew Cecilia felt perfectly safe in his arms, but the deadly tone in his voice caused the hand she still had resting on his arm to tremble slightly.

Dimitri walked across the room, stopping in front of Derrick. He stood there for a moment, and Mateo wondered how Derrick managed to remain so still in the face of such danger.

The Dominatrix had left him completely helpless, at their mercy.

After several long moments, Dimitri reached out and unhooked the ball gag, pulling it out of Derrick's mouth.

Mateo saw the shine of drool on his chin. Derrick's mouth closed almost painfully and he wondered how long the gag had been in. It looked like the muscles had been strained and it was taking them a moment to move naturally again.

Mateo still stood near the door, but his voice, when he spoke, resonated and filled the cold space. "Why?"

Derrick seemed hesitant to take his eyes off Dimitri, who stood too close and was clearly the more immediate threat.

"Untie me."

Dimitri shook his head. "Answer his question."

Derrick closed his mouth, his silence proving he wouldn't make this interrogation easy.

Mateo considered what they would do if he continued to refuse. It wasn't like Dimitri could beat the man with the whip. Given the deep red welts covering too much of his body, it was obvious he'd enjoy that technique.

Dimitri reached into the back pocket of his pants and pulled out his phone, handing it to Cecilia. "Record."

Cecilia lifted the phone, pointing it directly at Derrick before asking,

"Did you let the drone operator on the grounds of Triskelion Castle?"

Derrick's eyes flicked to hers, and she felt his disdain for her. She was clearly confused by that look. Mateo also found himself wondering about it. Cecilia had done nothing to Derrick, who still refused to respond.

Dimitri waited for sixty seconds, then reached into his other pocket, pulling out the lock pick he'd used to break into the room. He ran the sharp tip of it down Derrick's chest and stomach, then he ran it over the front of the leather underwear.

Dimitri didn't say anything. Cecilia stepped closer, moving so she had a better angle for the video. Mateo could read the curiosity on her face. Knowing their intelligent lady, she'd seen a thousand spy movies and read a million mystery novels where the bad guy was tortured for information, and she was actually viewing this moment as educational.

Dimitri glanced at Cecilia, and Mateo thought he saw amusement in his eyes, but it was there in a flash, then gone again.

Derrick snickered, giving Dimitri a derisive grin. "Do your worst."

Dimitri didn't reply. Instead, he lifted his leg and brought his boot down hard on Derrick's bare foot.

The man yelped, jumping awkwardly in his bindings. "Bloody hell!"

Dimitri raised his heel and smashed it down again. The sound of boot on flesh and bone was sickening.

Derrick shrieked, and tried to shift his weight to his good foot, but the spreader bar prevented that. "You broke my toes!" The words were a pained gasp.

"Probably. If not all, some. Ready to answer our questions or should I start on the other foot?" Dimitri glanced up at Derrick's bound hands. "Then I'll break your fingers."

Derrick's face had gone white, pain etched in the lines by his eyes and mouth. "Okay."

Cecilia was impressed and apparently anxious to become a part of the action. "Did you let the drone operator on the grounds?"

"Yes," he snarled at her.

"Did you taint the medicine that was given to the fleet admiral?" she asked.

Derrick's initial hesitance seemed to melt away. Now that he'd confessed to the first part, it was as if he was happy to suddenly be free to speak about his role. Not because he felt guilt or remorse, but because he was proud of his actions. He looked straight at the camera.

"I did."

"Where did you get the poison?" Mateo asked.

"I made it. You never knew about my talents as a chemist, Mateo. Always assumed I was nothing more than you. The muscle, the good foot soldier, the obedient warrior."

"Why?" Mateo asked.

"Because I should have been head of the Spartan Guard! My family has served as members of the guard for five hundred years, and yet I was second choice to *you*." He spat the last word at Mateo.

"Huh," Cecilia said quietly. "Josephine and Hugo were right. It was about the legacy guards. Remind me to tell them that."

"Who are Josephine and Hugo?" Dimitri asked.

"Err. Never mind."

Mateo stepped in front of Derrick. "Are you the Domino?"

"I recruited the drone operator. I have been instrumental in furthering our—"

Derrick's mouth was open to speak, but his lips pulled back in the parody of a grin. His body started to shake, his head rocking so wildly his chin hit the metal collar around his neck. His eyes rolled back in his head.

Cecilia dropped the phone and started to reach for him—he seemed to be having a seizure.

Dimitri grabbed her hands, jerking her back. "Find the control!" he shouted to Mateo.

"What's happening?" Cecilia asked.

"He's being electrocuted."

Derrick's body jerked roughly; his bowels released. Mateo dashed around the room. "There's nothing."

His former friend's body slumped but didn't stop twitching.

"There's nothing!" Mateo snarled, still searching desperately. If Derrick died, they'd never find the answers they were seeking.

"The woman!" Cecilia yelled. "She must have it."

"Dammit." Dimitri spun on his heel, racing for the door. "She's part of this."

Mateo started to ask how, but Dimitri was gone. Cecilia and Mateo followed him, watching when he grabbed the first club Dom he saw.

"Where is the woman who was in that room?"

The Dom glanced the direction Dimitri was pointing. "In the private room?"

"*Tak*," he said impatiently, before translating to English. "Yes!"

"Mistress Alicia left a few minutes ago."

"Alicia who?" Dimitri demanded. "She broke club rules. Abused her sub."

That seemed to be some sort of magic code, because the Dom looked shocked and pissed, whereas before he'd seemed reluctant to answer.

"Derrick is hurt? His top is Alicia Rutherford."

"Alicia…" Mateo felt ill.

The club Dom looked to him. "She's American, not a regular, comes to play here when she's in London on business."

"A.R.," Cecilia whispered.

"She killed her sub," Dimitri told the club Dom, whose eyes widened in shock.

Mateo whirled and headed back to his friend.

"What? Killed?" Mateo heard the club Dom saying.

"Inform your boss," Dimitri commanded loudly.

Mateo knew when they raced back into the room, not because he could hear them, but because he could *feel* them.

Mateo released Derrick, lowering him to the floor and started doing CPR.

"You shouldn't touch him," Dimitri said in Catalan.

"I couldn't just leave him hanging there," Mateo panted as he did chest compressions.

"The current could still be active."

"It's not." Mateo sealed his mouth over Derrick's.

"The collar?" Cecilia asked. "Is that what killed him?"

Around them, people were filling the room, exclamations of dismay and a few muffled sobs masking the sound of their lower conversation.

"Low voltage kills," Dimitri said. "Mateo, stop. You can't help him."

"You don't know that," he panted.

"I do. A collar like that wouldn't have been able to deliver a high enough voltage for him to be revived. Over 200 milliamps and you can restart the heart, but there are no burns on him, and there would be if it was that high. This was a low-voltage shock. Meant to kill."

Mateo sat back, breathing hard.

A woman in a rope dress pushed forward, dropped to her knees, and took over.

Dimitri grabbed Mateo and pulled him back, letting the crowd fill in the space around Derrick's body.

"Maybe..." Mateo started.

"No. That collar must have been modified. Normally electro play is only 10 milliamps. If it had been tampered with to deliver 100, 150 milliamps... I'm sorry. It stopped his heart."

"We should leave," Cecilia murmured. "There are too many people here. The authorities will arrive and they'll have questions."

"She's right." Dimitri still had his hand wrapped around Mateo's upper arm and used the hold to force Mateo back. "Where's the phone?"

Cecilia looked around, but too many people had come into the room. "I dropped it when he started convulsing."

"Find it," Dimitri said, pushing several people aside until he found it. Someone had stepped on it, the screen smashed. "Dammit."

"We need to report this to the fleet admiral," Cecilia said. "He confessed."

"And without that video, we were the only ones who heard it," Mateo said.

They looked at one another, each seeming to realize exactly how badly this had gone, and what the ramifications would be at the same time.

Cecilia looked distressed, but only for a moment. "Come on." She hooked her arms with each of theirs, propelling them toward the exit. "I know someone who will help us."

Chapter Seventeen

Mateo paced the waiting room, trying to figure out some way to convince Cecilia this meeting was a mistake. His head was pounding, the pain between his temples the result of no sleep and too much stress.

To make matters worse, he couldn't shake the image of the construction barriers they'd just passed in the hallway, blocking off the staircase that led to the floor above, to the large conference room where his father had been gunned down by the American sniper as Mateo had been across the Channel, reeling over his failure to protect Kacper.

He'd failed more than just the fleet admiral that day. His father had died in this building without him, his last parent struck down, Mateo helpless to save him.

Mateo rubbed his brow, trying to drive that dark feeling away. There wasn't room for that now. He needed to get a grip, to be ready to answer the admiral's questions. His life depended on it.

After leaving Red last night, Cecilia had made a call to her cousin, James, who'd met her at a small café near Piccadilly Square to retrieve the destroyed phone. He'd called this morning and set up this meeting with

Arthur today. He hadn't mentioned whether or not they could retrieve the video from the phone.

The three of them had returned to the hotel last night, but neither he nor Dimitri had slept easily. Dimitri had gotten up every hour on the hour, peeking out the window. Mateo wasn't sure what he was looking for, but it had added to his own anxiety.

Cecilia had been restless as well, but Mateo wasn't sure why. She'd seemed soothed after speaking to her cousin, and it was evident she didn't think they were in any danger where the Masters' Admiralty was concerned.

Mateo didn't share her confidence. Their traitor was dead and their only evidence of his misdeeds was a confession only the three of them had heard if the video couldn't be retrieved. Given that Dimitri had broken him out of the dungeon, and he and Cecilia had gone on the run with him, they weren't exactly reliable sources.

There was a very good chance the fleet admiral would assume they were lying to protect Mateo.

Cecilia insisted the fact that they'd discovered the name of the third member of Manon's affair would save them. Mateo wasn't sure that was enough. He'd wanted to go after Alicia Rutherford, try to find her, but Dimitri insisted that would be a waste of time and energy. For some reason, Dimitri was convinced that Alicia had been long gone the moment she'd flipped the switch on the bondage collar that had killed Derrick.

Derrick. His best friend.

A traitor.

"We shouldn't be here," he murmured again. Arthur had instructed the three of them to report to his office this afternoon, and Cecilia, the lovely, trusting woman, had agreed.

Cecilia was sitting in a brown leather chair, casually flipping through a magazine. Only the constant bobbing of her foot gave away her own nervousness. "We're fine. James would never put us in a dangerous situation."

Dimitri had been quiet since they'd left Red last night, and all damn day. Cecilia's confidence in their safety was only slightly less annoying than Dimitri's silence.

"Dimitri," Mateo said, repeating the name twice more before Dimitri even heard him.

"What?"

"What is wrong with you? I was telling Cece I think we should leave."

Dimitri rubbed his neck. "I think you're right."

Cecilia looked up in surprise. "*Et tu*, Brute? We're not in danger," she paused before adding, "from Arthur."

Mateo noticed the bounce in her foot was faster now. If the threat wasn't from Arthur or Eric, who...

Him.

Her nervousness wasn't based on what the Masters' Admiralty would do to them. She was worried about what would happen to their trinity. What *Mateo* would do to the three of them.

He had been so wrapped up in his concern about their evidence not being enough to clear him, he'd stopped considering what would happen if it *was*. The trinity would be dissolved. He would go back to his position as head of the Spartan Guard.

"It's not the admiral I'm worried about," Dimitri said, shaking his head. "I need to talk to the two of you about something. There's something I need to tell you bef—"

Before he could finish, Arthur's office door opened. A man wearing a trim suit with a regimental tie and a sword at his waist stood there. One of England's knights. Mateo remembered him. He'd been in that hotel room when they'd confronted Manon.

Cool, assessing eyes swept over them.

Mateo walked forward, holding out his right hand. "Percy. It's good to see you again."

Percy nodded, but didn't shake. Vaguely, Mateo remembered something about the knights not shaking hands with someone they didn't trust because it meant their sword hand was engaged.

Percy didn't trust him. Fuck.

"The admiral will see you." Percy stepped back and to the side, clearing the doorway.

Mateo waited until Dimitri and Cecilia were at his back before passing into the room. Then he stopped, Dimitri stepping up on his right, Cecilia on his left.

The admiral of England stood when they entered. "Have a seat."

Where most offices had one or maybe two visitor chairs on the other side the desk, it seemed the three chairs that had been here last time Mateo was in the office were permanent fixtures. Probably because Arthur had meetings with other trinities.

One way or another, they were never going to be a trinity. Either he was going to be branded a traitor and punished, or he would be cleared and return to the Isle of Man.

Alone.

Cecilia crossed the office, heading for the waiting chairs. Neither Mateo nor Dimitri moved.

She turned, and Mateo recognized the fear in her eyes.

"Cece," he said, wishing he could comfort her.

Arthur cleared his throat.

Mateo and Dimitri followed Cecilia to their seats, the three of them claiming the exact same seats they'd been in a week earlier.

Mateo couldn't believe it had only been one week. It felt as if they'd lived a lifetime together since then.

Arthur leaned back in his leather desk chair. "James said you discovered the name of the traitor."

"Yes," Cecilia said, nodding. "It was Derrick Frederick."

"And your proof?" Arthur's tone was cool. He looked like some gallant knight from a cartoon fairy tale—gold hair and handsome features. The sling that held the stump of his arm close to his chest didn't detract from his appearance. Instead, it gave him the air of a wounded hero.

Mateo remembered him when he'd been a knight. He'd been quiet, disciplined and utterly devoted to his duties. He was different now, maybe even different than he'd been when they saw him last week. It was as if becoming the admiral was hardening him a little more each day.

"He confessed," she said.

Arthur's expression barely changed. A slight frown made a line between his eyebrows. "To whom?"

It was just as Mateo suspected. He didn't ask about the confession, he asked who'd *heard* the confession. The Masters' Admiralty would never take their word for it without that recording.

"To us." Cecilia's response was sure, strong. Their lovely woman wasn't cowed by Arthur's questioning.

"James said he's dead."

"Yes," Mateo responded. "We found him in a sex club here in London. Red. He was bound, and his Domme had placed an electrical collar around his neck."

"I've seen the police report regarding what happened at the club. Nothing happens to a member of my territory that I don't know about immediately. And though he was a member of the Spartan Guard, Derrick

259

was first and foremost from England. I didn't see any mention of the three of you in the report, however."

"We didn't stick around to give a statement," Dimitri said drolly.

Arthur paused, scowling briefly. Rather than call Dimitri out, he continued his line of questioning. "What, exactly, did Derrick confess to?"

"He was the one tainting the medicine that was given to Kacper. Apparently, he's quite clever in chemistry." Cecilia took the lead in sharing what they'd discovered. Mateo was grateful for that. Her tone and posture left no doubt she believed they'd accomplished the task they had been assigned.

And while Mateo prayed that was true, he wasn't sure that would be a blessing. Because that outcome forced him to make a choice.

"He also recruited the drone operator," Cecilia continued. "Apparently, Derrick's lineage dates all the way back to the original Manx guards, who were replaced by the current Spartan Guards. He seemed to feel he had some sort of birthright that made him better suited to lead the guards than Mateo. I have some, er, friends checking out that claim, doing some research into Derrick's family tree."

Arthur didn't seem surprised by that piece of information. In fact, Mateo thought it felt as if a lot of what they were telling him had already been relayed to him. Mateo had been too preoccupied by Derrick's murder last night to pay much attention to Cecilia. All he could recall was that she'd left the hotel to give the phone to James. She also mentioned contacting a few other friends who could help. He hadn't had the presence of mind to question her about that at the time.

"Did he mention the Domino? Did he confirm the villain was Manon?" Arthur asked.

Cecilia shook her head. "No. He was electrocuted before he could say anything more."

Arthur rubbed his chin with his one good hand. "By the Domme?"

Cecilia nodded. "Yes."

"Why were you at Red?"

Dimitri reached into the duffel he'd been carrying and pulled out the whip. "Because of this. We found it in the stables of a rental property just outside Triskelion Castle. We believe it was where Manon met her lovers."

Arthur picked up the whip, examining the handle, cord, and then the tag. "I can determine who G.R. and M.K. are, but A.R.?"

"Alicia Rutherford," Cecilia said. "The club Dom said she was American, and we're assuming she's related to Griffin Rutherford. Wife, sister, something like that."

For the first time since they'd entered the room, Arthur showed a real spark of interest. Picking up a pen, he awkwardly jotted down the name with his left hand. The pad of paper he wrote on was held in place by a large paperweight in one corner. The briefest hint of either frustration or grief crossed his face as he finished the note, but then his expression returned to neutral and he pushed a button on his phone. "Lorelei."

"What do you want?"

"I have guests with me."

"Same question."

Cecilia looked a little scandalized by the woman's tone and glanced at Mateo and Dimitri.

Mateo had met Lorelei. He wasn't surprised by her tone. Only a very stupid person tried the oh-so-limited patience of the vice admiral of England.

"I need you to run a name for me. Alicia Rutherford. American. Get me everything you can find—"

There was a click as she disconnected.

"—immediately," Arthur finished with a sigh. He looked at Dimitri. "Where is Alicia now?"

Dimitri held still, but Mateo couldn't help but shift his weight in discomfort at the answer they would have to give. Beside him, Cecilia was making a face.

"We didn't realize who she was." Dimitri's accent gave his words a clipped authority. "Our primary objective was to question Derrick. She left the room...with the remote to the collar. I can only assume she was listening at the door. When it was obvious Derrick was about to say more than he should, she triggered the collar. It had been rigged to deliver a low voltage that would have stopped his heart almost instantly. By the time we realized it was her, she was gone."

Arthur sat perfectly still, his gaze focused in middle distance. When he finally spoke, his words were slow and measured. "You found Derrick in a compromising position, and let his companion leave without speaking to or questioning her."

"Yes," Dimitri agreed, with a hint of defensiveness.

"She murdered Derrick while you were in the room with him, and by the time you thought to look for her, she was gone."

"Yes." Dimitri was practically smiling.

"We can go after her," Mateo suggested a bit desperately. "Give us more time and we'll find her, bring her back here to you."

Arthur shook his head. "No. Your part in this investigation is done. You were asked to find the traitor in the guard and you did."

Mateo's lungs seized. "You believe me."

Arthur frowned. "Of course I do."

Mateo wanted to slump in relief. The feeling was short-lived. Just because Arthur believed him didn't mean others would. He and Arthur had forged a bond during the op that had led them to Manon and the American sniper. Mateo had felt a kinship with the admiral of England, but he didn't share that same comrades-in-arms bond with Eric Ericsson. "Will the fleet admiral believe me?"

"Why don't you ask him?" Arthur swiveled in his chair

A narrow door, which Mateo had assumed was to a closet, opened.

Eric Ericsson walked into the room.

Mateo hadn't spent much time with the man, and the last time he'd seen him, he'd been injured, so he was struck again by just how *big* he was. Like Arthur, Eric was blond, but while Arthur looked like a romantic hero, Eric looked like a barbarian, like a Viking. The Viking. The nickname was more than fitting. It wasn't hard to imagine him wielding a club or massive sword, his face streaked in mud, blood, or both, with his lips pulled back in a berserker's smile.

Even his thoroughly modern clothes—jeans and a shirt that strained at his shoulders—didn't detract from the impression of barely restrained brute strength. The one thing that did distract was the black sling supporting one arm. If the situation hadn't been so tense, it would have been almost amusing that Eric and Arthur had matching slings.

Mateo studied the man a second longer. Both his hands were bandaged in thin layers of gauze that made it look like he was preparing for a boxing match. His rugged face was paler than normal, but there was no missing the hard glint in his eyes and strength in his face that said pain was nothing new to him.

"Bernard."

Mateo stood and faced the fleet admiral. He had to bite back an instinctive reprimand. The Spartan Guard were the only people who had the authority to give the fleet admiral orders. That was necessary if they were going to protect him. Mateo wanted to tell him he shouldn't be here, ask who was with him, what security measures were in place, what provisions and backup plans had been made for his security while he was away from Triskelion.

Mateo had to clench his teeth and take a breath to hold back the questions. He wasn't the head of the Spartan Guard right now.

Right now, he wasn't the protector, he was the accused. He was here because he'd failed once. He was here because he was trying to, once more, prove himself.

He was grateful when Cecilia and Dimitri rose as well, flanking him as he awaited the fleet admiral's decision regarding his future. He'd done what was asked of him and he wouldn't cower before the man.

"The traitor was Derrick Frederick," Mateo said, perfectly aware the fleet admiral already knew that. Regardless, he'd promised to deliver the traitor, so he would. "He confessed and he's dead."

"Saw that part. Lorelei was able to retrieve the video. It ended abruptly when Derrick began convulsing. Died in the middle of a BDSM scene?"

"Yes, Fleet Admiral."

Eric snorted, tried to cross his arms, winced and settled for planting his good hand on his hip. "Red always was garbage. Though I can think of worse ways to die. Unless his dick was out. Wouldn't want to die with my dick out."

Arthur sat back. "I'm guessing it's not like the place we visited?"

"Places like Red are as different from The Garden as McDonald's is from fine dining. I told you if you want to engage in real power-exchange play, you need to talk to Damien."

Were they randomly discussing BDSM clubs? Mateo put that thought aside.

Eric's attention shifted back to him. He'd relaxed slightly while talking to Arthur, but now his expression was stony, and even with only one arm he looked dangerous.

"Do you believe Derrick was the Domino?" Eric asked.

Mateo shook his head. "No."

"The apprentice?"

Mateo considered that, then shook his head again. "Maybe. I believe he was easily manipulated and used when it became apparent he harbored ill will toward me for becoming head of the guard instead of him."

"Very well. You have served the Masters' Admiralty honorably, in bringing the traitor to justice." Eric's eyes slid from Mateo to Dimitri. "Both of you have."

Mateo glanced over his shoulder at Dimitri, who looked unsure and almost...scared...for the first time since they'd met.

What was going on? He was confused by his lover's sudden discomfiture. "Both of us?" Mateo asked.

Dimitri looked at Mateo. "I started to tell you before. You see, the..." Dimitri paused, and Mateo could see his lover stiffening his spine, taking a deep breath as if girding himself before saying, "The fleet admiral called me to the Isle of Man and informed me of this trinity. My task was to watch over you during the investigation…while doing one of my own."

It took a moment for the words, and their meaning, to penetrate. Mateo's temper erupted. "You were put in this trinity to prove I was the traitor!"

Dimitri nodded stiffly, clearly not surprised by Mateo's anger.

"This was never a real trinity," Cecilia whispered.

Mateo had been so focused on Eric and Dimitri, he hadn't considered how all of this was affecting her.

Dimitri moved toward her a split second before Mateo.

"Cece." Dimitri reached for her.

"No! Don't touch me. Either of you!" She took a step away from Dimitri, then her eyes narrowed as she looked at Mateo, her rage stopping him in his tracks as well. "This is done. I'm done with this."

Mateo felt the bottom fall out when she turned toward the door, clearly intent on leaving. "No! No, Cecilia."

"Cece," Dimitri said. "Please. Let me explain."

She whirled on them, furious. "Explain what? That for the past week, the two of you have been actively working *against* what I truly believed was…was special? Was right? I gave everything I had to this union, opened my arms, my heart. Gave you my trust and my…" She swallowed heavily, brushing away a tear before shoving her emotions deeper. "Submission," she whispered.

Mateo had never loved her beauty and her strength more than in that moment.

She backed up another step, and Eric reached out, putting a hand on her shoulder.

"Submission?" he asked quietly.

Mateo wanted to tell Eric it was none of his fucking business, but Cecilia raised her chin, as if daring Eric to pass judgment on her. "Yes."

"Then I'm sorry. Dominance and submission is something I take very seriously. Abuse of trust in a power-exchange relationship can do... If I'd known you were a sexual submissive, I might have handled it differently." Eric squeezed her shoulder.

"I'm not," Cecilia said through clenched teeth, her voice so soft, Mateo barely heard her denial. What she gave them in the bedroom was clearly meant just for them. She'd never allow anyone else to know how much she'd changed, came alive...gave them.

"Take your hand off her," Mateo snarled.

Eric very deliberately stepped in front of Cecilia. "She's not yours."

"Yes, she is."

Cecilia still looked pissed, but she darted around Eric, turning to address him. "Fleet Admiral, why was I placed in this trinity?"

Eric smiled. "You were the one I expected to actually solve the mystery. Mateo was my primary suspect, given his presence on the balcony and in the hotel room when the sniper killed Manon, and his access to the medication, Dimitri was the double agent, and you were the brains."

"Oh," Cecilia said.

Eric wasn't done. "Mateo might have used your time together to further cover up his crimes. I expected you to see through that. And if he was the traitor, Dimitri was in place to kill him." Eric looked up, meeting each of their gazes in turn, and there was no remorse or apology in his stare.

Mateo briefly closed his eyes, feeling sick.

The silence stretched long enough that he could hide in the darkness behind his eyelids. When he looked around, Eric had taken a step back and Arthur had turned his chair to look at the far wall, giving them the illusion of privacy.

"I don't want out of this trinity." Dimitri was the first to speak. "I haven't since that first night you took us to your bed. I love you." Dimitri glanced Mateo's way. "Both of you."

Mateo went weak as relief flooded him. He grinned...and realized he didn't have a choice to make after all. He looked at Eric. "I am stepping down as head of the guard, Fleet Admiral. My trinity comes first...they always will. If they will have me."

Eric studied his face for a long, uncomfortable minute, before nodding. "Very well. And I'm glad you're not a total dumbass. You're relieved of your duties."

Mateo smiled, ready to take Cecilia in his arms, but Eric moved, putting himself between them again.

Eric turned to Cecilia. "I'm the one who stuck you with these two, and you were the only one who didn't know this was—"

"A sham?" she snapped.

Eric grunted. "It wasn't ideal, but it was necessary. I won't apologize, but I *will* give you the choice. If you want, I'll dissolve the trinity."

"I thought it wasn't a real trinity anyway," she said.

"This was always a real trinity, Ms. St. John. If Mateo was innocent, I intended to finalize the marriage." He looked at Mateo. "One way or another, I would be looking for a new head of the Spartan Guard at the end of this." He looked back to Cecilia. "But the choice is yours."

Mateo sucked in a deep breath and held it. There was too much pain, too much distrust still lingering in her expression. He and Dimitri put it there, and he wouldn't blame her if she wanted to walk away.

It would kill him to watch her do it, but he would understand why. She'd done everything she said. Found a way to reach two stubborn, antagonistic alpha males and create something that was more than right.

It was magic.

"Leap of faith," Dimitri murmured, capturing Cecilia's attention.

Mateo smiled at his lover's plea. Cecilia had asked both of them for a leap of faith and they'd given it...sort of.

She narrowed her eyes briefly, but the request had worked. Her anger seemed to melt away, replaced by something that looked a lot like hope.

"I'll never betray your trust, your loyalty again, Cecilia," Mateo vowed.

"Nor will I," Dimitri said.

She studied both of their faces, not responding for a painfully long minute. Then she turned to the fleet admiral. "My trinity is ready."

"Very well," Eric said.

Mateo wasn't sure how he could tell the fleet admiral was pleased with her reply. God knew his expression was stern, his voice gruff. But there was something in his eyes that looked suspiciously like respect.

The fleet admiral stepped in front of Arthur's desk and gestured for the three of them to stand before him.

Arthur walked to a bookshelf, running his finger along some spines.

"What are you doing?" Eric asked.

"There's a book...here it is," Arthur pulled a thin old tome from the shelf. "It contains the script for the ceremony. Since this is your first—"

"Put that away. I don't need the book. I know the words. I remember, from..." Eric trailed off then grunted, in apparent self-directed disgust.

Arthur hesitated, then returned the book to its spot before coming to stand next to Eric.

With a nod of his head, the fleet admiral gestured for the three of them to link their hands. Dimitri reached out with his right hand. Cecilia placed hers in, and then Mateo rested his on top.

"I hereby bind you, Dimitri Bondar of Hungary, Cecilia St. John of Rome, and Mateo Bernard of Castile, in marriage.

"Your union will serve to better and protect the people of our proud and ancient society.

"It is your duty to love, protect and keep your spouses. I will hear your pledge to not only keep and protect one another, but to strive to better our world."

Mateo released their hands and knelt. "I pledge on my honor, and as your spouse, to love, protect and keep you, all of your days."

Cecilia was the next to kneel and take the same vow, followed by Dimitri. All three rose as one as Eric pronounced them married in the eyes of the law and the Masters' Admiralty.

"We did it," Cecilia whispered. "I thought...when we got here..."

"You thought I was going to choose the guard," Mateo said when it was clear she didn't want to share her fear lest it remind him of what he'd just given up.

She nodded.

Mateo reached for her, pulling her into his arms. "When I was a child, I thought my calling was medicine. After my parents died, I thought I could better serve the world as a protector. Now I know every step I've taken, every decision I've made was leading me to you." His gaze traveled to Dimitri, who was standing just behind Cecilia. "To both of you."

He kissed Cecilia softly, keeping it short and chaste, given the fact the fleet admiral and admiral of

England were still standing there. When he released her, he was surprised to find Dimitri taking her place, offering Mateo a hard kiss filled with promise and— God help him—challenge.

He and Dimitri were bound to spend the next fifty years or so battling for control. Mateo grinned when Dimitri's lips left his.

He couldn't wait.

Then Dimitri turned to Cecilia. "Cece, my sweet wife." He raised an eyebrow as he spoke, provoking the memory of him calling her both names in this office a week ago, Cecilia balking at both.

She knew he was purposely teasing her, but their lady never backed down. "My Dim...husband." Her pause gave her words the desired effect and Dimitri laughed.

"Kiss me, *koxaha*, my love."

Dimitri clearly didn't give a shit if they had an audience or not as he wrapped his arms around their wife and gave her a long, hot, openmouthed kiss that seemed to go on for hours.

Arthur cleared his throat as the fleet admiral snorted. "Perhaps now would be a good time for the three of you to take the honeymoon elsewhere. Arthur and I have business to discuss."

Mateo took one of Cecilia's hands, Dimitri the other.

"Thank you, Fleet Admiral," Mateo said.

Eric nodded, but said nothing more.

An hour ago, he'd expected to be imprisoned. Alone.

Now Mateo was free. And married.

When they reached the street, they glanced around, the action reminiscent of the previous week.

"Where to?" Dimitri asked.

"I want to go back to my family's B&B," Cecilia said, reaching for her cell. "I want the two of you completely to myself for as long as we can manage to avoid the real world."

Mateo gave her a kiss on the cheek. "Sounds like the perfect plan, *tesoro*."

Arthur closed the door to his office after Mateo, Cecilia and Dimitri left. While he was happy for the trinity, there was still a great deal of work to be done. Uncovering the name of the traitor had only unlocked a new mystery…Alicia Rutherford.

"There's something I want to discuss."

"My husband, wife and I have a very nice sex life, and I don't think we have time for a BDSM club membership."

Eric snorted. "Time is an issue. Though I expect we could both use the emotional relief." Eric looked Arthur over. "I can teach you to spank with your left hand. I trained for impact play with either hand."

"I…I can't believe we're having this conversation right now. But, er, thank you very much for the offer."

"That isn't actually what I wanted to talk to you about."

Eric reached into his jacket pocket, withdrawing two photographs. He placed them side by side, faceup on Arthur's desk. "Just between us, I started to question if Mateo was the traitor before my fall. I want you to look into something for me."

Arthur picked up one of the photos. "That's Mateo and—"

"The former admiral of Castile, Ricardo Garcia. He was Mateo's father."

Seeing Mateo with his father should have made that fact obvious from the first moment he'd met the other man. The resemblance was uncanny. However, he'd never heard that the admiral of Castile had any children.

His gaze drifted to the other photo. Mateo was in this one as well, a younger boy clearly flanked by adoring parents.

"Those are his other two parents, renowned surgeons in Seville. They were brutally murdered when Mateo was sixteen."

Arthur considered that, and the fact the admiral of Castile had been gunned down at the same time as his own admiral. "I had no idea Mateo had suffered so much loss, and one so recently."

"I want you to look into that first killing, the one that took the lives of both Doctor Bernards."

"The killer was never caught?" Arthur asked.

Eric shook his head. "No. I realize this has nothing to do with your territory. I'm asking anyway."

Arthur tried to connect the dots, tried to figure out why Eric was making this request of him. They were already trying to solve one mystery, track down the Domino. Why would Eric ask him to take on searching for another killer? Unless...

"You think that killing is connected to the Domino?" Arthur asked, suddenly wondering if that bombing in the Ottoman territory truly had been the initial crime.

"Just find out what you can. Covertly. I don't want anyone else to know about this. Not even the librarians. Understood?"

Arthur nodded, holding the fleet admiral's gaze, showing him he was a man who could be trusted with secrets...kept even from those he loved and trusted the most.

Chapter Eighteen

Dimitri stood by the wide expanse of windows, watching the sun set over the lake. The sky had faded from a pale shade of white to soft gray to dark slate in the matter of an hour, the colors of the lake matching the ever-darkening sky. A few scattered stars, too rare an occurrence in this country, had begun to make their appearance. Cecilia had remarked on the beauty of this room last week, but all he'd been able to think was the entire first floor of the place was a security nightmare.

Funny how he was seeing it from her point of view tonight. After years as a spy and a week spent chasing a traitor and racing the clock, it seemed as if his entire existence had flipped on a dime since this afternoon. Since he'd pledged his life to Cecilia and Mateo.

They'd made the drive from London to the Lake District after leaving the London headquarters. While Dimitri would have preferred to find the nearest hotel immediately after their wedding ceremony, he knew firsthand how special this place was…to Cecilia, and now to them.

They'd spent their first night together here, and tonight, they'd consummate their marriage in the same room. It was the perfect place to begin their honeymoon, their lives together.

Mateo and Cecilia were sitting on the couch, her bare feet resting in his lap, both of them sipping a glass of Merlot. For seven straight days, they'd done everything at a breakneck pace, racing from city to city—hell, from country to country—in pursuit of Derrick.

None of them was in a hurry right now, taking a few moments to just relax and savor the quiet time. However, he suspected his lovers were beginning to feel the same pull toward the bedroom as he. That suspicion was confirmed when Cecilia glanced toward the door to the hallway that led to the stairs.

He grinned, forcing himself to be patient. Last week, she had taken the reins, dragged him and Mateo upstairs in an attempt to make peace between them...with sex.

It had worked.

"Strategically, this place would be a logistical nightmare to defend," he mused, pretending his thoughts weren't solely on getting his lovers upstairs and undressed.

Mateo appeared surprised by his unexpected comment and glanced around the room. "I don't know about that. Obviously you would have to replace the windows with bulletproof glass, but there are also shades that could be purchased that would shield the occupants of the room. I had some installed at Triskelion Castle."

Dimitri shook his head, merely to be contrary. "No. You're wrong. There's absolutely no way this place could be made safe."

Mateo stood up and walked the perimeter of the room, clearly gearing up to strengthen his case. "I disagree. The fleet admiral's main rooms had a lot of windows, and we found some very successful ways to fortify them."

"Clearly I have more expertise in this area," Dimitri added, working hard to school his face, determined to project the unmistakable arrogance that had rubbed Mateo wrong at their first meeting.

Cecilia shot Dimitri an amused grin that she followed up with a quick roll of her eyes. His clever woman knew what he was up to.

Dimitri decided to up the ante. "This is the difference between a spy and a mere guard. There are intricacies to protection that you simply don't understand."

Mateo scowled, his fists clenching in an antagonistic manner. "Excuse me?"

Dimitri managed to maintain his superior expression for the count of three before turning away to hide his grin.

Cecilia stepped in. "That's it. It's clear the two of you are never going to agree on anything, and I'm not about to spend the rest of my life watching these pissing contests."

"Cecilia," Mateo said, still not in tune with their game.

Until she pointed upstairs. "So there's only one way to settle this. Sex."

She winked at Mateo as Dimitri chuckled.

Mateo snorted. "You got me."

Dimitri walked over and wrapped a strong arm around his husband's shoulders. "The two of you looked entirely too comfortable on that couch. I needed a way to get things moving in the right direction. Cece has made an excellent suggestion, and I think we should take her up on her generous offer of sex."

"For once, we agree on something."

Cecilia laughed when Mateo walked over and swung her up into his arms.

"I believe there's a tradition that involves the groom carrying his bride?"

"Over the threshold to their home," she corrected as he headed toward the stairs.

Mateo continued upstairs, Cecilia's hands clinging to his shoulders as Dimitri followed. "There's a threshold to the bedroom. I suspect that's the more important one."

The three of them headed toward "their room" in the inn, the one they'd shared the previous week.

Dimitri struggled to believe such a short time had elapsed. He had come to this room with distrust and reservations the first time. Tonight, he felt only joy and love.

Both emotions were foreign to him, yet they came so naturally, so easily when he was with Cecilia and Mateo.

Mateo carried Cecilia directly to the bed, setting her down on the mattress. He wasted no time unbuttoning her blouse.

Dimitri leaned on the doorframe, watching his husband strip the clothing from their beautiful wife. A man of action, he was surprised to discover the pleasure to be found in merely observing.

Cecilia, never one to remain idle, was working to get Mateo out of his clothes as well. The two of them spent a great deal of time touching and kissing as they disrobed. Both snuck surreptitious glances his way, but he dismissed their unspoken invitations with a smile that said he was very happy where he was at the moment.

Dimitri considered their trip to Red, and Cecilia's obvious interest in the things she'd seen there. Walking across the room, he stopped at the foot of the bed, his hand gripping one of the posts of the footboard.

Cecilia and Mateo were now naked and standing next to the bed.

"Turn around, Cece. Face the bed," Dimitri said, his voice thick with desire. He was aware it deepened the tone, made his words sound more like a command than a request. In this instance, that worked in his favor.

Cecilia sucked in a quiet breath, even as she did as he said.

"Bend over. Keep your upper body on the bed, your legs hanging over the edge. Mateo and I are going to test some limits tonight. See how strong your desire to submit is."

She shivered, but again, did as he directed without comment or argument.

Mateo lost no time running his hand over the bare skin of her ass, his eyes gleaming with appreciation. Their wife was truly beautiful, sexy, and the thick erection Cecilia had set loose from Mateo's pants proved his husband was more than ready for what came next.

Dimitri had set the night's adventures in motion, but Mateo didn't seek guidance or wait for instructions. Instead, he lifted his hand and brought it down firmly on Cecilia's backside.

She jerked, then sighed.

Mateo shared Dimitri's need to learn more about their inexperienced lover. While Cecilia had clearly had other lovers in the past—men whose names he'd never ask for lest he be tempted to hunt them down in some irrational jealous rage—their wife was new to BDSM, to the role she would play in their bedroom.

Because of that, they needed to take care, to initiate her slowly. Mateo continued to spank her, each slap varying in intensity and placement.

Cecilia remained as still as she could, but there was no missing the sexual need growing inside as she clenched her thighs together, her hips twisting in such a way that said her pussy needed stimulation. It was clenching, empty, hungry.

Dimitri was still fully dressed, something he didn't intend to rectify. Keeping Cecilia naked while his clothing remained would only heighten her feelings of being possessed, claimed by her Master.

Mateo broke up his spanking with gentle strokes on her now pink ass cheeks. Dimitri didn't need to touch her to know how warm—no, hot—the skin would feel.

"Please," she gasped, parting her thighs in invitation. "Please, Mateo. Touch me."

Dimitri placed one knee on the mattress next to her, slapping her ass sharply. "You haven't been given permission to speak."

She snorted. "Yeah. That's probably going to be a hard limit for me."

Dimitri laughed, despite his desire to appear stern. Her humor, her frankness, always caught him off guard, delighted him.

"Mateo can spank your ass until it's glowing red, but you balk at a demand for silence."

She looked at him over her shoulder, her brows raised, feigning disappointment. "It's like you don't know me at all."

Dimitri dug deep, needing to draw them back into the scene, so he unfastened his belt, sliding it from the loops in one quick motion, before bending the leather in half and slapping it against his palm in a menacing manner.

Cecilia never blinked an eye. More than that, he wasn't certain if he saw or merely imagined that she'd lifted her ass slightly in invitation. Dimitri's hand twitched, debating whether or not to move forward.

Mateo took the decision away from him, his large hand clasping Dimitri's wrist. "Perhaps we should move a little bit slower. We have an entire lifetime to expand on our repertoire."

He appreciated Mateo's patience. Dimitri felt his grip on control slipping. There was too much he wanted from her.

God, he wanted everything.

After a lifetime of living alone, and thinking himself happy in that existence, he found himself wanting to make up for that lost time all in one evening.

He dropped the belt on the floor, then reached for Cecilia, drawing his hand through her hair before clenching his fingers around it. He used that grip to direct her, moving her from the bed to her knees in front of him.

"Unfasten my pants and pull out my dick. I want it in your mouth in ten seconds, or not even Mateo will save you from my belt."

She hesitated for a split second, long enough to prove to Dimitri that the belt was something she definitely wanted to try. He catalogued that information, tucking it away for future use.

Cecilia lost no time freeing him from his jeans, his base of his cock firmly encased in her small hand as she guided the head to her mouth.

Dimitri sucked in, deeply, filling his lungs with air as she took him deeper, increasing the suction until he saw stars.

Mateo stepped up next to him, his thick erection a mirror image to Dimitri's. They were both hard, hurting.

Cecilia accepted Mateo's unspoken invitation, gripping his dick in her other hand, her lips moving from the head of one cock to the other, treating them both to a mind-blowing blow job.

Dimitri's hand remained in her hair, tugging it every now and again, enjoying the way the sting in her scalp had her eyes drifting closed in bliss, hot breath escaping in a sigh, tickling his cock.

Mateo cupped her neck, his thumb stroking her jaw, as she took him even farther into her mouth.

"Open your throat," Mateo murmured. "I want to come in your mouth."

Cecilia did as he asked, moving faster along their husband's dick.

"I'm close, Cece," Mateo said, the words sounding more like a grunt. "God. I'm coming, *tesora*."

Dimitri released Cecilia's hair, allowing Mateo to step more fully in front of her, holding her face with both his hands, adding his own forward thrust to her blow job. Cecilia never balked, never pulled away, even as Mateo took her mouth roughly.

Dimitri placed his arm around Mateo's lower back, unable to watch his lovers without touching them. There was something incredibly moving about watching his wife bring his husband to climax.

They were his.

He couldn't stop marveling over that fact.

His. They were *his*.

It took Mateo a couple of moments to recover enough to be able to move. He stepped back and Cecilia turned her attention toward Dimitri once more, clearly ready to offer him the same gift she'd just given Mateo.

Dimitri shook his head, reaching down to help her to her feet.

"On the bed," he murmured.

Cecilia looked toward the mattress, then back to him for more instructions.

He'd thought they would have to guide her through her submission. He was wrong. Cecilia was a quick study, their perfect counterpoint. Neither he nor Mateo was true Dom material, both of them more alpha than Dominant. The same was true of Cecilia. She would give them her obedience, but she would question things and test them.

"On your back, *koxaha*. I want to make love to you."

Cecilia smiled, then complied, claiming the center of the large bed, reaching up to him. "I want you," she whispered.

He recognized her wording. He could see from her flushed face, her tight nipples, the sheen of arousal on her inner thighs that she needed him. That was evident and wonderful, but nowhere near as special as the realization that she wanted him.

Dimitri climbed on the bed, coming over her, caging her beneath him even as he lowered his head for a kiss.

Her tongue darted out, meeting his halfway. They kissed for hours, maybe years, but Dimitri didn't seek more. Didn't need more than her breath mingling with his, her taste on his lips, her arms clinging to his shoulders in a way that said she'd never let him go.

Mateo had joined them on the bed, lying next to them, idly stroking Cecilia's breast, then running the same hand along Dimitri's side. Mateo appeared to feel that same need to touch.

Finally, Dimitri pulled away, the words he was thinking slipping out unbidden. "I want to make babies with you, Cece."

Ever practical, she laughed softly. "Perhaps we should deal with the issue of where to live first. Singapore? Spain? Ukraine?"

"I don't want to return to the Ukraine. My life there is done. I'm not going back."

"There's nothing for me in Spain. My family is gone, and I haven't lived there in many years. In truth, I think I'd like to return to school, to study medicine. I can do that practically anywhere."

Cecilia smiled. "Dr. Bernard. That sounds good to me."

"So...Singapore?" Dimitri asked. He'd visited there a couple of times, and while he liked the city, he wasn't sure how he felt about living there. Of course, wherever Mateo and Cecilia were would be home. The country mattered very little.

He was surprised when Cecilia shook her head. "No. I don't think I want to go back. If the two of you are making fresh starts, I'd like to do the same."

"Well then, I vote we stay here," Mateo murmured. "Right here."

Cecilia started to laugh again until she realized Mateo was being serious. "The Lake District?"

He nodded, then looked around. "You said your family owns this B&B."

"Yes. I have two aunts and an uncle who've split up the duties to keep it running, however, they're all getting older and have begun to ask me to take over more of the tasks. I was actually here, not in Singapore, when Arthur called me last week."

Dimitri looked around the room, considered all the improvements they could make to the inn. "My father was a carpenter. He taught me everything about building, wiring, plumbing when I was growing up. This place has a great deal of potential." His mind began to whirl with plans of ways they could improve and expand the B&B.

"Are you both being serious?" Cecilia asked, excitement sparkling in her eyes.

Dimitri considered the unrest in his homeland. "Our children could grow up in this beautiful, wild country. Safe. Happy."

"I'll call my aunt in the morning. Ask her if we could take over the inn now. I'm certain she will be relieved by the request. And in truth, James and I are in line to inherit it. When that day comes, I'll simply ask to buy his half."

Dimitri kissed her once more. "Now that that's settled, I'm going to repeat my previous statement. I want babies."

Cecilia laughed, then rolled her eyes when she glanced in Mateo's direction and saw the same earnest desire on his face.

"Fine. Children. But not tonight. Tonight is just for us."

Dimitri gripped his cock, guiding it to Cecilia's pussy, slowly pushing inside.

"Us," he repeated, once he was fully encapsulated in her wet heat.

"Us," Mateo added, kissing Dimitri's shoulder, his hand stroking his ass.

Dimitri did exactly what he'd wanted. He made love to Cecilia, taking her slowly, gently, as he took turns kissing her and Mateo.

They came together, clinging tightly, declaring their love.

Dimitri had come to this room last week seeking a villain, suspicious, prepared to kill if need be.

Instead, he'd found a family. A future.

Forever.

Epilogue

Antonio Starabba murmured his goodbyes to the security minister and ended the call. It was nearly midnight, and his official duties as a security officer for Rome were done for the day.

Now it was time to think about the dead.

The torture, murder, and mutilation of Nazario, Christina and Lorena had been attributed to the Domino. It was the first in a series of crimes that resulted in the death of the fleet admiral and two territory admirals, among many others. Tradition said the Domino always had an apprentice. That meant two people were responsible for the rash of crimes and murders that had rocked the Masters' Admiralty to the core.

Two people.

Yet they had caught, cornered, and killed more suspects than that. And none of the people tied to the crimes had conclusively been identified as the Domino.

And at the end of the day, Antonio's job, his duty, was to protect the people of Rome.

He wouldn't rest until he found proof as to who had killed three members of his territory. He wouldn't let Nazario's, Christina's and Lorena's deaths become lost amid the chaos the Domino had wrought.

Antonio walked from his home office to his bedroom, pulling off the black shirt he'd been wearing since waking at six a.m. and exchanging it for an identical clean shirt. Then he went back to his office, grabbed his laptop, and carried it to his couch. The concession he would make to working on this off-duty investigation was that he would sit on the couch rather than at a desk.

It was only after he sat that he thought about making himself a coffee, but then decided against it. Not that it was too late to drink coffee. There was no such thing as a wrong time to drink coffee.

He was just too tired to get up.

Antonio opened the custom-built database search software he had and started scrolling through that day's matches. He'd cross-referenced the methods of torture, tools, and exact causes of death for the three members of his territory with other crimes in Europe, using Interpol's databases. In addition to that, he had a standing request with the security offices of the other territories for information on missing persons and violent crimes committed against members. Before the death of the fleet admiral, people may not have been so forthcoming with information. Now, they were under siege, and most territories were acting accordingly.

He had information drops from everyone but Kalmar. He sent a reminder request to M. Virtanen, who had been his point of contact.

When he opened the message from Germany, his mouth tightened.

It was confirmed that Karl Klimek had gone missing. The knights in Germany had checked his residences and offices.

Just to be thorough, Antonio ran a facial recognition scan for Karl. He could only access high-quality video from airports and train stations in his territory—including Italy, Greece, and the areas bordering the Adriatic Sea. While that ran, he went through the other reports. Nothing stood out, so, for the one-hundredth time, he turned to the crime scene photos.

Every bit of evidence from that cave near his father's country estate had been analyzed and inspected. Still, he couldn't help but go back to it. Not to the obvious clues, but to the violence with which the trinity had been killed. The dichotomy of a criminal who would leave such elegant clues as precisely stacked ancient coins while also being a murderer who would dismember someone while still alive was revolting. He'd consulted with experts, knew it was possible for a high-functioning psychopath to exhibit both characteristics.

The search program pinged.

Antonio sat up, the laptop nearly sliding off his lap. He closed the images of death and suffering, pulling up the search result.

Facial recognition had picked out an image of a man that was a sixty percent match for Karl Klimek at a train station near the Italy/Slovenia border. That alone wouldn't have been enough to sound an alert.

In the same frame, facial recognition had IDed a man who was on Antonio's list of suspects. The list was hundreds of names long, and focused on anyone with a criminal history who had also purchased ancient coins or fine art within the past eighteen months.

"Ciril Novak." Antonio clicked, his fingers trembling though he wasn't sure it if was from exhaustion or excitement.

He opened Ciril's file and pulled up the still image facial recognition had flagged.

As soon as the image appeared, his heart stopped.

Karl Klimek was on a stretcher, a mask covering the lower half of his face. His eyes were closed. Ciril Novak, a security guard who'd spent time in prison after several violent fights put his opponents in the hospital, was dressed as a paramedic, escorting Karl's stretcher out of the train station to a waiting ambulance.

Antonio ran the video, heart racing as he watched Ciril load Karl into the back of the ambulance, then climb into the driver's seat and pull away from the station.

Antonio switched from the video to Ciril's file.

He had to find Karl, and he had to find him now, before Antonio found himself standing over Karl's corpse.

He was so focused on scanning Ciril's file for locations where he might have taken Karl, he didn't see the notice pop-up from Kalmar.

Kalmar security officer Leila Virtanen is missing.

Are you just dying to know what happens to Karl and Leila? Grab your copy of Pleasure's Fury right now!

And if you're new to Mari and Lila's secret society, be sure to check out the American counterpart to Masters' Admiralty, Trinity Masters, available now.

Elemental Pleasure
Primal Passion
Scorching Desire
Forbidden Legacy

ABOUT THE AUTHORS

Writing a book was number one on Mari Carr's bucket list. Now her computer is jammed full of stories — novels, novellas, short stories and dead-ends. A New York Times and USA TODAY bestseller, Mari finds time for writing by squeezing it into the hours between 3 a.m. and daybreak when her family is asleep.
You can visit Mari's website at www.maricarr.com. She is also on Facebook and Twitter.

Lila Dubois is a top selling author of paranormal, fantasy and contemporary erotic romance. Having spent extensive time in France, Egypt, Turkey, England and Ireland Lila speaks five languages, none of them (including English) fluently. She now lives in Los Angeles with a cute Irishman.
You can visit Lila's website at www.liladubois.net. She loves to hear from fans! Send an email to author@liladubois.net or join her newsletter for contests, deleted scenes, articles, and release notifications.

Look for these titles by Lila Dubois

The Trinity Masters, Erotic Ménage Romance
Elemental Pleasure
Primal Passion
Scorching Desire
After Burn (free short story)
Forbidden Legacy
Hidden Devotion
Elegant Seduction
Secret Scandal
Delicate Ties
Beloved Sacrifice
Masterful Truth

BDSM Checklist, BDSM Erotic Romance
A is for…
B is for…
C is for…
D is for…
E is for…
F is for…
G is for…
H is for…
I is for…

Standalone BDSM Erotic Romance
Betrayed by Love
Red Ribbon

New Adult BDSM Romance
Dangerous Lust

Undone Lovers, BDSM Erotic Romance
Undone Rebel
Undone Dom

Undone Diva

Glenncailty Castle, Contemporary Romance
The Harp and the Fiddle
The Irish Lover (short story)
The Fire and the Earth
The Shadow and the Night

Monsters in Hollywood, Paranormal Romance
Dial M for Monster
My Fair Monster
Gone with the Monster
Have Monster, Will Travel
A Monster and a Gentleman
The Last of the Monsters

The Wraith Accords, Paranormal Romance
Carnal Magic

Zinahs, Fantasy Romance
Forbidden
Savage
Bound

Standalone Paranormal Romance
Calling the Wild
Kitsune
Savage Satisfaction
Sealed with a Kiss

Look for these titles by Mari Carr

Wild Irish
Come Monday
Ruby Tuesday
Waiting for Wednesday
Sweet Thursday
Friday I'm in Love
Saturday Night Special
Any Given Sunday
Wild Irish Christmas
Wild Irish Box Set

Wilder Irish
January Girl
February Stars
Guardian Angel
March Wind
April Fools
May Flowers
June Kisses

Compass
Northern Exposure
Southern Comfort
Eastern Ambitions
Western Ties
Winter's Thaw
Hope Springs
Summer Fling
Falling Softly
Heaven on Earth
Into the Fire
Still Waters
Light as Air
Second Chances

Fix You
Dare You
Just You
Near You
Reach You
Always You

Sparks in Texas
Sparks Fly
Waiting for You
Something Sparked
Off Limits
No Other Way
Whiskey Eyes

Trinity Masters
Elemental Pleasure
Primal Passion
Scorching Desire
Forbidden Legacy
Hidden Devotion
Elegant Seduction
Secret Scandal
Delicate Ties
Beloved Sacrifice
Masterful Truth

Masters Admiralty, with Lila Dubois
Treachery's Devotion
Loyalty's Betrayal
Pleasure's Fury

Cowboys!
Spitfire
Rekindled
Inflamed

Big Easy
Blank Canvas
Crash Point
Full Position
Rough Draft
Triple Beat
Winner Takes All
Going Too Fast

Boys of Fall
Free Agent
Red Zone
Wild Card

Clandestine
Bound by the Past
Covert Affairs
Scoring
Mad about Meg

Cocktales
Party Naked
Screwdriver
Bachelor's Bait
Screaming O

Farpoint Creek, with Lexxie Couper
Outback Princess
Outback Cowboy
Outback Master
Outback Lovers

June Girls

No Recourse
No Regrets

Just Because
Because of You
Because You Love Me
Because It's True

Love Lessons
Happy Hour
Slam Dunk

Madison Girls
Kiss Me Kate
Three Reasons Why

Scoundrels
Black Jack
White Knight
Red Queen

What Women Want
Sugar and Spice
Everything Nice

Individual Titles
Seducing the Boss
Erotic Research
Tequila Truth
Power Play
Rough Cut
Assume the Position
Do Over

Printed in Great Britain
by Amazon